Journey from Exile

A Legion Archer

Book #1

J. Clifton Slater

A Legion Archer series and the associated books are the creation of J. Clifton Slater. Any use of *Journey from Exile* in part or in whole requires express written consent. This is a work of fiction. Any resemblance to persons living or dead is purely coincidental.

I'd like to thank Hollis Jones for her skills in guiding me through the story process. She has adjusted the structure, identified rough spots, and called my attention to overly long descriptions. Because of her, the novel exists.

And, I would like to thank the readers. You are the reason I can spend my days doing research and writing stories. A salute to you for being there.

If you have comments, contact me at
GalacticCouncilRealm@gmail.com

To follow my progress on the next book, read blogs on ancient topics, or to sign up for my monthly Author Report, go to my website.

www.JCliftonSlater.com

Journey from Exile

Act 1

In Rome, despite resistance from the Patrician class, Senator Gaius Flaminius pushed through a bill to aid veterans of the first war with Carthage. Qualifying men were given small plots of land to replace the farms they lost while away fighting. And even though it was nine years after the war, the Legionaries appreciated the grants and adored Gaius Flaminius. On the other hand, the nobility disapproved of the Senator and the handouts.

East of the Mediterranean Sea, King Seleucus the Second marched his Empire's army towards Persia. And like the Great Macedonian King Alexander, one hundred years before, the Seleucid army included a compliment of Cretan archers.

But King Seleucus' expedition fell into disarray when his army suffered defeat on Parthian spears at the border to Persia. After the battle, his mercenaries disbanded. Most migrated to new Monarchs with coins and a hunger to tame the world.

A number of the bowmen, however, chose to return to the Island of Crete. Some archers visited their villages to rest before hiring out to another warlord. Others raced to defend their cities from attacks by neighboring towns. And a few older, wiser, and tired of combat, came home to retire from mercenary service.

Welcome to 232 B.C.

Chapter 1 – Arriving Crete

Zarek Mikolas checked the ties on his two bow cases. Then he tested the knots securing the cases and other items to his long pack. Once sure nothing would fly off and land in the water, he hoisted the bundle and slipped the straps over his shoulders.

"Lieutenant Mikolas, let me carry your pack," Sargent Machaon offered.

As an officer of archers, Zarek could ask for and receive help with his load. But as a leader, he felt it was his job to set an example, even if only for this last time.

"I'll handle my load. You see to your Files," Zarek growled. "We've made it this far without archer Sim starting a fight with the sailors. Let's keep it that way."

"Yes, sir," Machaon acknowledged.

While the NCO went to check on his charges, Zarek stooped, slung the strap to a heavy box over a shoulder, and straightened. The deck under his feet rolled a little and he shifted to keep his balance.

Inside the box, the unit's logbook rested on a layer of gold. As the Lieutenant for a detachment of archers, Zarek was expected to keep track of his bowmen whether dead, injured, or alive, their ability to handle the toils of warfare, and the field pay dispersed to them while on the assignment. Additionally, he listed operations they took part in while away from Crete. As well, he rated the reliability of the principal who hired the Cretan archers. For the business of selling mercenary services to the highest and most reliable bidders, the Council needed to trust the persons hiring their archers.

Plus, with the bulk of the Company serving King Seleucus in the Persia campaign, having information from Zarek Mikolas' detached unit, helped the Captain manage his Company.

While the logbook had mass, the gold in the bottom of the box supplied the real weight. The logbook would eventually go to the scribes of the Council. But first, the gold payment for services rendered, would be taken to the offices of Eugen Admetus. As the Archon for Phalasarna, Admetus would see to the final payments for the archers, NCOs, and their officer. All done under the watchful eyes of representatives from the other Archons, to be sure equal shares would be sent to the other nine major cities of Crete.

A little wobbly under the load, Zarek Mikolas walked off the deck of the Rhodian merchant vessel and onto the dock at Phalasarna. Around him were the walls and still waters of a protected harbor. To the west, he gazed at the solid buildings and paved streets of the city and at the market to the east. Despite the weight, he smiled and took a step. Then the Lieutenant froze. Behind him, voices rose above the noise of the busy port. The smile fell away as quickly as a full sail in a sudden calm.

"And I say he took my coin purse," yelled a male voice.

His accent was that of a man from the Isle of Rhodes. Based on his origin and his anger, Zarek assumed the sailor had already drawn a sica. Rhodians were proud and did no shy away from a fight.

Zarek Mikolas tilted his head back and, without turning to look, called out, "Sergeant Machaon, do you require assistance?"

It might have been another culprit or troublemaker. But for the last six months while the one hundred archers fulfilled a contract to a king with a border problem, Lieutenant Mikolas' main source of aggravation had been Sim Admetus.

Big for his age and stupid for his actual years, the young man pulled a heavy war bow and consistently hit his targets. But he was lazy, liked to pick fights, and had the habit of taking items that didn't belong to him.

"Truly, a lazy and stupid thief," Zarek grumbled while waiting for an answer.

"Third File, draw and stand by," the NCO instructed. Eighteen long packs smacked the ship's deck. Steel swished from leather sheaths and hatchets scraped from holding rings. Sergeant Machaon continued. "Sailor, you have two choices. Withdraw your accusation, or bleed on your ship's deck."

A deep breath from a man, probably the sailor, told the story of the Rhodian's frustration. But the inhalation also informed Lieutenant Mikolas that the sailor would choose not to fight the Cretan archers.

Then Sim's vomited all over the situation.

"I'm not sure I'm prepared to excuse the insult," Sim Admetus announced. "My feelings are hurt. I think a silver coin would ease my broken spirit."

"But. But you have my coin purse," exclaimed the sailor.

***

Transportation for the mercenary units required buying passage on merchant vessels from other nations. If a crewman was killed in a street fight, that was one issue. Murdering a sailor on his own ship, especially a Rhodian, would make it hard on the next detachment to find a ride back to Crete.

"Sergeant Machaon. I asked you a question," Zarek reminded the NCO.

"Lieutenant, we have it handled," Machaon assured him. "Third File, disarm Sim and search him."

The NCO's instructions changed the focus from the sailor but didn't order the blades and hatchets to be put away. Zarek dropped both the long pack and the box, pivoted, and braced.

Murdering a Rhodian sailor was bad enough. Being the officer in charge when the son of Archon Eugen Admetus was killed by his own File would be worse.

After already losing bowman on the assignment, Zarek envisioned a blood bath on the merchant vessel and losing a couple more archers. He sprinted back to the ship.

Sim Admetus, true to his nature, backed away from his File mates and the Rhodian crew while slicing the air with his short sword.

"I'll cut you," Sim threatened. "Nobody is going to search me. Because…"

Zarek ran up behind the young archer, smashed the troublemaker in the back of the neck with his forearm, and followed Sim to the deck.

"Move and I'll bounce your head against the deck boards until you relax," Zarek warned.

While straddling the big youth with his knees, Zarek trapped the sword with one hand and held the back of Sim's head with the other.

"We're home and I don't recognize your authority, Lieutenant," Sim Admetus declared. "Get off me."

The announcement would have come out with bravado, except, the young man spoke into the deck. The slur from lips pressed into the boards lessened the malice. Between the intention of discarding the officer's control, the reality of being pinned to the deck, and the realization that the File was home, and no longer had to deal with Sim, the archers laughed.

When Sim realized he was the subject of the jest, he hunched his shoulders and arched his back. Lieutenant Mikolas lifted the youth's head and hammered his face into the deck. Stunned and disorientated, Sim Admetus relaxed.

"Search him and if he has an extra coin purse, give it to the sailor," Zarek ordered while climbing to his feet. Before turning back to the dock, he directed. "Someone, collect Sim's long pack and a few of you help him off the boat. As young Master Admetus stated, we are home. So, let's enjoy it."

***

Several blocks from the port and downhill from the government building, Zarek pushed through a gateway and entered a courtyard. The space was filled with Troops of older boys sitting in circles. He scanned the groups before focusing in on a Herd of eight-year-olds.

"I need my long pack guarded until I get back from meeting with the Archon," he notified the wide-eyed children. Then to their instructor he asked. "Do these bowmen know their dances?"

"Lieutenant Mikolas, the Cretan agoge welcomes you back," the teacher greeted Zarek. "This Herd is learning. But they have a long way to go before earning the title and taking their place in a File with Cretan archers."

The ten boys watched in awe as their instructor talked to an officer of archers. Then they stiffened at a request from the Lieutenant.

"I'd like to see a war-dance," Zarek remarked.

Without pausing, the instructor barked, "Cretan counter-march firing. Set the beat."

The ten eight-year-olds jumped to their feet. Several started a chant, "Mártios, mártios, step left, step right, mártios."

The call of march-step was soon repeated while the ten formed a single file. Then the first in the column positioned his arms as if holding a bow. And while he was still, the chanting and marching in place continued behind him.

"Your target is the far wall of the agoge," the instructor ordered.

The first in the File mimicked pulling an imaginary arrow from an invisible case, notching it on a pretend bowstring, and drawing back the string with his two fingers and his thumb.

The teacher moved to Zarek's side.

"They move pretty good for being so young," Zarek mentioned.

"Don't let the setup fool you, Lieutenant. As soon as they begin shuffling forward, the formation will fall apart," the teacher warned. Then to his class he instructed. "Your release sequence is the standard five arrows. We'll do two rotations. First position, begin."

The boy at the front mimed notching and firing five arrows in time with the march-step chant. Then, he rolled offline and rushed to the rear of the File.

To the rhythm of *mártios, mártios, step left, step right, mártios,* the next in line moved up. But he neglected to notch a pretend arrow before drawing the bowstring.

The boy behind him coached, "Take arrows from your case."

Another boy scolded the speaker, "Shut up."

"Stay with the chant and maintain your war-dance," the teacher prompted.

The boy at the front finished his five shots, peeled off to the left and the next boy in the column moved forward. This one remembered to run the loading drill before mimicking five releases.

All the while, the Herd chanted, "mártios, mártios, step left, step right, mártios."

"Thank you for the encouragement," the teacher remarked to Zarek. "Most returning officers want to go to advanced classes where they can be idolized by older boys in a Troop. This Herd barely knows they're in archery school."

"Half the time on assignments, I wonder if the archers remember the lessons from the agoge," Zarek replied before heading to the gateway. "I'll pick up my pack when I get back."

The straight column of eight-year-olds had transformed into a wavy line as boys leaned out to speak to friends behind and ahead.

"That's not a Cretan File," their teacher scolded.

Giggles and snickers arose from some of the other circles. Lieutenant Mikolas stopped halfway across the courtyard.

"Is there cause for mirth in the agoge? Has a farmer, fisherman, or an actor stumbled into the school by accident?" Zarek boomed. "In my day, we were too busy practicing our war-dances to laugh at a young Herd. Have things changed?"

No one replied to the officer. But shouting by angry instructors rousted the other Troops off the ground. In moments, all the boys were up and chanting, "Mártios, mártios, step left, step right, mártios."

While the teacher for the eight-year-olds had guided his Herd gently, the instructors for the older Troops managed with harsher discipline. Some kicked slower moving students into position. Others leaned in and demanded the chant be yelled at a throat ripping volume. And all the teachers struck students with their fists and elbows to force the future archers to be precise in their movements.

Lieutenant Zarek Mikolas nodded his approval at the controlled chaos, shifted the strap for the heavy box to a more comfortable position, and marched from the courtyard.

As he walked through the streets of Phalasarna, Zarek remembered his years in the agoge fondly and recalled joyously sharing the challenges with his Troop mates. And yet, he remembered the instructors as being meaner and harsher which seemed in conflict with his sympathetic memories.

***

Built of solid blocks of limestone, the seat of government for western Crete occupied the center of the metropolis.

From the roof, soldiers kept watch over the fortified harbor and the land around the port city. On street level, a crowd of people seeking an audience with the Archon stretched from a doorway to half a block away. Standing between the good order of the government and the masses was a Cretan soldier armed with a spear and a shield.

"Lieutenant Mikolas," Zarek told him. When the spear didn't move aside, the officer of archers proposed. "Tell you what. I'll go stand in line with the Archon's gold and wait. If I get robbed, I'll be sure to tell him you wouldn't let me in."

The spear popped to the soldier's side, clearing the entrance. As he walked by, Zarek noted the arm holding the shield. Old welts and scars marked the sentry's wrist and forearm.

"Couldn't make it as an archer?" Zarek teased as he entered the building.

Once the Lieutenant had gone, the soldier scowled at the remark by the arrogant officer.

***

In the great hall, the Archon of Phalasarna sat on a raised seat. Not so much for his glory, but to allow the magistrate to see his scribes and the representatives seated at desks around him. And conversely, the arrangement identified him to the citizens coming to petition the Archon.

"Lieutenant Mikolas, did you bring my son home safety?" Eugen Admetus yelled when the archer marched into the room.

"I have, Archon. But the archers of the Files work and play rough," Zarek warned. "It may take a day for Sim to sober up before he finds his way home."

"And what of the contract?"

"The raiders have lost too many men to continue raiding the Kingdom," Zarek reported.

"Not too many, I hope," Archon Admetus suggested.

"No, sir. They should be back to raiding by next year."

"My son is home, we have a satisfied customer, and the possibility for a future contract," Admetus exclaimed. Then he slipped into his orator's voice. "It is the duty of every citizen of Crete to be prosperous. Have you and your Files been prosperous, Lieutenant Mikolas?"

"We have, Archon Admetus," Zarek assured the Chief Magistrate. With effort, he bent his knees and straightened quickly. The coins in the box didn't cascade and jingle. Rather the weight of the coins lifted inside the chest and dropped down with a satisfying thud. "Indeed, sir, we have been prosperous."

***

The rest of the afternoon, Zarek went over the accounting sheets with the scribes. In turn, the scribes consulted the coin counting accountants. Finally, one of the accountants slung two sacks of coins over his shoulder and signaled a guard to accompany him. They marched to Zarek.

"Your books are in order," the accountant told him. "It has been agreed that the final payment shall be disbursed."

Lieutenant Mikolas escorted the scribe with the coins and the soldier from the hall, out of the building, and onto the street.

"You've always brought back coins from assignments," the accountant mentioned, "and most of your bowmen. With your record, you could petition for your own Company. Archon Admetus would back you."

"Not once he sees his son," Zarek commented softly, after thinking about pounding the son's face into the deck of the ship.

"Excuse me, Lieutenant?" the scribe inquired. "I didn't catch that."

"I said, this is my last contract," Zarek told him.

The three hiked down from the high section of Phalasarna. They marched quickly through the gates of the defensive wall, by Poseidon's Throne, and made good time crossing to the center of the coastal city.

At the gates to the agoge, Zarek waved for the accountant and guard to go ahead. Then he saluted the sentry on duty and followed the scribe and the bodyguard onto the drill field.

***

Gathered in a loose formation on the far side of the compound, the archers, and Sergeants from Zarek's expedition waited for their pay.

"Files, attention," the Sergeant of First File ordered.

From slouching, the seventy-five healthy archers snapped to attention. Behind them, the eighteen wounded saluted from their mats. The families of the seven buried in the far away kingdom would receive their pay by courier.

On a table, the accountant placed the sacks of coins, an ink container, a pen, and a list of what was owed to each archer.

Zarek slipped off to the side. He remained close enough to settle any disputes, but far enough away to avoid any chance of a payoff. Not that it happened often, but a dishonest officer could excuse an archer from dangerous or dirty duty in exchange for a bribe.

A relatively young man came from behind Zarek and stopped by his side.

"We have two contractors and a Captain looking for archers," Dario Pandarus advised.

Dario was the head of the agoge. One would assume the chief instructor of a military school would be old and wise. Not so, for the Cretan academy. To keep up with the students, the members of the Cosmos, the ruling body of Crete, gave the job to men able to keep up with the overland marches, night maneuvers, and the long days of training.

"I'm retiring, Captain Pandarus," Zarek informed him.

"I've heard," Dario allowed. "But you have knowledge and opinions about most of our archers. I just want you to sit in and help me judge the best men for the jobs. And the right archers for a newly formed Company."

"Will there be wine?" Zarek inquired.

"Yes, Lieutenant Mikolas," Dario assured him, "there will be plenty of wine and platters of food. We need to keep our customers, the new Captain, and our retiring archer happy."

"Then, Captain Pandarus, I'll be happy to drink your wine, and offer my opinion of the selected archers."

Chapter 2 – I Cannot Judge

At a house three blocks from the agoge, the main room glowed with candlelight. Delicious aromas from a feast hung in the air, and the space rang with merriment. Servants hurried to refill bronze goblets with wine and to move bowls of fruit to within reach of a hand, or away from an errant elbow. Much to the servants' irritation, archers by nature used their arms and hands to express themselves and to knock items off tables.

"Why is it, Zarek, you recommended young Sergeant Machaon over your First File NCO?" Tibalt Narcyz inquired.

"My First and Second File leaders are excellent NCOs," Zarek explained to the new Captain. "But Files Four and Five could barely get out of their own way. I put Sergeant Machaon on Third File so he could oversee Four and Five during combat operations."

"And he'll make a good officer?" Tibalt asked.

Zarek studied the Captain. He looked as if he'd just graduated from the agoge.

But, Tibalt Narcyz had worked with King Attalus in central Anatolia. After several years of raiding by the Celts, Attalus drew the barbarians into open combat at Pergamum. With the help of Lieutenant Narcyz and a detachment of

Cretan archers, Attalus defeated the Celts and ran off the horde. For a reward, the King made Narcyz a noble. With a built-in clientele, Tibalt was putting together a five-hundred-man Company to service Anatolia.

"Sergeant Machaon knows men, understands tact, and discipline," Zarek listed. "He'll make a fine officer. For example, I put my worst archer in his File. And after that, I had little trouble with the man until we docked."

"Until you docked?" Dario Pandarus said while laughing. "That has to be a story. Come, Lieutenant, tell the tale."

"Sir, once I got my pay, I am officially a civilian," Zarek explained. "Naming the archer would be bad for him and for me."

One of the contractors seeking Cretan archers for a civil war in a small kingdom sat up and pointed.

"Come on civilian Mikolas, tell us so we can avoid the bowman," he urged.

All through the meal, they had talked about archers from a list. Each was judged for his skills and any negatives were discussed. Based on the Lieutenant's candor in describing the archers, the four men knew they hadn't come across the troublemaker's name.

"Work with us," the second contractor begged. "We only want…"

The front door of the house flew open and slammed loudly against the wall. A few candles died, creating a dark aura around the frame. A big man staggered in from the black night.

"Lieutenant Mikolas, I have a problem with you," Sim Admetus bellowed.

"There's no Lieutenant Mikolas here," Zarek assured him.

"By the Goddess Apate, I am not fooled," Sim responded. "I see you sitting at the table with my own eyes."

Unfortunately, the young man's eyes were black and blue from contact with the deck boards, red rimmed from drinking, and glaring from his temper. Plus, his nose had expanded to twice it's normal size and each nostril showed a little blood from where it was smashed.

"Truly Archer Admetus, the Goddess of Deception has not fooled you," Zarek said trying to sooth the bowman. "Come have a glass but then you must go."

Sim swaggered to the table, reached across the top, snatched up Zarek's goblet, and took a drink.

"Who have we here?" the big bowman inquired. He blinked and focused on Dario. "Captain Pandarus? What are you doing here? Shouldn't you be off beating little boys?"

"Admetus, that's enough," Tibalt instructed. "You've had your fun. Now, get out and leave us to our business."

Sim wobbled and seemed as if he might fall into the table. But he steadied before extending a pair of fingers.

"I know what this is," he sneered while jerking the fingers in the direction of the four attendees. "This is an archer selection conference. And you brought in Lieutenant Mikolas to badmouth me. How many lies about me has he told? What crimes has he laid at my feet? Tell me, so I can defend myself."

"Your name hasn't come up," Dario assured him.

"So, even before I have a say, Mikolas has erased me from the roster," Sim exclaimed. "I am the best bowman in Crete. I put arrows on target with every draw. Ask anyone. They'll tell you."

"I'm sure you are," Tibalt agreed. "But now isn't the time or the place for a demonstration."

Sim scanned the serious faces and chuckled. Then he threw the goblet and stormed out of the house.

The goblet spun, spilling a rooster tail of wine in a wave of red. While the wine did no damage, the bronze foot of the vessel hit Zarek above his right eye. The eyebrow split and a spurt of blood joined the flow of wine. The liquid mixture landed on the tabletop and, a heartbeat later, Zarek Mikolas' head rebounded and splashed down.

"Ugh," he groaned while lifting his wet face from the spill. Zarek blinked, squinted as the pain cleared, and told the gathering. "That was Sim Admetus, the millstone around my neck for the last six months."

"Is he the son of the Archon?" one of the contractors asked.

"That he is," Zarek replied.

"It's no wonder you didn't want to name him," Dario said. He ran a finger down the list, then stopped on the second page. After dipping a finger in his wine, the Captain rubbed out a name. "Let's see, there seems to be a problem on this line. Smudged and unreadable. Let's continue, we'll just skip that name."

"Are you able to continue, Lieutenant?" Tibalt inquired.

"I've suffered more damage with my Troop in the agoge," Zarek insisted. "Although, I need more wine. My cup appears to be empty."

A servant rushed over with a fresh goblet and a rag for the cut. He filled the new one and removed the mug with the blood stain.

After settling down from the disturbance, the men resumed the evaluation process. It continued late into the night.

***

Dario Pandarus and Zarek left the candlelight of the house and strolled into a moonlit night. While rooms were supplied for the new Captain and the contractors, Zarek and Dario had to navigate the dark streets to their quarters at the academy.

"I appreciate your help tonight," Dario offered.

"My Files held a parting of the ways gala and wanted me to attend. Your invitation gave me an excuse to beg off," Zarek remarked. "I've lived with them and tried to set an example for half a year. Tonight, I had fun because I was free to relax, and didn't have to mediate any arguments."

"Except for young Sim," Dario pointed out. "After tonight, he'll never get another posting as an archer. Let's hope he's like his father and better at politics than…"

As if an enraged bull, Sim Admetus bellowed from an alleyway and charged at Zarek. The shape of his knife passed in front of the moon as he drove it downward at the Lieutenant.

With no time to retreat, Zarek Mikolas dropped to a knee. The movement gave him a foot in distance and a moment to pull his hatchet. Once free of the holding ring, he swung the handle up and caught it with his other hand. Holding it steady, Zarek leaned to the side and placed the hatchet handle in the path of the knife.

Once the sica struck the maple handle, Mikolas would hook the big man's wrist, twist it with the underside of the hatched head, and disarm…

Dario's sword came over Zarek's shoulder and the long blade plunged into Sim's unprotected chest. The tip no doubt penetrated his heart as the bellow stopped and the big archer dropped to his knees. He pitched forward and landed face down at Zarek's feet.

Dario froze in the pose of thrusting over Zarek and gasped.

"What have I done?" he muttered. "Phalasarna is my home. And I've murdered the son of my Archon."

Zarek felt Sim's neck but couldn't find an active blood vessels. Then he rolled the body over.

"You just stumbled into a street fight, Captain Pandarus," Zarek stipulated. "Now go. Send the city guard to investigate my claim of self-defense."

"But it was me…"

"No sir, you remember wrong," Zarek insisted. He chopped Sim's chest with his hatchet obliterating the sword wound. "I'm afraid you are fuzzy from too much wine."

"Thank you," Dario offered when he realized Zarek would take the blame for killing Eugen Admetus' son. "I'll be sure we have archers around to take you into custody if the guard Captain wants to hold you."

"For that, I'm grateful," Zarek acknowledged while cutting a defensive wound in the back of his hand. After wrapping the rag from his eyebrow around his hand, he placed Sim's fingers around the sica hilt. Lifting the hatchet, he chopped into the side of the young archer's neck. Once the evidence matched the story, the former Lieutenant tilted his head to Dario and declared. "I'm afraid, I'm in for a long day."

Dario was fifteen steps away when running feet caused him to turn. Five soldiers rushed to surround Zarek and the body.

"You're an archer officer?" one inquired.

Dario was midstride back, when Zarek answered.

"I am. And the dead bowman is Sim Admetus, the son of Archon Admetus."

"Was it an attempted robbery?" the NCO of the patrol demanded. "How many? Which way did they go?"

"Not a robbery. He attacked me, and I defended myself," Zarek replied.

Dario had taken another two steps when a soldier swung his spear. The hardwood end smacked the side of Zarek Mikolas' head, lifting him off his knees. As limp as the blood soaked rag, he crashed to the street and lay as still as a fragment of linen. Rather than insert himself into the violent situation, Dario Pandarus backed away before turning and fast walking from the scene.

***

Lightening flashed, the rumbling of a sick stomach shook Zarek's world, and a sudden bright light blinded him.

"Get on your feet," a voice ordered from the doorway.

In his attempt to follow directions, Zarek rolled onto his belly. Pain shot through his head, taking his breath away.

"I said to get up," the voice scolded. "I haven't got all day to wait for you."

To reinforce the urgency, the soldier kicked Zarek.

A change occurred. From the focus on a major headache, Zarek became acutely aware of the sharp agony of a broken rib. Gathering his hands under his shoulders, the archer pushed to a kneeling position and paused. Involuntarily, he flinched, expecting another kick.

"You two, get him up," another man instructed. "The Archon is waiting."

Hands grasped Zarek, jerked him to his feet, and walked him from the dirty storage room. To his surprise, the sun hung directly overhead. Somehow, he had misplaced half the night and half a day.

***

Rather than the front entrance, the soldiers pushed Zarek through a rear doorway. Once inside, they shoved him down a corridor and into the great hall from a side foyer.

"Lieutenant Mikolas, I am in a quandary for I cannot judge the man who murdered my son," Eugen Admetus announced. "Even as we meet here, his mother is at home bathing and oiling the body of her youngest son."

"It was an accident, Archon," Zarek pleaded. "We had a disagreement that got out of hand."

"I can't and won't dispute that claim," Admetus responded. "In the name of my deceased son, I intend to wrap up this sad episode quickly."

"Then I can go?" Zarek questioned.

"Go? No Lieutenant Mikolas. Not until justice is done."

"Sir, it was an accident in the heat of battle," Zarek asserted.

"My son's viewing starts this afternoon, and I will be there. Do not interrupt me again."

"Yes, Archon," Zarek said.

"After a review of your logs and statements from witnesses, I charge you, Lieutenant Mikolas, with accepting bribes," Eugen Admetus proclaimed. "Further, you stand accused of acts that endangered the archers in your care, and of criminally, sloppy bookkeeping that may cover fraud. For these crimes against the Council of Crete and the brotherhood of archers, I banish you from the western region of our island. For that is as far as my authority goes."

"Archon. The archers would like to hold Lieutenant Mikolas until he leaves the city," Dario requested from the back of the room.

"Captain Pandarus, do you take me for a fool?" Eugen Admetus inquired. "After his crimes against the archers, I'm commending Zarek Mikolas to the city guards for safe keeping. Then at dawn, while I lay my son to rest in his grave, Mikolas will be taken to the outskirts of Phalasarna and left beside the road. This is my final decision."

The Magistrate stepped down from his platform and headed for an exit.

From the rear of the room, Dario yelled to no avail, "Archon Admetus. Archon Admetus. The archers insist."

But Eugen Admetus ignored the Captain's request and a moment later vanished through a doorway.

"Remember me," a soldier whispered in Zarek's ear. He drove the edge of his shield into the back of Zarek's knees. The rear pressure collapsed the archer's legs and he dropped to the floor. Leaning over the archer, the soldiers said. "Yes, I failed the agoge. And now I'm in charge of you."

Zarek shivered at the anger displayed by the man's voice. Many children were asked to leave the archer's agoge for one reason or another. Some were happy to be out of the misery of constant training. Others carried a lifetime of resentment when they were marched from the compound.

"Get up, Lieutenant," the soldier sneered. "It's not my job to be your legs."

"Nor mine," another soldier added. "Arrogant archers think everyone should fawn over them and bow when they walk by. Get up."

On shaky legs, Zarek struggled to stand. But it wasn't injury, at least not yet, that caused the sick feeling in his stomach.

While the Archon couldn't convict Zarek of murder, he had found a way to get revenge for his son. Through doctored logs and false statements, the city's magistrate managed to ruin Zarek's record of service and his reputation. Now, Zarek faced an uncertain day and night until he was ejected from the city. And while the soldiers wouldn't kill him, they most likely had orders to make his journey away from Phalasarna as painful as possible.

***

With the sunrise came wailing and words of lament from the procession moving slowly to the graveyard. From another city gate, screams of agony rose from a hand cart.

"Hurts, doesn't it, archer?" a soldier teased. "You shouldn't have moved when I swung the club."

At a crossroads outside of Phalasarna, the guard tilted the cart and dumped Zarek into the grass. With a final chuckle, he wheeled the cart and strolled back to the city.

At the grave site, priests and mourners cried, prayed, and begged the Gods to hurry Sim Admetus' soul along on his journey. For the burial, funeral goers filled the air with their voices.

Alone near the crossroads, Zarek Mikolas cried, hugged his shattered knee, and coughed from the chest pain of a broken rib. Then, a soft whistle sounded from the tall grass on the far side of the crossroads. In response, ten youths popped up from the concealment and raced to the injured man.

"Hold still Lieutenant Mikolas," one instructed. He pried Zarek's hands from the knee and studied the damage. "I can straighten and stabilize it. But, sir, you won't know the real damage until the swelling goes down."

Two other boys stripped Zarek, and the medic noted the bruising around the ribs. He unrolled a bandage while the two washed the Lieutenant. After binding his chest, they dressed him in clean clothes.

"Are you hungry, sir?" another boy inquired.

"Thirsty," Zarek replied. "Who are you?"

"Third and fourth year agoge Herds, sir," he replied while holding a waterskin up to Zarek's mouth. "Compliments of Captain Pandarus. He said you got caught up in a powerful man's grip."

"Is there a lesson in that?" Zarek inquired.

"Yes, sir. Stay away from powerful people and don't aspire to be an officer."

"I can't argue with that," Zarek admitted. "Did you think to bring me a crutch? I don't know if I can walk without help."

"Captain Pandarus arranged transportation, sir," the medic informed him.

Braying came from another area and a donkey climbed to its feet. A little irate at being kept down, the animal shook to show displeasure. While a handler calmed the beast, a gang of boys assembled a cart.

Moments later, Zarek was lifted to his feet. Reaching out, he scratched behind the donkey's ear.

"Get me home girl," he promised, "and you'll always be treated well."

They eased him into the bed of the cart. His long pack and both bow cases were dropped in beside him.

"Sir, we must get back for the Prowess before we're missed. Do you need anything else?"

"No. Thank you."

The boys ran towards the city walls, then they vanished into the weeds. But the Herds hadn't performed a magic trick. Following their training, they were crawling like ants undercover of the tall growth.

Zarek Mikolas' head hurt, his knee throbbed, and his chest ached. But he was alive. And although exiled from Phalasarna and western Crete, he felt a small comfort because some in the agoge knew the truth.

Fighting off nausea, the former Lieutenant of archers scooted to a sitting position. With a snap of the reins, he put the cart in motion. They bumped onto the road and his vision blurred. Partially blind, Zarek guided the donkey onto the eastward route before passing out.

Without encouragement, most draft animals would stop, and graze. The donkey, however, glanced back at her unconscious passenger. Then she wiggled her ears, gathered her strength, and steadily pulled the cart away from the port city.

Chapter 3 – The Widow of Zoniana

Neysa Kasia shoved the three-pronged garden fork into the soil. Once the dirt lifted and crumbled, she grabbed a handful of stems and pulled up a bunch of carrots. After tossing the carrots into a basket, Neysa pushed the fork into another section.

"Neysa, I'm done and heading home," Dryas Kasia called.

The skinny teen stood shirtless with an ax in one hand and a serious expression on his face. Around his legs were pieces of split lumber.

Neysa's heart ached. Dryas resembled her dead husband so much, it hurt.

"If you start a new stack of firewood for me, I'll give you a second basket of carrots," she offered her young brother-in-law. "You can take one to your mother and sell the other one in the market."

His stoic countenance exploded into an adolescent's wide-eyed look of glee.

"I'll trade them for a new wooden bowl," he proposed. "I'll sell that for a bronze coin. Then I'll use the coin to buy a copper pot. And next, I'll make a profit from selling the pot. Who knows where it could lead? With my bartering skills, I may turn that basket of carrots into a fortune."

"Stack the firewood first, Master Kasia," she teased.

Dryas' older brother had gone to the agoge and graduated as a bowman. After a few foreign contracts, he came home to the city of Eleutherna with a sack of coins and a proposal on his lips. The older Kasia brother married Neysa and together they bought a farm in Zoniana. Then a year ago, archer Kasia died during a border dispute somewhere in Egyptian territory.

Having a dead older brother, who boasted the title of Cretan archer, left Dryas trying to live up to a myth. His mother had refused to allow Dryas to attend the agoge, trapping the boy at home. Now the teen helped his mother tend the family's olive grove and his father with the seal stone craft. And three times a week, he traveled five miles to the village of Zoniana where he helped his sister-in-law with her farm.

Although he was cherished by the family, Dryas hungered to go out and make his mark on the world.

"You know, I could be a city magistrate one day," he exclaimed.

"I've no doubt, a bright man like you could accomplish anything he put his mind to," Neysa assured him. "But first, *Odysseus*, stack the firewood."

"After the battle for Troy, King Odysseus traveled the world for ten years," Dryas related while picking up an armload of wood. "Imagine, traveling to exotic places for ten years."

"Or walking ten steps to the woodpile," Neysa coached before going back to harvesting carrots.

***

Fevered dreams of trees passing carried Zarek Mikolas eastward. Memories of the occasional stream and the snapping of reins to get the donkey moving were but flashes of remembrance. Nights under the stars, filled with discomfort and throbbing, seemed but endless bad dreams.

On the third day out from Phalasarna, the donkey cart met two men.

"What have we here?" one asked.

Zarek, curled up on his good side, eased his arm under his body. Before he could lift off the bed of the cart, the donkey broke into a gallop.

"Get back here," one of the strangers called while reaching for the reins.

But the donkey's sudden burst of speed took him by surprise.

The second man threw a rock at the racing donkey cart, and asked, "Did you see the two bow cases?"

"It would have been a nice find," the first acknowledged.

Zarek noted the rock and the attitude of the two men.

"I didn't like their looks either," he said to the donkey. "You need a name. Let me think on it."

He didn't think overly long. The donkey's pace soon left the pair far behind, but the agony of riding on a bouncing cart drained Zarek. He fell back into a stupor.

Late in the day, the cart stopped, and voices drifted to Zarek. Afraid the men had chased down the cart, he drew his knife and sat up. Dizziness washed over the archer, forcing him to put both hands on the cart bed to keep from falling over.

"She's young but an old soul," a man spoke from behind the cart. He held a ladle in one hand. "Supper is almost ready, are you hungry?"

"Who are you? Where am I? Who is an old soul?"

"Your donkey pulled off the road to greet my team," he replied. "I gave her some straw and let you sleep. My wife said to wake you for supper."

Zarek scooted to the end of the cart and groaned when his right leg fell over the edge. Ignoring the ache in his knee, he limped to a log beside a cookfire.

"Thank you for taking care of my donkey," he acknowledged the man's kindness. A middle-aged woman handed him a bowl of stew and he added. "And for feeding me."

"My uncle was an archer," the woman said while pointing at the cart. "When he died, we discovered that no one could pull the string of his war bow and hit a target with it. So, my father displayed the bow and the case on the wall of our dining hall."

"It takes strength and a few years of training to handle a war bow. I'm sorry for the loss of your uncle."

"We're heading home to Aptera," the husband mentioned. "You look like you could use a few days off the trail. Why don't you come home with us and rest?"

"I'm afraid Aptera won't do," Zarek replied. Then, changing the subject to avoid talking about his exile from the west, he asked. "What did you mean the donkey is an old soul."

"She strolled into our camp as if she'd been here before," the man answered. "Like she was immortal, and we're just visiting her in this field."

"Tansy would be a good name for a donkey," Zarek offered.

"The word for immortality is as good a name as any," the man remarked. "If you're the kind of person who names their work animals."

"I wouldn't have before this trip," the archer admitted. "But she's taken care of me like a sister. And a sister needs a name."

"More stew?" the woman inquired.

"Yes, please," Zarek replied. "Then, I'm going to try and unstrap Tansy and rub her down. She's been in harness for too long."

"I'll give you a hand," the man offered.

***

Dryas Kasia scrubbed the carrots until the vegetables shined and the green stems glowed. He walked into Eleutherna with the basket of produce, marched through town, and proceeded down the hill to the market.

As he entered the agorá, a vendor with a crowd around his stall announced, "See this linen. It's direct from Egyptian weavers and colored in their secret dyes. Come feel this linen."

Dryas chuckled at the description. The material was probably from cotton grown on the mainland and woven by a spinster in a neighboring village. After finding an open spot, he squatted behind his basket and waited for a buyer. Few noticed him, less looked at the carrots, and none stopped. Frustrated at being ignored, Dryas thought about the linen seller's speech.

"See the royal vegetable," he shouted. The light purple hue of the produce was hardly royal purple. But the portrayal drew the eyes of a few shoppers. "These selected carrots are the favorite snack of Pharaohs, and a delicacy in the feasting halls of barbarian Kings worldwide."

Oddly enough, his boast almost seemed true when compared to other vendors with carrots. While their produce still had dirt from the harvest, Dryas' carrots were cleaned and polished to reveal the color.

"Where did you get these?" a woman asked.

"A secret garden on Mount Ida," the teen whispered as if trying to keep the information confidential. "There the soil is dampened by the morning mist and the rows are tended by mountain spirits."

Several women gather around.

"How can that be?" one demanded.

"How could it not?" Dryas countered. "No crops grow up there. It has to be the garden of a nymph."

"I'll take a handful," a woman announced.

She shoved a bronze coin at the teen before taking a bunch. Seeing the first one buy, other shoppers thrust coins at the teen and grabbed carrots until the basket sat empty.

"Do you have more?" a disappointed customer inquired.

"Unfortunately, no," Dryas informed her. "The supply is limited because it's hard to steal from a nymph."

"It is indeed," she allowed before strolling to another vendor.

Dryas Kasia opened his fist and stared at the bronze coins. Forgetting about the bowl, and the copper pot, he grabbed the basket and ran home.

The youth had learned a valuable lesson. Many people had produce or products for sale. What separated the common vendors from the successful was a good story.

***

On top of the sadness at losing her husband, Neysa Kasia regretted they never had a baby. Of course, with a little one to care for, she couldn't handle the farm.

"Now there's an odd thought," Neysa commented while straightening her back and stretching. The hoe had a rough spot in the handle that produced a blister on her right hand. "Just when rotating the soil gets hard, I go looking for a baby to get me out of the work. Goddess Leto, if you were listening, I don't need or want a child."

Happy to have appeased the Goddess of Motherhood, Neysa returned to tilling the soil. Not long after the break, a familiar voice called from the trail.

"Neysa, I need more carrots," Dryas shouted. "I need more carrots. I can turn them into bronze."

He raced across the partially turned soil with a wide grin on his face.

"You can't eat bronze," Neysa warned. "My carrots are packed in sawdust and stored in the root cellar. If there's a shortage of the vegetable, I'm sure they'll only go up in value in a couple of months."

"No. No. It's not a shortage," Dryas assured her. "It's me. I can sell anything."

"If you can trade anything, why do you need carrots?"

The teen took a step back as if hit by a sack of grain. Then his eyes opened wide, and he gushed, "That's right. I can sell lots of things. What should I sell?"

"The radishes are almost ready for harvesting," she suggested. "But that will be in another week or so."

Seeing the teen sag from the recommendation, Neysa thought for a moment.

"Your brother's hunting bow is in the house," she told him. "I was saving it for when you were older. But you can have it now. Whether you use it or sell it, I don't care. If you're ready, the bow is yours."

Dryas dropped as if his strings had been cut. From sitting on the ground, he looked up at Neysa.

"I didn't know you were saving it for me," he admitted. "I thought you'd give it to Zarek."

"My brother is a master archer. If he needs a hunting bow, he can make one," she replied. "Do you want your brother's bow or not? Please decide. I have rows to hoe before dark."

"I'll take it."

***

The hill town of Eleutherna was nestled in the foothills about six and a half miles from the coast. Dryas Kasia had no intention of going that far. After a week of trading and buying, he had a stack of quality goods but no customers in his town for the items. Figuring the people in the villages along the route to the sea would be interested, he left home early in the morning.

On his back were copper pots, a few lengths of quality rope, some steel tools, and seal stones on consignment from his father.

Once he had the load balanced on his back, he complained, "If I knew being a trader would make me a pack animal, I'd have stuck to tending the olive grove."

But he had every coin he made from selling his brother's bow invested in the merchandise. It was not the time to give up on his chosen profession.

At the first village out of Eleutherna, farmers bought his rope. Farther down the trail, he sold his steel tools. At the next town, he traded in the copper pots for two she goats. Flush with cash, he thought about turning back. But he had the seal stones and two goats, so he continued northward.

On a rise before the land fell to the coastal plain, Dryas walked into the town of Kirianna. From the main street, he saw the sea for the first time.

"Maybe I should become a fisherman," he pondered while gazing at the blue haze.

Then a voice called, "Dryas. Dryas Kasia. Come here boy."

He turned to see a donkey, a cart, and Neysa's brother sitting under a shade tree.

"Zarek?" he asked.

"It is. And I need your help," Zarek told him. "I need a hot meal and feed for the donkey. Do you have any coins I could borrow?"

***

Neysa Kasia yanked a radish from the soil. After dusting it off with her hands, she inspected the coarse black skin. Once satisfied there was no sign of blight, the widow of Zoniana pulled a knife and sliced the vegetable in half. The color of fresh cream, the pulp was firm to the touch, crisp when she bit into the center, and pungent on her tongue.

"Dryas will have no trouble selling his share of these," she said while eating the rest of the radish.

With the crop ready, she separated two baskets, placed them beside the rows and began pulling radishes.

"Neysa. Come see what I found," the teen called from the house.

"That boy could interrupt one of Zeus' lightning bolts," she whined.

But he was a good soul. Putting down the hand shovel, she turned as she rose.

A donkey and cart sat in front of the house. For a moment, she wondered if Dryas had bought a cart for his trading business. Then, Zarek sat up, smiled, waved at her, and slid to the rear of the cart.

When her big brother crashed to the ground, Neysa squealed and sprinted to help him.

***

The night fell and a fire crackled in the fireplace. Neysa and Dryas sat listening to the rough breathing of the archer. When it stopped, they tensed, waiting to see if the breathing would continue.

"Neysa. I'm sorry to come home all broken up," Zarek muttered. "I'll leave once I've healed."

Neysa and Dryas looked at the shape under the blanket. Although neither noticed the other, they both smiled. But only Neysa said the words the brother-in-law and sister-in-law thought.

"At least you made it home, big brother," she assured him. "You can stay as long as you want."

To Zarek Mikolas the words were garbled as he drifted off to sleep. But the soothing tone and reassuring voice of his sister let him know he was safe and among family.

Act 2

Chapter 4 – Leto's Gift

During the warm summer months, Zarek's ribs healed, and he regained his strength. Unfortunately for the archer, his knee remained stiff and the leg limited to partially bending. While the injury made getting down and up and walking a problem, it's didn't stop him from chopping down trees.

"We can't plant in the shade of that hill," Neysa remarked.

"But we can use the lumber to build an addition to the house and to fill out our stack of firewood," Zarek informed her. He rested the ax handle on his shoulder and pointed at the steep grade. "And the hill will stop the arrows."

"You're building a range," she guessed. "I'm sure you'll need to stay in practice for your next contract. But why leave those two trees?"

Neysa reached out and patted two trunks that stood in the middle of the cleared area.

"Those are maple," Zarek answered. "I plan on an occupation beyond being your crippled fieldhand."

"You're my brother. You can stay forever," Neysa proclaimed. Then she thought about what he said. "What occupation?"

"Maple trees," he explained while tapping the bark. "As part of the addition, I want to build a work shed. Once I can keep the maple dry, I'll harvest these two, and let the wood season in the shed."

"Bows? You're going to make bows," she guessed.

"And Dryas is going to sell them."

"What a marvelous idea," Neysa said. "Does that mean you're staying."

"Sister, I've been telling you all summer, I'm retired."

"I know. But until now, brother, I didn't believe you."

***

On his next trip to the farm, Dryas Kasia brought the donkey and a load of grain.

"I'm returning Tansy and the cart," he told Zarek as he lifted a sack. "She's levelheaded and easy to work with. But I need more pulling power for my new vendor's wagon."

"We can use her to help drag logs," Zarek said. He pulled a sack from the cart and placed it on his shoulder. "Tell me. If you had bows to sell, which kind would you want?"

The archer took three steps and stumbled. Off balance on the bad leg, he would have fallen except the donkey moved. Her side and back provided a stable surface for Zarek. He steadied and shifted the sack of grain to better distribute the weight.

"That donkey is smart," Dryas noted.

"She's saved me more than once," Zarek declared. "What about those bows?"

"Few people want to buy a self-bow. They don't see the value of the craftsmanship for a single piece bow. However, everyone wants a hunting bow for game and protection. So, there's a big customer base for those," Dryas described as the two walked to the house. "But a lot of craftsmen make hunting bows for birds, hares, and deer. That keeps the prices down and the quality of the bows low."

"What about war bows?" Zarek inquired as they dropped the sacks into a bin.

"There are less customers, but they will pay handsomely for a bow that can take down a wild pigs or a man," the young businessman listed. "Especially for farmers with wolf and mountain lion problems. But there's a bigger shortage in that profit center."

Neysa stood in the doorway watching them.

"Where did you learn to talk like that?" she interrupted. "Just yesterday, you were a boy spouting dreams. Now, you sound like a man of property."

"At every market I attend, I talk to the other sellers," Dryas replied. "I listen and learn while I sell my merchandise."

"What did you call it, a profit what?" Zarek inquired.

"All items are categorized," he answered. "And every item in a category is ranked by their trading value. For bows, the types and quality of the bows bring different prices. But another part of the weapon's category are quality arrows. They are in demand. Thus, arrows bring a decent price which makes them a profit center."

"We'll need to catch, clip, and start raising geese," Zarek muttered as if his mind was far away.

"You want to add birds to the farm?" Neysa questioned.

"I can get you a fair price on laying chickens," Dryas offered.

"Chickens would be fine," the archer told them. "But their feathers are too short for arrows. We need goose feathers for the fletching on our shafts."

"It appears, we'll need another building on the farm," Neysa informed her brother.

"Another structure? Whatever for, sister?"

"We need a temple to the Goddess Artemis. And instead of drawings or sculptures symbolizing her interest, we'll have real bows, arrows, and quivers, to honor the Goddess."

"This sounds like a good business plan," Dryas exclaimed. "When will you start?"

"You and I will start in the morning, right after breakfast," Zarek replied.

"Start what?" the young man asked.

"Building a shed," Neysa told her brother-in-law.

***

Pine wood seasoned and aged quickly allowing Zarek to construct arrows first. Although the iron ore for the arrowheads presented more of a challenge. The ore mines were located in the hills above the town of Kydonia in western Crete. And while Zarek was forbidden to travel there, Dryas Kasia developed trading stops along the route. By late winter, the arrows sold by vendor Kasia were developing a following.

"Who is making these for you?" an archer inquired while balancing an arrow across the back of two fingers. "The weight is good, the spines are uniformly stiff, and the arrowheads and shafts are consistent. I don't even have to sort them when I draw a handful from my quiver."

"I'll tell you. But you must keep it a secret," Dryas confided in the bowman. "A shepherd discovered an ancient temple dedicated to Artemis in the foothills. When the Goddess visits, some of her arrows spill out. The herder brings them to me."

"Do you expect me to believe these are arrows from the Goddess?" the archer demanded.

"I'm not expecting you to believe anything," Dryas commented to the man. "Just look closely at the glue near the feathers."

The archer spun the arrow, examining the spaces between the fletching. Stamped in the shaft near the rear bindings was the name Artemis.

"If they aren't from the Goddess, they certainly are dedicated to her," the archer announced.

"Please, sir, let's keep this between us," Dryas begged. "If more archers knew, I'd be swamped with customers."

"You can trust me," the bowman assured him.

***

On his next trip to the town, ten archers rushed the wagon and Dryas quickly sold out of the fine arrows. But he didn't worry, the crowd also bought his other wares.

"It's going to rain," a bowman offered while peering at a bank of clouds. "I'm glad we aren't at sea."

"I remember that contract and the storm," another in the group commiserated. "We almost drowned."

"We made it back to port. But another of our merchant ships crashed on rocks. Miles of cargo washed up on the beach but no bodies. Or, so I've heard."

"The thought of being eaten by a sea monster makes my skin crawl."

Even while he bought, sold, and traded, Dryas Kasia listened to the archers talk. He didn't think much of sea monsters, but the idea of merchandise washing up on shore intrigued him.

Then clouds closed in, and the sky opened. Drenched, the shoppers ran for shelter and Dryas snapped the reins on his mule team.

One lesson he learned, *"Once you finish trading, get out of town. Too many unsavory people know you have loose coins. If they can find you, they will help themselves to your profits."*

As he drove through the pouring rain, he made a commitment. If the God Poseidon was going to wash merchandise up on a beach, Dryas would drive the coastal route, looking for the God's rejects.

***

Unknown to the trader, the storm raced down the Adriatic Sea and into the Ionian. Once it cleared the Ionian Sea of shipping, the squalls lashed Lacedaemon with torrents of rain and high winds. It plowed into the Mediterranean and, freed from land obstructions, the unhindered winds swirled in a left-handed direction. In years gone by, the winds would have pushed ships away from the Island of Crete. In any other year, the storm wouldn't have raced to the coast of Africa, allowing the left turning winds to circle the Sea of Crete.

In the grasp of gusting winds and surging waves, a Roman warship rolled and pitched but survived. Even when she turned sideways, the oarsmen fought to out row the storm. In spite of their heroic struggles, before the crew could regain control, the rocks on the northern coast of Crete punched in the starboard side of the hull. For a few moments, the ship hung motionless. Wind howled across her stationary deck, blinding rain drenched the crew and passengers, and the sea ebbed just below her keel. Then, as if the vessel offended him, Poseidon sent an enormous wave to dislodge the ship.

On the slick deck, the wave knocked adults off their feet. Weighted down by their years and size, they fell and rolled. The wave as if fingers raking sand clawed them into the sea. But one body, that of a child, wasn't tripped by the deluge of water. Lifted from the ship's boards, the small boy rode the crest up the tilted deck, through the air, and down onto the beach. The water that deposited the youth on the sand, returned to the sea, transporting the warship and its passengers into the depths.

***

The litter on the shoreline was a clear sign of a recent shipwreck. Mostly composed of long oars made of fir, a rolled section of sail, pieces of wooden decking, and tatters of cloth. To the trader's eyes, Poseidon's rejects had little value.

But Dryas Kasia started his business with a basket of carrots. No matter the value, any trader with that humble legend for a beginning couldn't ignore free merchandise. He guided the team to the side of the trail and halted the mules.

"I guess I could sell the oars and the sail rig to fishermen," he mentioned while tethering the animals. "The rest at best is firewood."

Picking his footing carefully, Dryas worked his way through tall grass until he reached the beach. Starting from the last oar, he picked up an armload, and carried the long fir poles to his wagon. On another trip, he hoisted the sail rig to his shoulder and hauled it to the transport. Another jaunt to the shoreline produced a few more oars and broken pieces of pine.

"I think we've picked the beach clean of anything of value," he declared. Before untying the legs of the mules, he scanned the beach a final time. As he turned, a movement and a flash caught his eyes. "It appears, we might have missed a coin. Perhaps a sack or a chest of gold."

Attracted by the enthusiasm of their master's voice, the mules looked at Dryas.

"What? It could happen. I could find a treasure on this very beach."

The mules turned away and Dryas moved towards the shoreline.

He discounted the movement as a drying piece of cloth blowing in the soft morning breeze. It was the brief reflection of the sun he wanted to investigate. Following the same path through the grass, Dryas reached the sand, and strolled to the pile of fabric. It moved and something metallic reflected the sun again. Rushing forward the last ten steps, Dryas Kasia stopped and looked down at a toddler.

Dryas glanced up and down the beach, trying to see who had dropped a child on the sand. On the little one's chest, a bronze medallion on a silver chain reflected the sun as if the Goddess Leto was winking at him.

"I don't need a brat," he announced. Then he thought for a moment and said to the sky. "But my sister-in-law does."

Scooping the small body off the sand, Dryas carried the child to his wagon.

"So, you're a boy," he discovered while stripping the damp tunic off the child. "Someday, you'll be able to help around the farm."

Before dressing the boy in warmer material, Dryas lifted the chain and medallion and dropped them into a pouch.

"My finder's fee," he uttered while holding a waterskin to the boy's mouth.

Dressed in clean dry clothes, and his thirst sated, the boy fell asleep. Dryas untethered the mules, and soon they pulled onto the trail.

As the wagon rolled away, Dryas peered over his shoulder at the beach.

"How could a small child be the only survivor of a shipwreck?" he pondered. ***

Zarek leaned on Tansy's neck as the donkey started down the steep hill. On flatland or even on gradual mounds, the archer managed. But for steep elevations, he found leaning on Tansy helped propel him up and down the inclines.

Over the donkey's shoulders were a quiver of arrows and a war bow. Draped across her haunches was the reason for the climb.

"Venison? That's where you went this morning. Need I remind you, there's smaller game closer to the farm," Neysa Kasia pointed out. Then she noted the exhausted state of her brother and the proud set of his shoulders. "We can use the hide for a blanket and salt the venison for later. After we feast on our fill of deer meat, of course."

"We will feast, but there'll be no blanket," Zarek informed his sister. "I need the hide and sinew for the bows."

In the shed, stacks of pine shafts dried while waiting for final shaping and assembly. Beside them, large wedges of maple logs dried and aged on a stand.

"You're going to start a bow," Neysa exclaimed. "I'm so happy for you. We need to do something to mark this momentous occasion."

"If Dryas ever brings me the kri-kri horns, it'll be a special day," Zarek remarked. He elbowed Tansy forward. "I'll start dressing the deer. If you bring a container, we'll save the intestines."

"You cut and I'll catch," Neysa commented. They both turned at the sight of Dryas' wagon and mule team coming through the trees. She suggested. "Maybe he has your goat horns."

"You never know what that boy is bringing," Zarek remarked. "From the look of him, it'll be something special. I've never seen him so animated."

***

Dryas reined in the mules, stood on the seat bench of the wagon, and bent at the waist. Sweeping his arm in a low arc, he straightened and held both arms above his shoulders as if receiving recognition for a heroic deed.

"I am possibly the greatest trader in all the world," he announced.

"Finding me a set of kri-kri horns is hardly earth shattering," Zarek responded to the boast.

"The Kasia Trading Group..."

"Now you're a Trading Group?" Neysa questioned.

"As I was saying, the Kasia Trading Group proudly announces our newest partner," Dryas proclaim.

Neysa searched the area. Not seeing another person, she inquired. "Is he invisible?"

"No, he's right here," the trader announced.

Reaching behind the seat, he lifted the boy and held him at arms' length.

"It's a toddler," Neysa declared. "What are you doing with a child. Dear Goddess, don't tell me you're trading in children. That's terrible."

"No, no. I found this one washed ashore at a shipwreck."

"Surely there were other survivors," Zarek offered.

"Nope. Just this little guy laying wet and cold in the sand," Dryas responded. "I thought to sell him at the market, unless..."

Neysa ran to the wagon, snatched the child from her brother-in-law and scolded, "You'll do nothing of the sort, Dryas Kasia. This is a gift from Leto."

While his sister strolled away cooing at the child, Zarek smirked at Dryas.

"How about you get a container and help me dress out this deer."

"Absolutely. Anything is better than taking care of a child."

"You weren't really going to sell it, were you?"

"I hear children bring a good price."

"Better than kri-kri horns?"

"Now mountain goat horns are hard to come by."

"I thought you were the greatest trader in all the world," Zarek remarked.

"I'm working on the horns," Dryas promised. "Let me unharness the mules and get a bucket. Then we'll take care of that deer."

Chapter 5 – Jace's Choice

Early spring found Neysa on her knees, digging a channel for planting.

"Jace Kasia, leave that alone," she scolded the active child.

"Tansy," he said, holding up his dirty hands.

"No. Tansy didn't lose that," Neysa instructed. "That's manure. We'll put it into the trench with the roots."

Jace grabbed a double handful and dropped it on top of the strings of asparagus roots.

"That's the idea," she coached. "But a little less on each plant."

When she scooped water out of a container and sprinkled it on top of a buried root crown, Jace watched carefully. At the next plant, he slapped the surface of the water and a portion spilled out of the bucket and over the roots.

"Again, you are very helpful," she coached. "But a little less water. A farmer does everything in moderation."

"Moderation," Jace said tripping over the syllables. "Everything."

"That's right," she agreed.

***

Two years later, Jace Kasia bent, snapped off an asparagus stalk, and placed it in a basket.

"Remember, we only pick the ones high enough to fit in my pot," Neysa told the six-year-old.

While she harvested one row, the boy picked from the neighboring row of plants.

"I know that," he insisted. "When is uncle coming?"

"Dryas is very prosperous," Neysa replied. "He's managing three trading wagons. And that keeps him busy."

"He needs to learn moderation," Jace stated as if he had just discovered the concept.

"That's not a word I'd use to describe Dryas," she remarked.

They picked and moved down the rows for part of the morning. When the sun hung between the horizon and noon, a wagon came through the trees.

"Uncle Dryas is here," Jace shouted. "Uncle Dryas is here."

"I have eyes," Neysa told him. "Finish the row and take the asparagus to the house. Then you can go visit with your uncle."

As fast as his little hands could snap off stalks, Jace picked and tossed them into the container. After the last bunch, he struggled to lift the basket of stalks. Gritting his teeth, the boy held the handle with two hands, pulled the rim to his stomach, and walked bandy legged to the house.

"What do you have there, little man?" Dryas inquired.

He hopped off the wagon and stood by the mule team.

"I've been picking asparagus," Jace got out between hard breaths.

"No, no, not simply asparagus," the trader corrected. "What you have there are spears of passion. A fine representation of a vegetable that would make the Goddess of Love, Aphrodite, blush."

"Dryas stop teaching the boy to sell," Neysa reprimanded him. "Not everything is a commodity."

"Ah, but there, sister, your superb intellect falls short of reality," Dryas corrected her. "You see everything is a product. Either for personal consumption or as a profit center if it can be built, transported, and sold. Take for example this load of rich iron ore. From this Zarek will create arrowheads. Then he'll affix them to shafts, use hide glue to attach goose feathers, and create arrows dedicated to the Goddess Artemis."

"The only connection to Artemis is the stone stamp your father made for you," Neysa snorted. "Those marks in the glue hardly make the arrows unique."

"It's the story that sells," Dryas explained. "People need to buy. But to make them buy my merchandise, they must have an emotional connection to the product."

"Emotional connection," Jace repeated. "It's what people buy."

"See, the little man understands."

"You two are impossible," Neysa complained. "Jace, carry the Goddess' spears to the house. Then you can go play with the boys."

"We'll be shoveling ore, the source of all things iron," Dryas boasted. "It's not play, woman, it's men's work."

"You go do whatever it is men do to waste a day," she said. "Then clean up and come enjoy the fruits of my labor."

"Yes, ma'am," Dryas agreed. "Oh, remind me later, I have a gift for Jace."

"For me? What?" the boy asked.

"Later. First get those beautiful spears to the kitchen," the trader instructed.

Neysa and Jace carried their baskets to the house. Taking hold of the harness, Dryas walked the mules and wagon around back of the shed.

"About time you got me more ore," Zarek commented while he worked a sharp blade back and forth on an arrow shaft. With each scrape, small shavings came off the pine rod, fell to the floor, and pooled at the archer's feet. "I'm deliberating if I should start a war bow this afternoon. What do you think?"

Dryas pulled a cover off the back of the wagon to reveal rocks with wide bands of reddish material.

"I can sell a war bow for a fair price," he assured the archer. "But you're going to have to make stiffer arrows for it."

"That I know," Zarek informed him. He put down the rod and blade. "I heard you say you brought something for Jace."

"It's a numbers chart so he can learn to count and report quantities," Dryas told him. He reached behind the driver's bench and lifted out a scroll. "He'll need that skill when he comes to work with me."

"You think he'll give up farming to follow you into business?"

"I do."

"Do what, Uncle Dryas?" Jace asked.

He came from around the shed, trying to look calm. But Dryas and Zarek could tell he ran from the house by the rising and falling of his chest.

"Read a numbers chart. Now you sit over there and study it while the archer and I unload the ore."

"I can help."

"Maybe when you get bigger. For now, you study."

***

Two years later, Dryas walked another wagon load of ore around the shed.

"How about a little help?" he asked.

Eight-year-old Jace sat on a stump with the well-used scroll in his hands.

"That wagon is *gamma* by *epsilon,* and you have about a *beta's* worth of ore," Jace declared. "Am I right?"

Dryas beamed at the boy.

"You are correct, little man," he acknowledged. "The wagon bed is three by five feet, and the ore is two feet deep. But you know something else?"

"What's that uncle?"

"The ore isn't going to unload itself. Grab a shovel."

***

After supper, Neysa, Dryas, and Zarek sat around the fireplace while Jace practiced his letters on a sand tablet.

"Jace put that away for now and come over here," Neysa requested.

Carefully, so as not to spill any of the fine sand, he put the tablet on the floor and slowly pushed it under his bed.

"Yes, ma'am, I'm here," he said as he approached the fireplace.

Neysa slipped an arm around his small waist and hugged him.

"You're eight years old," she noted. "It's time you decided on a trade. If you want to be a farmer, I'll buy you some goats, and give you a plot of land. You'll continue to help me, but the profits from what you grow and the cheese you make will be yours."

Jace hung his head, rubbed his hands together, and shuffled his feet.

"That's one choice, Jace," Neysa assured him. "You don't have to be a farmer."

"You can come to work for me," Dryas offered. "You'll learn the routes, see most of the island, and meet interesting people. I'll teach you to sell and, in a few years, I'll buy you a wagon and a team. You'll be my partner in business. How does that sound?"

Jace bit his lip and stared at the fire so hard, the three adults glanced at the flames to be sure nothing was burning outside the fireplace.

"What is it, dear?" Neysa asked after long moments of silence.

"I enjoy helping you on the farm. But moderation isn't, ah, to my liking," Jace explained. "Uncle Dryas, oh, the stories you tell. And the wisdom of how to use words to get what you want is wonderful. Your language has surely been passed down from the Gods on Mount Olympus."

"That's an excellent expression, little man. But I've a feeling you're selling me something?" Dryas suspected. "Are you afraid you'll miss Neysa and the farm? We can make more stops here if that's what's bothering you."

"No, sir," Jace replied. "Trading goods and counting coins maybe a respectable job. But it's not for me."

"Well, if you don't want to be a framer or a trader, what do you want?" Neysa inquired.

"I want to be an archer, like Uncle Mikolas."

"No, absolutely not," Zarek exploded. He jumped to his feet and stormed out of the house. As the door closed behind him, they heard him repeat. "Absolutely not."

Jace stood crestfallen and dejected.

"Do you really want to be an archer?" Neysa inquired.

"I do, oh, I most certainly do," the boy gushed. "I want to be a master archer like Uncle Mikolas."

"You've asked for the one thing I can't help you with," she explained. "Archers have their own ways, and they keep the mysteries of the bow to themselves. But I know this. If you want it, you'll have to motivate Zarek to take you on as an apprentice."

"I'll do anything," Jace assured her.

"It's not me you need to convince," she informed the boy while pushing him towards the door. "You need to persuade Zarek that you're worthy."

Jace ran to the door, opened it, and raced after the master archer.

***

Zarek stood facing the workbench. His broad back to the entrance of the shed, he worked on shaving an arrow's shaft.

"I want to be an archer," Jace stated.

"You don't want to go through that much pain, boy. Be a farmer, be a trader. Or go into Eleutherna and apprentice to be a potter or a leather worker."

"I want to be an archer," Jace insisted.

"Go to the range and stand there," Zarek instructed without turning around.

"Why?" Jace inquired.

"You don't want to be an archer."

"I do. Teach me."

"Go stand at the range."

For an eight-year-old, the simple direction without context seemed absurd. Yet, the second time Zarek said it, Jace realized that following orders was important for an archer. Jace left the shed and marched to the range.

Trees had been cut, leaving a long, narrow clearing that ended at the face of a slope. There were no arrows in the dirt. Zarek removed them after his daily practice session. Jace spun, looking at the trees, the lane, the steep hill at the end, the farm, and back to the trees. Concentration for a boy of that age wasn't easy.

Neysa watched her little dear from the porch of the house. Seeing him confused and alone made her heart ache. If he would come to her, she would hug him and tell her treasure from the sea that everything would be alright. But the boy remained at the range.

When the shadows grew long and the sun touched the top of the mountain, Zarek appeared. He limped to the range, bent down, and spoke to Jace. A few moments later, the archer shambled to the house, leaving Jace standing at the range.

"Isn't Jace coming in for supper?" she asked.

"He will when he gets hungry enough, or bored, or scared," Zarek revealed in her. "Sometime before morning, he'll come to his senses and give up on being an archer."

"You know he has bad dreams on rainy nights," Neysa informed her brother. She peered across the farm at the set of Jace's face, his small fists, and his straight back. Zarek's plan to break Jace of his desire to be an archer was cruel and hurt her heart. Then she advised. "Yet, he doesn't cry out in fear. He wakes up mad."

After four years of sharing farm chores with the boy and comforting him on bad nights, she knew him well. And Neysa wasn't sure the harsh treatment to discourage Jace would work on the little survivor.

***

In the morning, Neysa selected a basket and left the house. Her destination was the cucumber patch, until she saw Jace. Taking a detour, she went to the range.

"Good morning, dear. Did you have a good night?"

"It got cold."

"I know. If you come inside, I'll fix you a hot meal," Neysa offered.

"I can't. I'm a stick," Jace stated.

"A stick? The last time I checked, you were a boy."

"Yes ma'am, I'm that too."

"Why are you a stick?"

"Zarek said all potential archers are sticks. Pointless, aimless, and misshapen," Jace told her.

"I'm not sure I like that description."

"It's okay," Jace disclosed. "Now that the sun's up, I'll be released from the training."

"How is standing here all-night training?"

"Cretan archers can attack at dawn, while the enemy is still sleeping" Jace informed her. "Because the archers train their eyes to see in low light."

Neysa caught sight of Zarek ambling from the shed with his war bow and a fistful of arrows.

"Good morning, sister," he acknowledged her while ignoring the boy.

For a moment, Zarek squared his shoulders with the range. Then in a snap, he dropped his right foot back, putting his shoulders perpendicular to the lane.

He held the bow between the thumb and forefinger of his left hand and the arrows in the other fingers. It seemed awkward. Most people would have dropped the arrows or allowed the shafts to spread and disrupt the notched arrow. But Zarek held them in line with the bow.

In a smooth draw that mitigated the strength needed to pull the war bow, Zarek brought the bowstring across his chest to his jaw line. Then he released the arrow. While it was in flight, the master archer notched a second arrow and sent it downrange. One, two, three, four, and five flew almost faster than the mind could grasp. Despite the speed of the archer, the arrows formed a straight line on the hill.

"Go collect the arrows and take them to the shack," Zarek instructed. "Then for the rest of the morning help Neysa. I'll be in the work shed this afternoon."

"I'll see you then," Jace declared.

Zarek walked away and Jace looked up at Neysa.

"What are we doing?" he inquired.

"After you finish with the arrows, meet me in the house," she replied. "You'll have a bite before we harvest cucumbers."

"Yes, ma'am."

Neysa Kasia studied the marching steps and arm swing of the boy. He had grown a lot since Dryas found him on the beach. But he was still so small. She couldn't understand his desire to be an archer. She only knew how helpless and powerless she felt at not being able to protect him from the training.

Chapter 6 – A Deadly Answer

"There are two reasons we use sections to construct the core of our hunting and war bows," Zarek described. "First, it's much easier to find perfect grain if you use shorter lengths to build the bow. Often, even in a nice-looking long piece of wood, you'll discover a knot or an imperfection on a self-bow. By using separate pieces for the limbs and the belly of our bows, we can be sure the maple is flawless."

Jace shook his head, not quite understanding the explanation. But he wouldn't admit it.

"The second reason the bow is constructed of individual pieces," Zarek continued, "is the ability to repair the bow. With the right amount of heat and steam, we can disassemble a bow and replace any damaged parts."

"I thought archers just had to hit the target," Jace commented.

"A good archer hits his targets and takes care of his bow," Zarek responded. "A great archer hits his target, takes care of his bow, and can repair or build another."

"Where do I start?" Jace asked.

"You sweep the floor, sorting the shavings and trimmings into different containers," Zarek replied.

"But they're all wood shavings."

"You can leave anytime you want."

Jace went to a corner of the shed, grabbed the broom, and began sweeping the floor. He managed, after a fashion, to form a pile of maple dust and shavings and another of pine. It would have gone easier if the broom wasn't twice the height of the boy.

***

Four years later, Jace Kasia swept the maple shavings and slivers of wood into a pile. While he cleaned up, Zarek leaned over two carved pieces of maple. Wider than they were high, as long as a man's arm, and tapered from thick to thin on the far end, the pieces had no rough spots, knots, or indentions.

"They'll make nice limbs," the archer judged. "Tomorrow you can start carving the belly. In a day or two, we'll bend the limbs."

"Yes, sir," the twelve-year-old acknowledged. "The other split log has nice grain as well."

Zarek picked up the log selected for the center of the bow. He rotated the piece, examining it for flaws. As he studied the segment, he inquired. "And you've finished the bundles of arrows for Dryas?"

"I checked with Neysa about harvesting more feathers for fletching," Jace said. He scooped up the shavings and dropped them into the container for hardwood scraps.

"And what did my sister say?"

"She said, we'll have goose for dinner tomorrow," Jace replied.

"Just be sure you keep the wing feathers together," Zarek reminded the teen.

"Yes, sir, always right wind feathers or left wing on an arrow," Jace repeated the lecture. "We never mix wing feathers for our fletching. Opposing feathers will throw an arrow off."

"Very good. When is Dryas due back?"

"He should have been here last night," Jace answered. "I can't imagine what's holding him up."

***

Bettina, the village girl, had dark brown hair that captured the sun. When she moved, it appeared as if an aura of light crowned her head.

"You're invited to dinner if you want," she said timidly. "Would you like to come to dinner?"

Dryas Kasia was torn. He wanted to act worldly and not reveal the pounding of his heart. But she had visited his trading wagon three times that day. And on every occasion, he had not been able to take his eyes off her.

In reply, the normally glib trader could only choke out, "Yes."

The girl started to run away. Ten feet from the wagon she stopped, slapped her forehead, and spun around.

"I'll send my little brother to fetch you."

"That would be nice," Dryas admitted.

He stared even when the girl vanished from sight.

"Excuse me," a woman demanded. "How much for this fabric?"

Coming back to the present, Dryas realized he had a line of customers with coins to spend.

"That, madam, is material made from sheep raised in the shadow of Mount Olympus," he told her while pulling the fabric out of her hands. "It seems a little blessing from the Goddesses wash down in the creeks where the sheep drink."

"Are you saying this wool is touched by the Gods?" the woman inquired.

"I would never say that," Dryas assured her. "But I've been told, clothing made from this fabric brings luck to the person wearing it."

She bought half the wool he had in stock. The next customer selected a copper pot and a wooden ladle. For the rest of the day, he talked and sold merchandise. But unlike other days where he was focused on the buyers, he kept an eye on the position of the sun. It seemed to be moving very slowly.

When a boy with dark brown hair arrived and stood at the back of the shoppers, Dryas lowered his prices just to clear the last few customers.

"How old are you?" Dryas inquired while pulling a tarp over his goods.

"I'm nine," the boy replied.

"My nephew is just a few years older than you. Jace enjoys numbers, do you?" the trader asked. He climbed onto the driver's bench and reached into a chest behind the seat. "Hop up and show me the way. I'll park in the area."

As the wagon rolled through the village, he handed Bettina's brother a numbers scroll.

Following directions, the wagon moved away from the market and rolled towards the cute girl's house. Unfortunately, for the first time since he began trading, Dryas Kasia didn't leave the village after he finished selling for the day.

***

In the moonlight, Dryas checked the tether on the mules and the cover on the wagon. With everything secured, he lit a fire and sat to reflect on the evening. He felt good after a meal with Bettina and her family. If things worked out right, he would begin buying her father's barrels, giving him a reason to see more of…

The club glanced off his shoulder before scraping by the side of his head. While it didn't knock him out, the swing ripped his earlobe. With blood flowing into his eye, he rolled onto his belly, trying to get to his feet. A boot in the ribs dissuaded him of the notion.

"Stay down," a gruff voice ordered.

With one hand cupping his ear, and a throbbing pain in his side, Dryas couldn't think of a reason to argue.

"Where's your coin purse, peddler?" the voice demanded. When he hesitated, the man added. "We can kill your mules and burn your wagon. Or you can hand over the coins."

"Fine. Let me get to my feet."

"Do it slowly."

From prone and hurt, he came to his knees. The movement made him nauseous. He heaved but nothing came up.

"Not that slowly," a second voice barked. "We haven't got all night."

Fearing another kick, Dryas pushed to a squat. Then, after standing, he stumbling to the wagon. Behind the driver's bench, the trader moved items before reaching down.

"I'll take it from here," the first voice directed.

Dryas stepped back, his hand still covering his ear. He counted five armed men in the light from the campfire. None had come by the market during the day, at least he didn't recognize any of them.

This time, the club came at him level with his face. But Dryas caught the motion and managed to lean away. The club missed but the sudden jerk backward sent the trader spiraling to the ground.

"That'll keep him out of our way," the man with the club bragged.

"I've got his coin chest," the thief at the wagon announced. "What about the peddler?"

"He's out. Let's go."

Single file, the five marched off into the woods. A short ways in, they intersected with a wide trail. Moving swiftly, the robbers traveled to a bend before turning off the main pathway. Climbing a slope, they vanished into the dark night.

Dryas Kasia dropped to the ground next to the trail to catch his breath. He might not know where they were going. But he had a general direction for when he returned to hunt them.

***

The tube of green bark swayed gently over the pot of boiling water. Stream rose inside the tube heating and moistening the two pieces of maple suspended inside the bark housing.

"We move fast once I pull the limb from the steam," Zarek directed. "I'll do the initial lash down, you come behind me with tight loops."

"Yes, sir," Jace acknowledged.

On the bench, a block of wood appeared to be solid. But, when Jace lifted the upper part, a cut resembling the outer edge of a bird's wing showed where the top and bottom joined.

Zarek pulled the string for a limb and drew it up and out of the steam. He put the damp wood on the block and pressed down until the warm, moist limb conformed to the wing shape. Then Jace pressed down on the upper part to lock the limb in place.

The archer tied the blocks together quickly. Then he stepped back while Jace circled the halves with closely spaced loops of twine. Once done, the block of wood firmly held the bow's limb in the proper wing shape.

"Ready for the second one?" Zarek inquired.

Jace pulled a second form to the middle of the workbench and pulled the pieces apart.

"Ready," the teen replied.

***

After a meal of baked goose and greens, Zarek took Jace to the range. Using a self-bow with a light draw, the archer had the teen notch an arrow then pull and hold the bowstring.

"Imagine a straight line across your shoulders and extending to your left hand," Zarek instructed. "The line of your stance will affect the flight of your arrow. Draw the bowstring to your chin so the arrow is in line with your eye."

"My fingers are slipping," Jace warned.

He held the bowstring between the sides of his first two fingers and his thumb.

"Don't lean away from your target. It stresses your bow unnaturally by widening your draw. And keep your head centered."

After moments of gripping the string, the tension was winning.

"Hold your stance and keep your grip."

Then, the bowstring parted his fingers and thumb, and the arrow flew downrange.

"I'm sorry, it just slipped through my fingers," Jace apologized.

"Every release should come as a surprise," the archer told him. "If you're forcing the hold on the bowstring, you're probably squeezing the belly tightly. All that makes you shake which influences your aim. The tension should be in your bow, not in your body. Notch another and hold your draw."

They practiced until the sun sank low and the hillside became a dark mass.

"Go collect the arrows. Sort out those with damage for disassembly and set the rest aside."

"Yes, sir," Jace acknowledged.

He ran to collect the shafts and Zarek limped to the house.

"He doesn't seem to be making any progress," Neysa observed. "You keep showing him and he keeps releasing arrows too soon."

"Sister, the hardest thing to teach is a relaxed release," Zarek informed her. "And although I won't tell him, Jace has one of the lightest touches I've ever seen."

"So, he'll make a good archer?"

"Right now, he's a good early Herd technician. But he needs a few years to build enough muscle to pull a war bow. In the meanwhile, I have to learn if he has the ability to fight and to kill."

"He had no trouble killing the goose," Neysa offered.

"Butchering a bird or an animal for food is different than slaughtering another human. There are moral holds on most people that prevent them from taking the life of another individual."

"And Cretan archers don't have these, ah, holds."

"Not after weapons training."

"You mean with the bow and arrow?" Neysa inquired.

"No. With the shield, hatchet, sword, and knife," Zarek answered.

Before Neysa could ask about the danger of blade training, a wagon came from the trees. Unlike Dryas' usual dramatic arrival, the mules plodded along as if they were simply wandering to a familiar place to get fed.

"Something's wrong," Neysa mentioned while standing.

"Jace. Bring the wagon in," Zarek shouted.

From a casual walk, the teen sprinted from the shed to the mules. He noticed a bundle of cloth on the bench. After recognizing it as the shape of a man, Jace slapped the lead mule. Then he ran alongside the team.

"Someone is hurt," he bellowed.

At the house, he pulled the mules to a stop and climbed onto the wagon. The bundle of cloth moved, and a hand uncovered a bloody face.

"Hello little man. It's good to see you. Can you help me down?"

***

At the table, Zarek washed his hands in vinegar before rinsing off Dryas' ear.

"That stings, you know," the trader moaned.

"It's just the start of your pain," Zarek whispered. "Tell me what happened while Jace sews up your earlobe."

"Jace is going to stitch my ear?"

"And it'll be painful because he's nervous and his hands will shake," Zarek informed the trader.

"Do I have to?" the youth questioned.

"An archer gets very close to his File mates," Zarek explained. "When one gets cut, his closest friend does the sutures. There's no better training for that than sewing up your Uncle."

"Isn't Neysa available," Dryas asked.

"She's not in training," Zarek told him. "While the boy works, tell me who attacked you."

Between groans and ouches, Dryas related the tale of the dinner and the ambush. How he followed the bandits, and about the weakness that forced him to stop. By the time he finished, Jace had cut the thread at the last stitch.

"In the morning, I need to go after them," Dryas said.

"You'll sleep in tomorrow," Zarek instructed. "I'll handle this."

"No offense, but you're a cripple, and the robbers are in the hills," Neysa suggested.

"Jace will be my legs and eyes," Zarek informed her.

"Is Jace ready for this sort of thing?" Neysa inquired.

"That's a good question," Zarek admitted. "We'll know the deadly answer by the time we get back, if we get back."

"When do we leave?" Jace inquired.

"Unharness the mules, rub them down, and feed them," Zarek instructed. "When the strongest mule is rested, we'll leave. In the meanwhile, I'll pack our war gear."

Act 3

Chapter 7 – Reduce the Population

The donkey cart rode at a steeper angle than when pulled by Tansy. But with the bigger mule, the transport easily hauled Zarek, Jace, and their bow cases and packs.

"How can you tell where we're going?" Jace questioned.

While the trail glowed in the moonlight, the night hid all the other landmarks.

"I was raised around Eleutherna," Zarek replied. "When we were younger, Neysa and I rode all over on an old mule. The village is an easy day's ride from the city."

At the rate they traveled, they would cut a big slice of time from the day's ride.

"Why rush? It'll still be dark when we arrive," Jace pointed out. "And we don't know where the bandits are camped."

"There are two ways to hunt bear," Zarek replied. "You can track one to its den and hope the animal comes out before smelling you. A raging bear makes for a hard target. Or, you can place bait and set an ambush along the bear's trail."

"But we don't know the trail the robbers used."

"I wasn't talking about their path," Zarek corrected. "I was referring to the bait used on Dryas."

"Of course, he was hunted," Jace remarked, "by the bandits."

"Cretan archers serve in far off places," Zarek explained. "We get targeted for information, our coins, our weapons, or just to end our lives. If they come at us directly, we will fight. But if they put out honey, like a hunter would use to attract a bear, the archer will walk right into the ambush."

"What bowman would be tempted by a jar of honey?" Jace asked.

"It's called a honey trap. But the tactic has little to do with sweets from a hive," Zarek told him. "In most cases it's a pretty woman luring the archer into a bad situation."

"You think Uncle Dryas was lured into a trap?" Jace gasped.

"The girl asked him to dinner which caused him to stay in the vicinity of the village overnight. Something he never does."

"Maybe she's just sweet on him," Jace suggested.

"Or a sweet put out for him. We'll know more when we get to Bettina's house."

"And we want to get there before the village wakes up."

"Now you understand the rush."

***

There was no hint of sunrise when Zarek reined in the mule. At a slow walk, they reached the market square. Following Dryas' directions, they rolled through the commercial area and left from the opposite side of the village.

"That's where he was attacked," Jace guessed when they passed an unplanted field.

A large shed for drying barrel wood identified Bettina's house. When Zarek guided the mule off the road and up beside the stacks of logs and wooden staves, Jace suggested, "Shouldn't we sneak up on them?"

"It's much easier to question a suspect when they come to you," the archer replied. Then he pulled the hood of his jerkin up and called out. "Iphis, barrel maker, you have a customer."

A candle flared to life in a window before a man stuck his head out of the doorway.

"It's not even light," he complained.

"By midday, I hope to be at the market in Eleutherna with a load of barrels," Zarek lied. "So come out here and take my coins."

Grumbling, a middle-aged man shuffled from the house. His head down, he seemed resigned to whatever the fates decided.

"Do I know you?" Iphis asked.

"You don't," Zarek assured him. "I heard about you from Dryas Kasia."

Lurching on his bad leg, while examining stacks of wood, made the archer appear frail.

"Oh, the traveling peddler," Iphis replied. "He was here the day before yesterday."

The craftsman lit candles and hung them around the shed.

"He's not very memorable, is he?" Zarek teased.

Jace shot a glance at the archer. Iphis' answer would tell them a lot.

"No, he's not. How many barrels do you want?" replied the man whose daughter was supposed to be smitten with Dryas.

Zarek stumbled, stepped forward, and collided with the barrel maker.

"Get off me...," but a blade against his throat stopped the complaint. After a couple of silent moments, Iphis continued. "You're too late. I've already been robbed. There's no money left."

"That's fine. I don't want your coins. I want the robbers. Tell me about them."

"Five Rhodian soldiers showed up in the village last week," Iphis related. "They took coins from a few of us. Then when we begged them to leave us something, they offered a deal. Set up vendors for them. What could I do? I have a young son and daughter. I couldn't fight five soldiers."

"You never expected someone like me to show up?" Zarek inquired.

"Like you how?" Iphis asked.

"Someone looking for revenge. Where are the soldiers?"

"They're staying in a cabin just off the trail about a mile south of here," Iphis replied.

Zarek pushed the barrel maker away, waved at Jace, and hobbled to the mule.

"The thieves being soldiers is both good news and bad news," the archer said as he sat on the cart.

"Bad news because they know how to fight?" Jace questioned.

"No. Bad news because they'll have a guard posted," Zarek informed him while snapping the reins. "But good news because the flame will help us locate their cabin in the dark."

"Soldiers know how to fight," Jace offered. "Isn't that bad?"

"That fact will make it easier for you to draw them out into the open," Zarek stated, "and for me to put them down."

The cart returned to the main trail, turned right, and headed uphill and away from the village. Behind them, the barrel maker noted the bow cases before the cart left the light from the candles. Iphis might not be able to recognize the faces under the hoods. But an early morning visit from a crippled Cretan archer was a memorable occasion.

Higher up the trail and after thinking for a while, Jace asked, "How am I supposed to draw them out of the cabin?"

***

Jace Kasia crept towards the campfire. A figure, obviously a man on guard duty, sat beside the low blaze. At a stump designated by Zarek, Jace placed the hunting bow and the quiver of arrows with the leaf shaped arrowheads. Reluctantly, he eased away from the weapon, and continued dodging from stump to bush, making his way to the sentry.

At an uncomfortably close distance, he sank behind a brush to wait for sunrise and a sign. As he sat, Jace glanced to his right, looking for his mentor. To the archer's credit, Zarek blended in with the dark trees. Even as morning brought illumination and individual trees became identifiable, the archer remained lost in the dark branches.

A sound resembling a pair of fingers swishing away a speck of dust from a tabletop came to Jace's attention. But, as if a bird had winged by in full flight, the sound vanished. Returning to the front, he noted the guard was stretched out sleeping. Except, an arrow extended from his chest. If not recognizable from the audio, the body and the shaft signaled Jace to call out to the soldiers.

Running put his heart in his throat and he found it hard to catch his breath. Jace approached the corpse. As with most untrained people, he feared the dead. Circling the man's feet, the young teen approached the door.

Thoughts raced through his mind. What if they were waiting for him? What if he knocked, the door opened, hands grabbed him, and pulled him into the rustic cabin? With his bones rattling, he reached out and knocked on the door.

No one called out or answered.

His nerves frayed, Jace stood staring at the wood, petrified and unable to will his hand to rap on the door again. Just to do something, he glanced over his shoulder at the fire and the body. A herding club rested next to the stone fire ring.

In three steps, he snatched up the club, and before the fear overcame him, he hammered on the door.

"Get out here you cowards," he shouted. "You attacked a vendor in the dark. Come outside and try that in the daylight."

A thud came from behind the door and Jace ran. Diving into the hiding place, he pulled the bow to his chest, then peered over the stump.

Two men burst through the door. Spotting the dead man, they called something into the house, before rushing to check on their comrade.

A pair of soldiers came out of the building holding shields. Quickly, in a well-oiled maneuver, they locked the shields together and formed a barrier for the first two men. The four squatted for a moment around the sentry's body.

***

An arrow smacked the ground, cut a shallow trench before bouncing off a rock, and climbing under a shield. A man screamed and fell to the side. The sudden ejection of a shield from the tight formation revealed another Rhodian.

The next arrow streaked from the tree line. Jace noted the fingers swishing away a speck of dust noise again, confirming the sound was that of an arrow. Another soldier toppled over, knocking the last shield out of position.

A third arrow impacted the shield, leaving a shaft jutting from the wood.

***

The remaining two soldiers righted the shield and backed towards the doorway. If they made it inside, Jace and Zarek would have to wait them out.

Fearing the tension of lingering at the cabin while expecting armed men to come out to fight, Jace Kasia notched an arrow. Drawing the hunting bow, he brought the arrowhead to bear on the ribs of one of the soldiers. Then Jace shifted to aim behind and in the path of the man. When the bowstring touched the side of his jaw, he released the arrow.

Carrying more tension in his shoulders than he should, Jace led the man too much while anticipating the backward steps. When the man stopped, the arrow flew straight but low. It entered one of the soldier's butt cheeks. The leaf shaped arrowhead cut through the muscles of one cheek, slipped across the man's butt crack, and lodged in the flesh of the other buttocks. With the shaft of an arrow cramping his lower extremities, the man's legs locked up. He screamed and fell face first to the ground.

His partner turned to check on the violent reaction from his comrade. Zarek Mikolas sent a bronze warhead into the side of his neck. The man dropped, choking as he died beside the one shrieking about the pain and spasms in his backside.

Angry at his missed shot, Jace notched another arrow and sent it into the ribs of the screamer. The screeching and whining of the soldier stopped.

***

"You're a cruel little stick, aren't you," Zarek mentioned as he limped up to the carnage.

"I didn't mean for him to suffer," Jace pleaded.

"It wasn't a criticism," the archer assured him. "His agony brought the other one from behind the shield."

Zarek pulled a knife, bent over a moaning soldier, and sliced his throat.

"Make sure none are still alive," the archer instructed.

"Isn't cutting the necks of wounded men harsh?" Jace asked.

"And pull our arrows," Zarek said without acknowledging Jace's question. He limped into the cabin and appeared a moment later. "Run and bring up the mule cart. I'll handle the disposing of the trash."

Jace sprinted to where they left the mule and transport. By the time he returned, the bodies were gone. Taking their place outside the cabin were coin purses and Dryas' money chest.

***

Zarek sorted arrows, placing the heavy spined ones with the bronze broadheads into his quiver, and the iron leaf-shaped biblades into Jace's quiver.

"Never start a fight you don't intent to finish," he instructed.

Jace leaned against the cart looking down at the blood on his hands.

"I didn't expect," the twelve-year-old stammered.

"It's never easy," the archer acknowledged. "But in the end, it was their lives or ours. Would you have a different outcome?"

"No. This had to be done. I knew that after sewing up Uncle Dryas' ear," Jace admitted. "Should we dig graves and offer prayers for the dead?"

"Whenever possible, cover your tracks and erase all the evidence of your campsite. The goal is to leave as little a trace of our activities as possible. For a File of archers on an assignment, it helps hide how many bowmen are present, and their direction of march. For us, burning the cabin and the bodies, like collecting the arrows, hinders anyone coming after us."

"Someone might come after us?" Jace asked.

"We just murdered five soldiers of Rhodes," Zarek remarked as he tied the straps on his quiver. "Surely they have friends, relatives, comrades, and commanders."

Jace's hands shook as he shoved the hunting bow into its case.

"You stack wood around the cabin while I start the fires," the archer instructed.

***

Behind the cart, flames crawled up the walls of the rustic cabin. At the road, Zarek guided the animal away from the village and onto the trail rising to the higher elevations.

"Not a bad day's work," he commented as the burning cabin fell farther behind and below them.

"Work?" Jace asked. "I thought we were avenging Uncle Dryas."

"We did or rather, we were," Zarek informed him. "But it's the duty of every Cretan citizen to make a profit. Once we settled the debt of honor and found the extra coins, we stopped being magnanimous defenders of the family."

"If we weren't getting retribution, what were we?"

"We were Mercenaries," Zarek declared. He reached back and felt the coin purses next to Dryas' chests. "And well-paid ones at that."

On the high trail, the mule took the eastern leg when the path split. Jace didn't question the direction. Because now, he understood the need to avoid the village in daylight and being identified as a murderer.

***

By twilight, the farmhouse came into view. Neysa and Dryas stood on the porch waving at the cart.

"Is Jace alright?" Neysa shouted when she didn't see him. "Please tell me he's not injured."

"I'm fine," Jace said coming to his knees behind Zarek. "And we have Uncle Dryas' coins."

Zarek pulled the reins and stopped the mule.

"Help me get the coins, bows, and packs inside," he directed. "Jace, take the cart to the corral and feed the mule."

Neysa and Dryas helped the archer move the items to the table. As soon as they finished, the trader sat in front of his money chest. He opened it and dug down into the coins.

"Checking to see if the bottom is still there?" Neysa teased her brother-in-law.

With a serious expression on his face, he fished out a medallion. While he was occupied, Neysa spoke to Zarek.

"How did Jace do? Did he get in the way?"

"I have proof of his ability to reduce the population," Zarek replied. "The boy definitely can get beyond the morality and deliver death."

"I don't know how I feel, knowing my little fieldhand is a killer."

"How about your big brother?"

"You don't count," she said with a wink.

"Why don't you count?" Jace asked as he came in the door.

"We'll leave the counting to Dryas," Zarek answered. "My share, Neysa's share, and your share."

"My share?" Jace questioned.

"You did the work of a man, you get a share," Zarek informed the boy. "Isn't that right Dryas?"

The trader held up the medallion.

"What's that?" Neysa inquired.

"When I rescued Jace from the beach, he had this around his neck," the trader confessed. "I should have given it to him earlier, but I kept forgetting. Now, I think Jace should have it."

"What's on it?" Zarek asked.

Dryas placed the medallion on the table. An imprint of a she-wolf baring her teeth was stamped into one side. Flipping it over, he translated the Latin.

"A fisherman explained the letters. They spell out, The Romiliia Household with bravery and the fierceness of wolves."

"But what does it mean?" Jace asked.

"When you came to me, I gave you a name," Neysa replied. "Now it appears, Kasia is no longer your last name.

And you may have family somewhere in the Roman Republic."

"Or his parents were servants in the Romiliia family household," Dryas suggested. "With bravery and the fierceness of wolves could be a family motto or words to identify a heroic deed by a household guard."

"With your share of coins, Jace, you can leave Crete and sail to the Republic," Zarek suggested. "And search for your real family."

"If it's alright with everyone here," Jace requested, "I'd like to stay with the family who raised me. At least for now. If that's alright?"

Neysa Kasia, Dryas Kasia, and Zarek Mikolas draped their arms over Jace Romiliia Kasia. Each hugged him until he had tears in his eyes.

"After we get our shares," the boy asked, "can we eat? I'm starving."

"While Dryas counts out the coins, I'll fix plates of food for my warriors," Neysa declared. "I don't think my brother-in-law will try to cheat me."

"I wouldn't. But have you considered going into business with me?" Dryas offered. "With the extra coins, we can buy another cart, hire an associate to sell and…"

Chapter 8 – One, Select a Shaft

Jace repositioned the ribbon of sinew on the block of wood. With a wooden hammer, he pounded the deer tendon until it separated into strips. Then, wrapping his fist around a bird's talon, he used the sharp claw to further shred the sinew.

"Make them as fine as you can," Zarek directed. On the workbench in front of the archer, a copper mug rested over burning scraps of hardwood. Slowly, he fed pieces of hide into the vessel. As the bits of hairless skin entered the mug, they melted into a thick gooey substance. "The hide glue is almost ready."

Once he had the sinew as fine as straw, Jace spread the strands on the workbench and combed them as Zarek pored hide glue over the sinew. After a few passes with a comb, the tendon material resembled wet hair.

The archer selected long pieces and carefully stretched them over one face of a hunting bow. Then, he brushed on more glue to form a strata of connective tissue and hide glue. It was the third and final layer for the hunting bow. Working from one end to the other, he completely covered both limbs and the belly with the wispy hairs of sinew.

"You sure do that tenderly," Jace observed.

"The material will keep the bow from cracking and breaking when it flexes," Zarek replied. "Plus, it'll protect the bow from rain, if an archer gets caught out in bad weather."

"I would never leave my bow out in the rain," Jace boasted.

"Sometimes, you don't have a choice," the archer warned. "While it dries, we can get in some target practice. Chant while you clean up the workbench."

"One. Select a shaft, and a two, notch your arrow. And, a three," the twelve-year-old sang while scrubbing the glue from the workbench, "pick your target. And, a four, draw. And, a five, release."

Zarek listened to the broken rhythm as he selected a war bow for him and a hunting bow for the boy.

***

Four years later Jace chanted in a driving cadence, "One. Select shaft, and-a-two, Notch arrow. And-a-three, Pick target. And-a-four, Draw. And-a-five, Release. And-a-six, and-a-seven, and-an-eight, and-a-nine, step-up."

Zarek pulled a single hunting bow from the wall and a basket with two hundred arrows.

"Are you ready?" he inquired.

"The bench is cleaned, and the hide pot scrubbed," Jace assured Zarek.

The sixteen-year-old stood as tall as the archer. And while both had wide shoulders, where Zarek carried thick muscles from a lifetime of pulling a heavy bowstring, Jace hadn't filled out, yet.

"After we practice, I'd like to whittle more on the belly for that new bow," Jace remarked.

"Maybe later," Zarek told him. "We're going to be busy until morning."

"Morning? You, the Cretan archer, are taking a day off," Jace laughed. "Say, you've only taken one bow. We need to test that new hunter. I'll get it."

"Jace Romiliia Kasia, I would advise you at this point to go to the farmhouse, have breakfast, and stay there with Neysa," Zarek advised. "Walk away from the shed."

Jace sensed something ominous and questioned, "Are you saying, if I leave, my archer training is over?"

"Walk away," the archer repeated. "Or walk with me and survive the test, if you can."

"I've learned how to build a bow from trees I harvest and animals I hunt," Jace listed. "I've learned the history and lore of Cretan archers. I can march the war-dances and sing the songs. And I can hit a target with any bow from any angle. I am not about to step away now."

"It is, as they say, your funeral," Zarek commented.

The archer carried the basket and bow out of the shed. Jace walked a pace behind him.

***

At the range, Jace found stakes in lines with a shoulder's width between them. The archer placed the basket behind the last stake.

"You have two hundred arrows," Zarek explained. "You start at the head of the line. Shoot five arrows to the rhythm, then march to the rear pole. Keeping with the chant, you will unstring your bow, select your next five arrows, then restring your bow, and moved in time back to the shooting line."

"I understand," Jace acknowledged. "That will take forty rotations. Should I rush and try to finish early?"

"Would the rest of your File understand why you were hurrying your shots?" Zarek questioned.

Jace reached out and took the bow. Then he went to the basket, sorted out five arrows he felt were evenly matched, and stared at Zarek.

"One. Select shaft," Zarek stated while waving Jace forward to the first stake.

The teen shot five arrows while chanting. He hit the target with each release, then he rolled left to clear the space for the imaginary archers behind him. At the rear by the last stake, he placed his leg between the bow and the string, hooked the back of his leg with the end of the bow, and bent the weapon.

"One. Select shaft," he sang while removing the bowstring. Then he sorted out five more arrows. "And-a-two, Notch arrow. And-a-three, Pick target. And-a-four, Draw. And-a-five, Release. And-a-six…"

He restrung the bow and stepped up and between the next set of stakes.

Two repetitions of the cadence later, he again stood at the front. And as the chant instructed, he selected an arrow from the five in his hand. Notched the arrow, looked downrange at the targets, brought the bow up, and drew the string back. Then he quickly sent the arrow to the target. "And-a-six."

When he finished the last arrow of the set, he stepped aside. The sequence completed two rotations. Jace felt good and the callouses on his thumb and fingers were solid. Plus, his shoulders were just loosening up.

***

Neysa noticed that Jace and Zarek had been at the range most of the morning. Taking two mugs and a pitcher of water, she started towards them.

"Your kindness is noted," Zarek informed her. "But we require no drink or sustenance. Our hearts are full of pride and that's all an archer needs."

Puzzled at the brush off, she huffed, and marched back into the farmhouse. Once inside, Neysa slammed a hand on the countertop.

"I'll bet you'll be begging me for dinner around dusk," she snorted while pouring herself a glass of water. "Maybe, just maybe, I'll tell you I require no hungry mouths to cook for. And that my feet are tired, and you can fix your own food."

As Neysa had her snit, Jace felt the first twinge in his shoulders and saw blood from a blister under a callous. He had lost count of the rotations, but the basket appeared to be just as full as when he started.

"...and-a-three, Pick target. And-a-four, Draw. And-a-five, Release," he sang with a hoarse voice while stepping by another stake. "One, Select shaft..."

***

Just prior to noon, the bowstring became coated with blood making it harder to hook the string on the ends of the bow. Jace's draw was less deep and, the arrows that had whooshed to the target, now flew with a slight arc, and less authority.

'At least the basket is emptying,' he thought.

The positive emotion was fleeting as he chanted, "One. Select shaft. And-a-two, Notch arrow..."

No one except a dedicated bowman could ignore the cramps, the aches, and the mess made by bleeding fingers.

Plus, the best arrows had been at the top and selected first. The bottom layer in the basket were warped, had shafts that varied in length, and spines of different stiffnesses.

"You miss a target, and you will hustle down there, collect fifty, and continue until you place every arrowhead where it belongs," Zarek growled.

Afraid of missing, Jace wanted to slowdown and concentrate. But the rhythm of the chant controlled the tempo.

One, Select shaft, and-a-two, Notch arrow, and-a-three, Pick target, and-a-four, Draw, and-a-five, Release…

A bowstring slick with blood, his vision blurry from focusing, and a shaft that should have been kindling, combined to send an arrow as high as the treetops and off to the left. It wobbled in flight, turned sideways, and seemed lost. Then in a lucky twist of fate, the arrowhead straightened, and flew to the center of a target.

Jace stood opened mouthed.

"Chant," Zarek urged. His voice was soft. Still amazed, he looked at the little arrow that shouldn't have been in the basket, but now stuck proudly in the target.

"One, select shaft, and-a-two, Notch arrow, and-a-three," Jace sang as he unstrung the bow. Then he stared at the basket before picking up the last of the arrows. "Pick target, and-a-four, Draw, and-a-five, Release."

He struggled to restring the bow while chanting his way to the front stakes with the last five arrows.

***

"Store the bow in the shed," Zarek ordered after the last shot. "Then catch up with me."

"Where are you going?" Jace inquired.

"To the hunting lodge."

Three years ago, they built a cabin seven miles from the farm and higher on Mount Ida than the village of Zoniana.

"I'll be right there," Jace confirmed.

"There's a pack beside the workbench," the archer instructed. "Strap it on and bring it with you. And don't take anything from Neysa."

Without another word, Zarek limped to a trail that took him up the hillside and above the range. The shafts and feather fletching of Jace's two hundred hits jutted from the hill. But the archer didn't look at the arrows, his eyes were on the shed and the front porch of the house.

***

Relief washed through Jace in such a physical force that he staggered. After recovering, he laughed at the weakness in his knees.

"Two hundred arrows, downrange, and on target with a hunting bow," he boasted to the shed. In his enthusiasm, he tapped the weapon. The pain in his forefinger felt as if someone had swung a log and impacted the fingertip. He jerked and the jarring sent a spasm down the muscles of his back. "I'll take it easy from here on out. Things can't get harder than two hundred arrows."

He unstrung the bow and set it on a pair of hooks beside the workbench. Then he reached for a big pack. On the first pull, it didn't move. Only when he used two hands and a hard jerk did he manage to get it to the top of the workbench.

"Jace. I don't know what's going on?" Neysa scolded while slipping into the shed. "But you've had enough of this nonsense. Come to the house and let me fix you lunch."

Jace backed up until the edge of the workbench hit him in the lower back. After slipping two straps over his shoulders, he stepped away from the bench. The weight of the pack bent him forward.

"I can't Neysa," he told her. "Zarek wants this at the hunting camp."

"Then use Tansy and the cart. That's too much weight for you."

Jace winked, took a step, and lurched to the side.

"I need to get it balanced," he said as an excuse.

With effort, the teen stumbled out of the shed. Neysa moved to the opening and watched her young charge struggle to climb the footpath into the hills.

***

In short unsteady steps, Jace caught up to the limping archer.

"What's in this thing?" the teen inquired.

Rather than answer, Zarek ordered, "Tell me about the Macedonian King."

Jace traveled a few more paces before offering his rendition.

"Early in his reign, King Alexander embraced, tested, and in most cases rejected undependable units of fighters.

During the battle for Thebes, the King noticed enemy troops on a low section of road. He ordered Eurybotas, the Captain of the Cretan archers, to move forward. Although the Captain was killed in the fighting, Alexander learned the heart of the Cretan archer," Jace replied between deep breaths. The pathway was little more than an animal trail with bad footing, making it difficult for someone carrying a heavy load. But the teen focused on putting one foot in front of the other while keeping his mind occupied with telling Cretan history. "When the great King moved his campaigning to Anatolia, he took the brave Cretan archers with him. As he did across Persia, and up to and over the Hindu Kush Mountains. For a King who only hired the finest troops, the Cretan archers were among his best."

Seven miles from the farm, Jace and Zarek arrived at the hunting lodge. The 'lodge' nickname was a nod to grander accommodations, not to the one room shack. Tucked into the shadow of a foothill at the base of Mount Ida's peak, the land acted as a wind break in winter. Yet while the wind whistled around the structure, the snow fell on its roof.

"I'll start a fire," Jace offered as they kicked their way through a foot of powder.

"Dump the pack on the table and stand by the door," Zarek directed.

While the archer unpacked dried vegetables, waterskins, cooking pots, and dried meat, he took nothing for himself, nor did he offer anything to the teen.

Jace wanted to eat and warm his exhausted body by a roaring fire. But the archer had him standing near the door waiting for what he didn't know. A little anger warmed his chest and put a flush on his face. When Zarek lifted four big stones from the bottom of the pack, the little anger burned hotter.

"Have you recovered from the stroll?" Zarek asked before Jace could say anything about the extra weight.

"I have," the teen answered truthfully. The anger had sent blood to his weary extremities and warmed his body.

"Do you remember the mountain pond at the higher elevation?" Zarek inquired.

"The one north of here, below the long slope?"

"That's the one," Zarek stated. "I want you to run there. I'll meet you."

"It's only a mile or so," Jace remarked.

"Not if you run to the south, and approach it from the other side of the mountain," Zarek told him. "Or you can stay here, and we'll cook a nice meal and eat beside a blazing fire."

Jace opened the door and stepped outside quickly before the lure of warmth caused him to quit. With stiff legs and a sore back, he jogged away, hoping the run would loosen his muscles.

***

The mountain stream gurgled as it cascaded down the rocks before collecting into a deep pool. In summer, its waters refreshed and soothed. Hunters and hikers, fortunate enough to locate the pond, discovered the water to be a wonderful solution to a parched throat.

But in winter, ice needed to be chipped away from the edges in order to fill a waterskin. And, the freezing water was sure to bring shivers to the hands that held the container. For the teen submerged in the frigid water, his tremors far exceeded simple shivers.

"Jace, stay with me," Zarek urged in a soothing voice. "Still your breath so your hands are steady. Calm your heart so your eyes are clear. Focus your mind on the task. Tell me of General Xenophon's archers."

The blue lips were shades of gray in the moonlight. While the sixteen-year-old had no color in the dark, if someone held a torch close to him, they'd see he had no color in his cheeks anyway. Beyond the almost deathly pale, the quiver of his voice and the clattering of his teeth were obvious signs of partial hypothermia.

"On the left bank of the Euphrates River, two great armies fought," Jace stammered. Pausing, he inhaled rapidly three times as if he had run sprints. "When the day ended, Cyrus the Younger was dead, his mercenary army fled, and..."

A fit of shaking sent out waves that washed back and splashed Jace's face. He jerked his head away from the dampness. As the only part of his body not submerged in the freezing pond, he attempted to keep his head dry.

"Focus, breathe," Zarek instructed. He looked to the east and searched the sky for signs of the morning. But there was nothing in the black heavens. So, he continued to offer what help he could. "Fled, and?"

"And to their dread, the Persian army sought and caught the Hoplites," the boy got out in fits and spurts. "Supplies were naught, but for the flights of arrows from Persian bowman. Plucking the spent arrows from the wounded and the ground, Cretan archers returned the gifts. With accuracy and sacrifice, the archers held back the Persian cavalry with the Persian shafts. The Cretans died with honor so the ten thousand could flee to the sea."

"A fine rendition," Zarek complimented. "Stay awake boy. Don't let your body betray you."

Jace opened his mouth to yawn but his jaw rested too close to the waterline. In mid shiver, his chin dipped, and water flooded his mouth. Coughing and spitting, he threw his head back and screamed into the night.

"Enough. I've had enough," he bellowed in rage.

Despite his cries, Jace Romiliia Kasia remained in the water. With only his head showing above the surface, his body convulsed while gratefully, the feeling left his feet, shoulders, and hands.

By the end of the run around the mountain, his legs wobbled, and he hobbled. Before then, the two hundred arrows with a hunting bow were more than enough to cramp his left hand. With so many pulls of the bowstring, the skin on the thumb and the fingers of his right hand were shredded and raw. And due to the repetition of pulls and releases, the muscles of his shoulders had burned as if on fire.

But now, there were no cramps in his legs, or pain in his hands, or fire in his shoulders. The cold had overridden all other sensations.

Yet, Jace did not try to crawl out of the water. He remained in the pond at the foot of the mountain stream, because he had the heart of a Cretan archer.

Chapter 9 – War Bow Trader

The winter sun offered light to the surface of the pond and the boy's stiff, cold face. And while it didn't offer warmth, its appearance offered relief.

Zarek kicked away the ice from the edge, waded out, and lifted Jace from the water. Dragging his limp form to the shore, he sat him on a fur wrap and vigorously rubbed the boy's arms, chest, and legs.

"Wait, what are you doing?" Jace questioned.

"Open your eyes and you'll see," Zarek suggested.

Slowly, Jace lifted his eyelids and peered at the sun.

"I, did it?" he asked before falling back on the animal fur.

"Almost," Zarek told him. "Now it's a simple hike to the cabin."

"That's easy for you to say," Jace mumbled.

With help, he got to his feet. But then he tilted dangerously to his left.

Before he toppled over, Zarek said, "Still your breath so your hands are steady. Calm your heart so your eyes are clear. Focus your mind on the task."

Jace managed to pull the wrap around his shoulders then took a cautious step. In several unsteady paces, he moved to the trail and stumbled down the path in the direction of the lodge.

Zarek's old injury caused him to limp, but he stayed behind the boy. With a wide grin on his face and his chest expanded, the archer hobbled with pride. And despite his handicap, he managed to stay close, in case Jace stumbled.

***

By full sunrise, they reached the hill above Zarek's hunting lodge. Down in the yard, a donkey sensed their presence and peered upward.

"Look, Zarek, Tansy's here," Jace observed. Still groggy from the overnight ordeal, he lifted his eyes following a line of smoke drifting from the chimney. "Do you suppose Neysa is here, as well?"

"I don't think the old donkey came up here on her own," Zarek offered. "And if it's not my sister burning my firewood, the stranger better have coins."

With a sense of urgency, Jace shuffled down the path. Even in his exhausted state, he outpaced the old archer. At the bottom, Tansy greeted Jace. Almost as if the donkey knew he was hurting, she walked beside him letting Jace lean on her back. At the doorway, Jace and the donkey strolled into the cabin.

"Out, get out," Neysa Kasia shouted. With an apron, she shooed the intruders back.

Jace and Tansy retreated from the fierce woman.

"No, not you, Jace. Get yourself in here and have a seat," she instructed. "I was talking to that stubborn donkey."

Jace shuffled to a rough framed chair and slowly lowered himself down. Moments later, Zarek appeared in the doorframe.

"Look at the boy," Neysa growled. "He's done in and looks like death. It's a wonder you didn't kill him. Going hunting in the dark. And coming back empty handed."

Silently, Zarek limped to a storage box, untied the leather bindings, and lifted the lid.

"Are you hungry?" Neysa inquired. "You must have gone out early. You both look hungry. Come brother, sit and I'll dish out a big bowl of my pork and celery stew."

Zarek didn't address his sister. After a few more moments with his hands in the crate, he lifted out an object and turned to face the table.

"You've been tested in the ways and thrived in the adversity," Zarek exclaimed. He extended a Cretan war bow at shoulder height. Seeing the weapon and realizing the meaning of the words, Neysa Kasia brought her fits to her mouth to stifle an emotional outburst. "Today, you are no longer a boy. No longer a fieldhand or a fisherman. Today, Jace Kasia, you are a Cretan archer. To signify your right to the title, I present to you your first war bow. May it keep you safe, fed, and employed."

Jace's mouth hung open and he stared at the beautiful bow. Composed of wood, bone, and sinew, the weapon could be mistaken for a polished work of art.

From behind her hands, Neysa coached, "Jace, you should take the bow. Yes, now."

With tears in his eyes, Jace stood and accepted the weapon.

"When you came to me," Neysa cried between the words, "you were a squalling little Latin child. Still wet from the sea and exhausted from the shipwreck. Now you are a Cretan man, an archer."

"But I haven't been to the agoge," Jace protested. "Don't you have be Cretan to attend the school? To become an archer?"

"It's true you must be born of Crete to be accepted in the agoge," Zarek admitted. "But the school is no more than a place for group learning. You, Jace, have passed the tests alone, and without companions to comfort you."

"Yes, yes," Neysa exclaimed while drying her eyes. "Now sit, both of you while I dish out some stew for my men."

Jace collapsed into the chair, leaned back against the cabin wall, and closed his eyes. In a heartbeat, he fell asleep. But even in slumber, he didn't release the war bow. That, he hugged to his chest.

"Should I wake him?" Zarek asked.

"Let him rest for a while," his sister replied. "I'll warm him a bowl later."

She dished out bowls of stew and they sat at the table and ate. And as Zarek Mikolas and Neysa Kasia had done for the last twelve years, they watched over the Latin boy who washed up from the sea.

***

For the rest of the winter and into spring, a few things changed for Jace. He started each day with archery practice using the heavy drawing war bow. Following the act of putting deep holes in targets, he performed farm chores as he had done for years. But now, after tiding up the pens, outbuildings, and corrals, the teen archer strapped a small shield onto his left forearm.

The blade work proved humiliating because, although Zarek limped, he didn't have to contend with a battlefield. He simply had to navigate his way around a fighting circle.

"The shield isn't just to stop a blade," Zarek instructed. Sprawled on the ground, Jace peered up at the master archer. "When I hooked and turned aside your shield with the hatchet, you attempted to defend against the hatchet."

"And you hit me with your shield," Jace said finishing the lecture.

"Get up," Zarek stated, "and defend yourself."

On his feet, Jace spread his legs for balance, and swung his left forearm around to block a chop from the hatchet. Deflecting the hatchet's head, he smiled at moving so quickly. Obviously unable to get through Jace's defense, Zarek hammered his shield into Jace's. The shields locked together and Jace put weight on his forward leg to help win the pushing match.

Almost as soon as he shifted his mass, Jace's left foot shot out from under him. He toppled forward. From the solid feel of a foe's shield against his forearm, his shield angled downward in an attempt to cushion his fall.

But there was no softening the landing. Zarek's shield pounded him to the ground.

"Target fixation," Zarek instructed. "In a fight, some archers will focus on a single threat to the exclusion of other dangers. You thought the pushing match of the shields was the primary contest. While you pushed like a mighty

Spartan, I hooked your ankle with the backside of the hatchet."

"And punished me for it," Jace responded.

He rubbed the knot on the back of his head while struggling to his feet.

"What's the lesson for today?" the master archer demanded.

"The shields, although small and unsharpened, are as much of a weapon as the blade or the hatchet," Jace ventured.

"No," Zarek countered. He held up his arms displaying the shield and the war hatchet. "The lesson is that anything in your hands can be used as either an offensive or a defensive weapon."

"I understand," Jace acknowledged. "One hand attacks while the other protects."

"That is the lesson. Tomorrow, we'll work with swords again. Now put away the weapons then wash up," Zarek directed. "Neysa wants to talk to us over lunch."

"Is something wrong?" the teen inquired.

He unstrapped his shield before collecting Zarek's shield and hatchet.

"She didn't sound worried, if that's what you mean."

"If she's not upset, then neither am I," Jace offered. "Neysa is the center that holds everything together."

"Are you comparing my sister to the heavy infantry?" Zarek inquired.

"More like the command staff," the teen said while walking away.

"If Neysa is the General, I suppose Dryas is our quartermaster," Zarek pondered. "If those are true, what am I?"

"You are, as you've always been," Jace answered, "the man protecting our flanks."

"But I thought I was in command."

Jace laughed all the way to the weapon's shed.

***

Neysa stood on the porch watching the archers' stride as they crossed the yard. She recognized the cat like prowl in the teen. Before his knee injury, Zarek moved with the same fluid motion. Now it was Jace who seemed only a leap away from attacking a prey animal. As they got closer, she noted an expression of amusement on the boy's face.

"What's so funny?" she inquired.

"It's nothing," Zarek scowled. "Let's eat."

The two broad-shouldered archers walked through the doorway and went directly to the table.

"Before I feed you," Neysa announced, "I have something to say."

"Is it bad news?" Jace asked.

"No, it isn't bad," she assured him. "The cities of Knossus and Polyrrhenia have formed a Cretan League. Every city has been asked to join. Most have, except for Eleutherna and the Spartan colony of Lyttos."

"Not surprising," Zarek suggested. "Did they think the Spartans would roll over and offer their bellies to the rulers of Knossus and Polyrrhenia."

"From what you've told me, the men from Lacedaemon are strong willed and keep their own borders," Jace stated. "So, while I understand why Lyttos is holding out, tell me why Eleutherna isn't joining the League?"

"Magistrate Timarchus is considering joining," Neysa reported. "But first he wants to consult with the citizens of the city and the farmers."

"It seems plain to me," Jace stated. "With all of Crete against a single city, Eleutherna has to join the Cretan League."

"I'm leaning towards that outcome," Neysa admitted. "But let's ask a warrior with more experience. Tell me brother, should Eleutherna join?"

"Absolutely not," Zarek replied while placing three mugs in a line on the tabletop. "Knossus sits between Eleutherna and Lyttos. If the Cretan army fails, and they will, the Spartans will slaughter everyone in Knossus before marching on Eleutherna and slaughtering us. When they're done, they'll have created a thirty-mile perimeter of desolation around Lyttos."

As he mentioned the fall of Knossus, the archer knocked over the center mug. When he described the Spartans attacking Eleutherna, he tipped over the mug on the left.

"Surely one city can't survive and overcome the army of Crete," Neysa declared. "You've often said the Cretan archer is the best fighters in the world."

“But he’s often acknowledged the Spartan warrior as the second best,” Jace remarked. “With the militia from other nations as being inferior by magnitudes.”

“Except for Jace and I, most of Crete’s archers in this area are old or away on contracts,” Zarek said. “We should not join the League.”

“Then it’s a good thing we’re going to the main market on the first day of next month,” Neysa told them. “Magistrate Timarchus needs to hear this side of the argument.”

“I don’t like going to the city,” Zarek grumbled. “Too many people packed into too small a space. There’s barely enough room to draw a bow.”

“We’re going to the market to sell, not to go to war,” Neysa remarked. She moved to a pot hanging over a pile of hot embers. “Besides, Jace has only seen the square with Dryas on trading days. He’s never seen a full market and a public meeting.”

“Not like Magistrates actually listen to the crowd,” Zarek complained. “We elect those men and then they become power hungry dictators.”

“Magistrate Timarchus is different,” Neysa argued. “He takes care of the citizens and the city.”

“We’ll see,” Zarek commented.

“Can we eat now?” Jace asked.

“Of course, dear,” Neysa told him while ladling soup from the pot into a clay container. She handed him the bowl and told him. “When you’re done, there’s more where that came from.”

***

The sun had yet to rise on the first day of the month. Although chilly, the cool spring night would fade once the sun appeared.

"Here are the arrows for the market," Jace said while placing a basket on the donkey cart.

"Go see what Neysa needs from the root cellar," Zarek directed. "I'll get the rest of the hunting bows."

The youth rushed to help Neysa, but she appeared in the dark.

"Take these," she instructed while passing him a basket of walnuts and almonds. "Did you get the goat cheese and sausage from the drying shed?"

"Yes, ma'am," Jace confirmed.

"In that case, it's off to the market we go."

***

The farm was a mile south of the village of Zoniana. And the city of Eleutherna rested in the lower foothills five miles northeast of the village. Tansy wasn't about to rush and Zarek appreciated the pace. Shortly after sunrise, they reached the outskirts of the city. Houses of wood and stone marked the boundary. Soon, the small party was following narrow streets along with other citizens heading for the main square. All hauled goods to sell or trade and most talked excitedly about joining the Cretan coalition. Few included a discussion of the attack on their city if it refused the League, or the possibility of war with Lyttos if the Spartans didn't join.

After crossing the city square, they traveled out of the city and down a sloping street. At the toe of the hill, the land opened to a wide flat clearing. Tents and stalls dotted the landscape. Their configuration created temporary lanes between the rows of vendors.

"There's Uncle Dryas," Jace announced when he noted the trader standing on his wagon and waving.

Leading Tansy, the teen walked the donkey and cart away from Zarek and Neysa.

"It's good to see people again," she exclaimed.

"Too many people," the archer whined.

A flatbed wagon pulled by a draft horse rolled from the city. At the base of the hill, it turned right onto the grass, and stopped.

Magistrate Timarchus accompanied by his advisors strolled down the road behind the transport.

Zarek noted the people looking at some activity behind him. Turning, he watched the leaders of Eleutherna gather around the flatbed.

"Your favorite Magistrate is here bright and early," he remarked.

"I imagine he wants to get the opinion of the citizens first thing," she offered. "That way, the council can debate the issue and make an announcement before the market closes."

"If he'll listen," the archer insisted.

She tapped his shoulder playfully then opened her fist and rested her fingers on his upper arm. In response, Zarek placed his hand protectively over her hand.

"He will listen, I'm sure," she told him.

***

Rather than go directly to Dryas and Jace, the brother and sister strolled along rows of vendors. As natives to the area, they knew many of the sellers. In no rush and assuming they would soon be heading to the flatbed to hear the Magistrate speak and field comments, they stopped frequently and talked to old friends.

"Zarek. Zarek," Jace said as he ran to the archer.

In his hands, he carried two war bows and a pair of quivers.

"What's the matter?" Neysa asked. "Is Dryas ill?"

"No, ma'am," the teen answered. He shifted to face Zarek. "There is a barrel seller on the back row. Uncle Dryas said he recognizes Bettina."

"It's fine, the family is allowed to sell their product at the market," Zarek remarked.

"Maybe, yes," Jace agreed while leaning close to the archer's ear. "It's just that Iphis, her father, isn't with his family. Another vendor told me a group of soldiers were here at dawn. They helped unload the barrels. Then they escorted Iphis into the city."

"Two questions," Zarek remarked. He reached out, took the quiver, and tied it around his waist before grabbing the bow. "Was he escorted or arrested? And who were the soldiers?"

"According to the vendor, Iphis was guided into the city by several soldiers from Rhodes."

Crowd noises caused them to look around.

"Should I string the bow?" Jace asked.

"No," Neysa replied. "There's no threat."

"Do it," Zarek told him.

He looped the string around the bow tip then placed that end of his bow behind his left leg. Flexing the bow around his right thigh, Zarek hooked the loop of the bowstring into the opposite bow tip. Jace did the same.

The flat bed backed up to block the road. Once the horse stopped moving, Magistrate Timarchus and a man dressed in the tunic of a Rhodian Admiral climbed onto the bed.

"Citizens of Eleutherna, today we have a decision to make and a guest to help with the choice," Magistrate Timarchus announced. "Admiral Polemocles will assist me with understanding your positions. Step up and let your voices be heard."

Vendors and shoppers moved forward and soon crowded around the wagon.

"The citizens of Knossus and Polyrrhenia have formed a partnership and they want every citizen of Crete to join them," Timarchus exclaimed. "I want to hear the pros and cons of joining with our sister cities. But first a word…"

Only because Zarek and Jace were searching did they identify the spearmen. Although not in the uniform of the Rhodian Navy, their stiff postures, and the outline of their spears, making depressions in the grass, gave them away.

"I have four spearmen on my side," Jace whispered.

"Four more on my side blocking access to the path up the hill," Zarek reported while untying the cap on his quiver.

"Five more coming from the city," Neysa added.

"…please give a warm welcome to Admiral Polemocles."

The naval commander nodded to the crowd and turned to Timarchus.

"I'm afraid I lied to you, Magistrate," Polemocles declared. "Although I have been hired by Polyrrhenia to blockade the colony of Lyttos, I wasn't authorized to visit your city."

"If you don't represent the alliance, why are you here?" the Magistrate demanded.

His words reached the crowd and they made menacing sounds, but none moved.

"I'm here to arrest a rogue bowman and his associate," Polemocles replied. He glanced around and spied his soldiers coming down the hill. As they closed with the flatbed, it was obvious their formation escorted a civilian. "There is a witness."

"Jace. What is the color of Bettina's hair?" Zarek inquired.

"Dryas said it was dark brown," the teen answered.

From the wagon, the Admiral continued, "But I learned last night the name of the murderers. Will someone kindly point out Zarek Mikolas and his student to me. There is a reward."

"Just a second, Admiral," Timarchus complained, "I didn't agree to a manhunt."

"No, you didn't," Polemocles replied. The knife came out of its sheath, and in a smooth arc, it rose to the Magistrates chest and plunged into his heart. "But I didn't ask your permission."

Horrified at the murder of their Magistrate, the crowd and council stood in silence. In a moment, they would have rushed the flatbed wagon. But a voice rose up before the mob surged forward.

"There they are," a familiar voice shouted.

Jace and Zarek spun to face Dryas Kasia. The Uncle, the brother-in-law, the family trader stood with an arm extended and a finger pointing at Jace and Zarek. Behind him, a pretty girl with dark brown hair waited with a smile on her face.

"Those two," Dryas said doubling down on his accusation, "are the murders of the Rhodian patrol."

People moved away from the three forming a circle. Shocked by the betrayal, neither Jace, Zarek, nor Neysa moved.

"Kill them," Admiral Polemocles ordered from the wagon bed.

Spearmen snatched their weapons from the grass and four threw.

"No," Zarek screamed as he tackled Neysa, landing on her upper body.

Seeing the woman who raised him only partially protected from the spears, the teen leaped onto her legs and her lower body.

Every animal, when struck a fatal blow by an arrow exhales. Not a sigh or a quick expulsion of air, but an outbreath that comes from deep in the lungs. Hunters knew the sound. It signaled that the hunt was over, and the animal would run no farther.

Tears came to Jace's eyes when he heard Zarek utter his final breath. Then a voice came to him. From under the archer's carcass, the voice that sang him to sleep at night when he was four years old and having a nightmare about a raging sea.

"Run, Jace," Neysa ordered. "Get to the cabin, gather a long pack, and get to Phalasarna. From there, sail away from Crete. And remember, I love you. Now run!"

Jace removed a handful of arrows from Zarek's quiver.

As he came to a knee, he notched an arrow and said, "And-a-three, pick target."

Act 4

Chapter 10 – Flight of the Archer and the Arrows

Jace came up, drawing the bowstring. The arrow flew into the thigh of one spearman.

A soldier, adjacent to the wounded man, threw his spear. But the screaming of his squad mate unnerved him, and the spear went wide.

Jace had jogged left while notching a second arrow. Dropping to his knees, he allowed the spear to pass over his shoulder. Then he returned the favor by releasing the arrow.

The spear thrower fell with a shaft in his ribs. Seeing two of their mates down, the remaining pair from that side of the field deserted their positions. As they charged forward the spearmen left a footpath leading uphill unguarded.

Coming to his feet, Jace shifted right. Even as the pair advanced, he turned his back on them and notched another arrow. Immediately, he picked a target, drew, and sent a shaft into a spearman on the other side of the field. As the soldier doubled over and fell, the other three charged from that side.

With five soldiers rushing towards him, Jace Kasia seemed to be trapped. But his selective shooting had sent a message to Admiral Polemocles. In fear of the rampaging archer, the Rhodian commander instructed his five soldiers to mount the flatbed and surround him. To Jace's benefit, they would not join in the apprehension of the archer's student.

Excluded from the formation of shields, Bettina's father, barrel maker Iphis, squatted in fear to the rear of the Admiral's screen.

Although it seemed haphazard, with only three arrows, Jace Kasia had managed to reduce the number of Rhodian soldiers pursuing him from thirteen to five. But, the five were close.

A war bow had a heavy draw and used that force to warp stiff spined arrows around the belly of the bow. Generate enough power and big arrows would fly downrange and impact the target with authority. But right now, Jace didn't have the luxury of a deep draw and a long flight.

Running away from the flatbed wagon seemed to be the obvious direction to everyone. In response, the five soldiers cut across the field to intercept the archer.

Jace notched a stiff spine on the string. At half draw, the arrow wouldn't flex around the bow. It would fly off to the right. To nullify the archer's paradox, Jace flopped the bow onto its side, lowered his arm, and released the arrow. True to the mechanics, the shaft shot off to the right of the belly. But due to the angle he held the bow, the right meant up. It struck the throat of a soldier.

Jace noted the height and the narrow target of a neck. While pulling a second short draw, he lowered his arm a little more. The stiff spine left the bow and zipped quickly into the second Rhodian's chest.

With the pathway uphill unguarded, Jace ran between the downed spearmen and sprinted to the escape route. The three Rhodians from the other side of the field adjusted, but they were too far out of position to reach Jace.

Halfway up the slope, he stopped. Notching an arrow, Jace selected the fastest Rhodian soldier on the field. Then pulling the bowstring to the side of his jaw, he released.

A feathery section of the shaft jutted from the front of the soldier's stomach, while a short section with the arrowhead poked out of his back. Seeing the result of an arrow shot from a powerful war bow, the last two soldiers sprinted away from the path and the hill.

Looking over the marketplace, Jace fingered a shaft but didn't lift it fully from the quiver. The Admiral remained behind the shields. Zarek Mikolas lay pinned to the earth by a spear through his upper back and Neysa Kasia stood defiantly over her brother's body. A few yards behind Neysa, Dryas Kasia was motionless with an arm draped over the shoulders of Bettina.

Calculating distance, height of arc, and depth of draw, Jace Romiliia Kasia considered dropping an arrow into the head of Uncle Dryas or Admiral Polemocles. Neither was a difficult shot. And inflicting death on one or the other might ease the burning in his heart. Then he thought of the years of training and lessons from Master Archer Zarek.

"Never let your emotions rule the situations. But if it's necessary, still your breath so your hands are steady. Calm your heart so your eyes are clear. And focus your mind on the task."

In honor of his teacher's phrase, *if it's necessary,* Jace parted his fingers and allowed the arrow to slip back into the quiver. Then he turned and sprinted up the hill. Escape, not revenge, was the task at hand.

***

Once on the far side of Eleutherna, Jace ran. Not jogged or trotted but ran at a bone jarring pace.

One lore of the archers was of King Alexander hiring Persian archers from the conquered territories. Their composite bows of wood, sinew, and bone far outperformed the self-bows used by the Cretan bowman of the age. And while the great Macedonian king had thousands of cavalrymen and as many Persian bowmen, he kept his dependable Cretan archers nearby. Used as couriers, Cretan archers ran the miles between units of Alexander's large army to deliver orders. And archers carried the King's messages to far flung towns and forts.

In keeping with the tradition, Jace ran, and his feet flew over the five miles to Zoniana. From the village, he sprinted through the last mile to reach the farm. Even if the Admiral wanted to chase him on horseback, the soldiers would still be gathering their mounts when Jace walked into the shed.

***

According to Zarek, collecting pieces for a long pack was an art. Things to consider included weight, distribution, balance, and personal endurance.

Beyond food and clothing, a Cretan archer needed small items for cooking and bedding. Jace added bow making tools to the weight. Once he had the items assembled, he stuffed them into a leather pack, then strapped a war hatchet, two bow cases, and three quivers to the outside.

At the farmhouse, he pried loose the boards hiding Neysa's stash. Taking only his share of coins, Jace Kasia reset the boards. As he rocked back on his heels, the Romiliia Medallion slapped against his chest.

"I guess you'll find me a new home," he said while squeezing the only link he had to the Roman Republic.

Outside, he hiked by the range and took the trail to the top of the hill. At the crest, Jace wanted to take a few moments to say goodbye to the farm. But, fearing the Rhodian soldiers would be arriving at any moment, Jace turned his back on the fields and buildings, and marched westward.

If he knew about the riot in Eleutherna, he could have spent the night in his own bed. As it happened, he would spend the night in a thunderstorm.

***

Once he trekked around the curving slopes of Mount Ida, the elevation began to drop as did the clouds. At first Jace thought it would be a sprinkle. But the day darkened, forcing him to stop and pull an oiled skin from the pack. Wrapped in the tarp, he continued westward. Then the heavy rains started, and he had to seek shelter under a canopy of trees. The gray day fit his mood.

Zarek Mikolas had been like a father to him. To have the man's life taken by a lucky, or rather unlucky throw of a spear seemed wrong. Then a stream of water slipped through the branches and trickled into an opening in the oiled skin. He sat with his back against a trunk, feeling as miserable as the dreary weather.

Sometime in the afternoon, the sun set, and the gray day faded into a black night of thunder, lightning, and rain. Jace huddled under the tarp and slept.

Interspersed with the sleep, stints of anger from the nightmare caused him to shudder.

The rain came down so hard, it made each breath a wet cough. Sloshing seawater coated the deck, forcing passengers to perform an impossible dance while trying to keep their balance. Beside the boy, an adult held his hand. Then a wave slapped them, and the boy's fingers slipped from the adult's grip. Sliding, he clawed uselessly at the boards. A pair of calloused hands snatched

him from the deck and shoved him at a rail.

"Hold onto that, boy," the man ordered.

He vanished and Jace, with his arms locked around the low handrail, howled with the wind.

Then the rail rotated to the sky and a wave lifted him up and over, stripping apart his intertwined fingers. Screaming in rage, he rode a water horse across the sky. Tumbling over the crest, the boy crashed to the sand and screamed himself to sleep.

Gagging on an imaginary mouthful of water, Jace came awake spurting and seething.

"Who are you?" he whispered.

But no matter how many times he asked after the dream, he couldn't put a face or a name to the adults on the doomed ship. With rain and dark around him, he settled back to wait for morning.

***

It felt like a different world. The wide creek bed wandered between steep tree lined banks. Dodging low hanging branches, Jace hopped from rock to rock until reaching another gravel bar. Then he strolled for a while before jumping on another rock. All the while, birds sang, and the water rippled over stones giving the place an aura of being enchanted.

It was cool and pleasant, and he would have continued following the stream. Except, the gentle grade began to fall drastically, and other streams merged into the creek. The water began to deepen and rush around his feet. Grabbing a branch, Jace pulled himself out of the water and away from the rocks.

A rushing sound came to him as he climbed the embankment, but Jace couldn't place the noise. Breaking from the trees, he reached the top of the bank and stepped onto a bare hump of land. Only then did he notice the big lake far below him and identified the roaring as the creek cascaded down a steep cliff.

"That would have been an ugly fall," he scolded himself.

"What would have been ugly?" a voice behind him asked.

Spinning, he noted an old man struggling up the rise, holding an ancient, cracked hunting bow.

"I'd say that bow of yours," Jace blurted out. He'd been on the farm with Neysa and Zarek and they were plain spoken people. In horror, he added. "My apologies, I meant no insult to your equipment."

"Son, this old bow has been my companion for a long time," the man offered. "I'm afraid she can't reach out for my winter provisions any longer. I'm thinking about using her for firewood. So, I don't think she'll take offense at your words."

"What will you use to hunt when she's gone?" Jace inquired.

"That does present a problem," the hunter confessed. "But, with her limited range, I almost have to be on top of the meat before I shoot, anyway. I could always just grab hold and hang on."

"Do you mind if I take a look?" Jase asked.

The old hunter handed him the unstrung bow. After examining the joints by twisting and tracing clearly visible cracks, he wedged a thumbnail under the horn backing and pried one section off.

"Oh, now look what you've done," the old hunter complained. "You've peeled off a piece of my girl."

"Where is your camp?" Jace inquired.

"You've broken my bow," the old guy whined. "Are you going to dismantle my cabin as well?"

"These cracks are from stress not signs of broken wood," Jace explained. "Feed and shelter me for two days and I'll rebuild your hunter."

"You can do that?"

"I can. Provided you have hide and tendon material."

"The hide I have," the old man said. "And I think there's some dried sinew from the last time she pulled hard."

"Jace Kasia."

"People call me, Baruch," the old guy responded. "My cabin is down the hill on the edge of the woods."

"Why on the edge? Why not under the trees for shade?"

"Because if I built it any lower, I'd have to pay taxes on that shade," Baruch sneered. "Come on young fellow, follow me. Imagine meeting a bow maker out here on the trail."

"Surely there are other bow technicians around," Jace suggested.

"Lots of fake Cretan archers," Baruch grumbled. "But none with the skills to fix my girl."

"How do you know they're fake?"

"Because they brag too much and do too little," Baruch replied. "Not like you, who showed his specialty right away."

As they started down the winding path, Jace turned over what the hunter said about fake archers. According to Zarek, Jace had the training and skills, but no way to claim a place among Cretan archers. But as a bow maker, he didn't need to prove all the skills, just one.

***

Baruch paced back and forth in the small cabin. Occasionally, he'd stop, bend, and look around Jace's shoulder.

"You can come up beside me and watch," Jace invited.

"Not with my girl in that condition," the old hunter told him. "I can't bare to look at her."

Jace held the joint of the belly and the upper limb over a boiling pot of water. As the steam soaked the hide glue, it softened the connection. After a few moments, the young archer applied pressure until the belly slid from the notch in the limb.

"Oh, oh," Baruch cried. "My poor girl."

He went to the far end of the structure and buried his face in his hands. Jace used a thin plate of steel to scrape away the glue and sinew that clung to the wood. After a few passes, he held the limb up to the light of the window and turned the piece over.

"Just as I thought, the cracks were in the glue," he announced. "But I see one problem from…"

Baruch raced across the room, stopped, and stared at the bow limb.

"What is it?" he begged. "Please tell me it's not terminal."

"It's the tip of the limb," Jace informed him. "It's rubbed down from years of looping the bowstring. I'll add a piece of bone to the bow tip with a channel for the string. That'll stop the abrasion."

"And then you'll put her back together?"

"Not until I take her, ugh, now you have me doing it," Jace complained. "Not until I scour the pieces down to bare wood. You know what we don't have?"

"What? What?"

"A couple of pieces of big horn."

"You will," the old hunter promised.

He ran out of the door and down to the village deeper in the woods. While he was gone, Jace worked the steel scraper back and forth over the wood of the belly. After removing years of hide glue, his hands stilled, and he gazed at letters scratched into the maple.

"Z. Mikolas," he read.

Slowing, Jace took more time cleaning each piece. He didn't know how long ago his teacher made this bow. But the young archer swore that when he finished, the bow would last at least that many years more.

***

It took two extra days to assemble, glue, and coat the hunting bow. After the glue set and the sinew dried, Jace presented the bow to Baruch.

"Ah, Jace, she's all done up in new clothing," the old man gushed. "Not a crack or a wobble in her frame."

"That bow will last a hundred years, if you treat it right," Jace explained.

He settled the copper pot into his long pack and followed it with the smaller copper container.

"You can stay here. We'll go hunting."

"I need to be moving onto Phalasarna," Jace told him. "Find some work, earn me some coins, and then catch a ship to the Republic."

"Getting off Crete, right now, is a good idea for any young man," Baruch said. "You'll find plenty of work in the port city. Between the comings and goings of archers, and the broken bows from the agoge, a man with your skill can make a fortune."

"That doesn't sound right," Jace argued. "A Cretan archer loves nothing more than his bows. To receive a gift of a weapon is the highest honor."

"Maybe in an ideal world," Baruch suggested. "For boys assured of employment in the future, their training bows are just toys."

"How could you know that?" Jace demanded.

"Years ago, I bought my girl from a Cretan archer. He only asked if I would treat her good," Baruch told him. "The archer said he would rather a hunter have the bow than a careless boy. That's what he said. It was."

The latter comment came as a reaction to the disbelieving look on Jace's face. Zarek had drilled the ideals, behaviors, and beliefs of a perfect Cretan archer into Jace. For years, he insisted on perfection and adherence to the highest standards. Now, faced with testament contrary to those values, Jace had no frame of reference for the change in perspective.

"I'll have to check that for myself," Jace stated as he tied the cases containing his war bow and his hunting bow to the side of the pack. "Any advice for the road before I go?"

"Head south from Amari Lake then follow the main trail west to the town of Kanevos," Baruch responded. "From there, it's three miles to the bay. It'll be quicker and you won't get drafted into any militias."

"What? Drafted into what?"

"Every small and medium sized town on the trail between here and Phalasarna has committed to sending soldiers to the nearest big city," Baruch told him. "It'll be safer for you to travel by boat. Sailors are notoriously reluctant to join armies. When you get to the bay ask for my cousin, Danaus."

"Oh, you're talking about the attack on Lyttos," Jace guessed.

"Lyttos? Nobody is going to attack the Spartan colony. Polyrrhenia and Lappa signed a pact with Lyttos after Eleutherna declared war on the Island of Rhodes," the old hunter explained. "It seems a Rhodian admiral murdered a citizen, and the council issued a statement of war."

"Then everything is settled?" Jace questioned.

"Oh no, my young bow maker. Now that the Cretan agreement has broken up, every city is trying to capture the other," Baruch told him. "It's civil war and you need to avoid being pressed into a militia."

"So, I should take a ship to the port city?"

"No, no. You work your way there on a shore trader," Baruch corrected. "That's one good thing about a civil war."

"What could be good about a civil war?"

"It creates a shortage of young men with strong backs," Baruch responded. "You'll have no trouble working your way to Phalasarna."

Chapter 11 – He Had No Choice

Jace left the cabin and headed south. After several hundred paces, he stopped, looked over his left shoulder, and contemplated returning to the farm. It would be nice to say a proper goodbye to Neysa. Although while there, he'd be tempted to hunt down Dryas and put an arrow in his heart. And no doubt, while messing around on a foolhardy mission of revenge, he'd get pressed into the Eleutherna militia.

"When I go to war," he swore to the trees, "I'll do it as a Cretan archer and get paid for my skills."

With that thought in mind, he continued the hike until he reached a crossroads. Halting in the center of the intersection, he paused for a moment. Then, Jace squared his shoulders, turned right, and marched to his fate. Or rather, he hiked to the town of Kanevos, his first stop on the road to his fate. That's if he didn't count Baruch's cabin. Confused, his mind leaped around ideas even as his feet took steps.

For all his training, skills, and learning, Jace Kasia had never been without the counsel of Zarek, Neysa, or even Dryas. And truthfully, in his current situation, he was lost on a journey along an uncertain road.

***

Thirteen miles to the west, Jace strolled into the village of Kanevos. A single street made up the commercial district. A sign over a shed read Galip Metals. Spying a metalworker pounding on a lump of hot iron, he strolled to the work shed.

"That would go faster if you had a second hammer," Jace suggested.

"What?" the metalworker questioned while shoving the iron into the fire.

"Whenever my master had a pretty chunk of iron like that," Jace told him. "he'd call me over to help."

"Can you keep a pace?"

"Try me," Jace said while dropping his pack.

The man handed Jace a hammer. Then he pulled the hot iron from the forge and tapped the glowing lump with his hammer. As soon as the man lifted his hammer, Jace brought his down. They went in turns until the glow faded.

"You had a good teacher," the man complimented as he shoved the iron back into the fire. "Are you a metalworker?"

"No, sir. We used the iron for arrowheads. I'm a bow maker."

"Don't say that too loud," Galip warned. "The militia will kidnap you for their war."

"Their war?" Jace inquired. "Isn't it yours as well?"

"Neighbors fighting neighbors, a son dies, then another," the metalworker lectured, "pretty soon there are feuds that kill descendants, long removed from the current civil war."

"That's a harsh description," Jace pointed out.

"No son, that's the truth of the matter. Why are you here?"

"I'm looking for Danaus. He's the cousin of a friend," Jace said. "I need a boat ride to Phalasarna."

"He docks his trader at the bay, three miles south of here," the metalworker told him. He lifted the bright iron from the fire. "Hit it."

They pounded the piece into a working form that could be shaped into different items. Then they put the hammers on a bench.

"You've earned lunch," the metalworker declared. "Come with me."

"What about Danaus and the boat?"

"You've got time to eat. He won't be here for another day or so."

At lunch, Jace discovered Galip had a wife and a house full of children. Unfortunately for the metalworker, they were all too young to help around the forge. After a long meal under the shade of a tree, Galip returned to the shed while Jace trekked southward to the bay.

***

A half mile outside of Kanevos, the trail met a slow flowing river. Then the reason for the calm surface became apparent. While the trail meandered down old goat trails, the Kotsifos River flowed into a basin before the water fell a hundred feet to a shallow pool. From the pool, the river moved without much change to a beach on the Mediterranean Sea. And while the fresh water ran straight, Jace walked a winding path to the lowland.

At the beach, he located a tall tree, dropped his pack, and sat looking out over the swells. Birds glided between dives to catch fish, far off clouds drifted across the sky, and the afternoon breeze blew gently across his face. With his belly full, thanks to Galip's wife, and no sign of Danaus or his boat, Jace closed his eyes with the intention of letting the afternoon drift away.

It felt as if he just dozed off when the crunch of feet on the sand and gravel alerted Jace to the arrival of another person. He thought nothing of it until two sharp objects poked him in the ribs.

"You, boy, have just volunteered for service in the home guard of Gortyna," a bear of a man announced.

Crumbs and drippings clung to his bushy beard. Above the hair, bright veins on his bloated nose and cheeks revealed his love of wine. Despite the slovenly appearance, the man had big arms and a broad chest.

It was his unhurried footsteps that awakened Jace. But the sound didn't alert him to the danger of two spearmen coming silently from behind the tree.

"Who are you?" Jace inquired.

"Lieutenant Acestes, at your service," the big man answered. "I'm the procurement officer for the City of Gortyna. And you have just volunteered for the city's militia."

"Where is Gortyna?" Jace asked while pushing to his knees. The tips of the spears followed as he moved.

With his war hatchet less than an arm's length away, Jace calculated his chances. Then a fourth man stepped from around the tree. Four against a single hatchet, settled any thought of battle.

"Gortyna is inland from the Bay of Matala. That's about thirty-five miles east from here," Acestes told him. "You'll love the city. It's beautiful this time of year. Ah but, come to think of it, you won't see much of the city."

"And why, Lieutenant Acestes, won't I see much of the city?" Jace inquired.

"Because new recruits are sent to the stone quarry," Acestes answered.

"You aren't really an officer in the city's militia, are you?" Jace challenged. "You're nothing more than a slave trader."

"Not since the civil war started," Acestes boasted. "Now, I'm a procurement officer for the City of Gortyna and these soldiers are my squad."

The three spearmen laughed at the description. Then one jabbed Jace in the ribs. Responding to the sharp hint, the teen came to his feet.

"What about my pack?" he asked when one of the soldiers began wrapping a leather thong around his wrists.

"I don't care about your pack," Acestes said.

"Lieutenant, those are bow cases strapped to it, and the hatchet is good steel," a spearman noted. "If you don't want the pack, I'll take it."

Acestes glanced at Jace's pack then up at the teen. Discounting the meaning of a youth having a Cretan archer's long pack was his first mistake.

"Have one of the other's carry the pack," he instructed. "I don't want my youthful conscript to get any ideas."

Jace turned around. On the trail behind the tree, five men shuffled into view. Tied at the waist onto a length of wagon rein, they looked dirty, exhausted, and half starved.

"Move it," a spearmen ordered. With a shove, he nudged Jace to the trail. As they neared the procession of prisoners, the soldier called out. "Bring up the wagon."

A mule and cart guided by a sixth man rolled to the hostages. That's when Jace knew he was dealing with men experienced in the trading and selling of human flesh. Before the wagon stopped, the teamster pulled a length of heavy harness from the bed.

In moments, the thick leather encircled Jace's waist and after a few knots it rested snuggly on his hips. The final step was to affix the waists harness to the length of rein. Jace's long pack ended up on the shoulders of the detainee at the front. He sagged under the weight that Jace carried on the trail.

For the second time, Lieutenant Acestes missed a sign that he was dealing with a Cretan archer.

***

Where the trip down the goat trail had been an easy hike, going up with men falling to their knees and dragging the others to their hands and knees made the going slow. Adding to their misery, Acestes' thugs prodded with the ends of their spears.

"Get up. Get moving," they bellowed while ignoring the difficulty of men linked together trying to navigate a twisting path. "Move it or I'll give you a reason to whine."

Of the six bodies tied to the thick wagon rein, the teen didn't complain or cry out when he was pulled to his knees. Rather than grumble, he helped the man in front of him back to his feet. After the challenges of the archer's test, bloody knees barely registered as pain. None of the slave traders noticed the youth's stoic nature.

At the top of the falls, the trail leveled and ran alongside the lazy river.

"I need a drink of water," one of the prisoners announced.

"We need to wait for the wagon," Acestes said. "Give him a drink. Give all of them a drink."

The two henchmen at the front swung their spear shafts, knocking the first detainees into the river. In a chain reaction, the first man jerked the second towards the water. Their combined weight snatched the third off the trail. Violently snapped from the path, the fourth and fifth men sailed bent in half before splashing into the surface. The guards were laughing so hard, they failed to notice the youth brace his legs before leaping with the fifth man.

Jace landed upright in the river where he cupped his hands and calmly took a drink. The other five were sputtering from near downing and struggling to get their feet under them.

"That's enough water for their likes. Get them out and get them moving. I want to get to Kanevos and have a drink," Acestes instructed. Seeing frowns on the faces of the guards, the Lieutenant added. "We will all have wine to celebrate the success of our recruitment drive."

Slipping and climbing, the first men up the riverbank suffered strikes from the spear shafts. The punishment worked as they quickly pulled the rest of the prisoners from the river while getting out of range from the spears.

"Get accustomed to the motivational sticks," Acestes told the captives. "Until you learn your place and obey instantly, you'll sample the sticks a lot."

Two miles from their dip in the Kotsifos River, the caravan of desolation entered the town of Kanevos. Jace looked for Galip, but the metalworker had left the shed. How long ago, the youth could only guess because the embers in the forge still glowed red.

"Now, out of the goodness of my heart, I'm going to give you trainees the night off," Acestes announced. As he talked, one thug strolled to the wagon. "But often, a new man will take advantage of my generous nature. So, before you turn in, I want you to have a taste of what's in store for anyone trying to leave the service tonight."

Returning, the soldier handed a club with a fist sized knot on one end to the Lieutenant. Stepping to the head of the line, the big trader swung the club.

The first detainee wasn't quick enough. The club smashed him in the face. The second got his hands up, but his fingers were speared. The club broke two fingers on one hand. After witnessing the savagery, the third man got his fists up and managed to absorb the strike with only a deep bruise to one wrist. Trembling in fear, the fourth and fifth men buried their faces in the palms of their hands. As if a tanner beating a hide to soften the material, Acestes flexed before smashing one man to the ground. Then in a move that seemed impossible for a big man, he spun and cracked the other just as hard. With five men withering on the ground in terror and pain, he stepped to the teen.

"This is a reminder of my mercy and my wrath," he exclaimed while bringing the club around with force.

Jace rotated his writs towards the slave trader and positioned the meaty part of his right arm in front of his face. When the club connected with the hard muscle of the archer's forearm, the impact resembled the wet sound of a butcher attempting to break the ribs on a side of beef.

Reacting to the sickening thud of the club, the other slave traders groaned.

"So what? He'll be a one-armed worker for a few weeks, but he'll recover," Acestes said, excusing his overzealous use of the club. Then to his downtrodden charges, he declared. "You'll have bread in the morning. For tonight, crawl into the bird pen. And remember, anyone trying to escape will get another round of my punishment stick."

Bent over his right arm, as if it was truly injured, Jace shuffled forward. What the slave traders didn't see was the calloused fingers of an archer already untying the straps of the waist harness. He followed the others as they entered a large enclosure.

Posts forming a short stockade kept out predators by sealing the bottom of the bird coop. Above the ring of sticks, several continued up and over creating a mesh to keep the birds in the enclosure. A healthy man could easily kick his way out of the bird enclosure. But the noise would draw the attention of the thugs. And they would come swiftly, bringing the spears, the club, and the pain.

Jace understood the idea behind controlling with pain. Zarek explained that administering agony conditioned men to quickly follow orders. But through training, a Cretan archer conditioned himself to use the pain to accomplish his own goals.

While his arm was bruised and tender, the muscles that for years had pulled and held ever increasing difficulties of bowstrings, worked just fine. Soon he went from unraveling the waist harness ties to holding it up, so it didn't fall off his hips. Then Jace sat on the ground while working out his escape plan.

***

The chuckles and tantalizing aromas drifting from the slaver traders' camp were opposite the moaning of the hurting men, sprawled in the dirt and bird droppings of the coop. And while one got ever louder from the consumption of wine, the other area quieted down as the evening darkened.

"Just a reminder, recruits," a thug said from outside. He drew something along the stockade wall creating a thump, thump, thump sound as he circled the pen. "Anyone trying to leave the service of Gortyna, will have a really bad day on the march tomorrow."

His threat brought howls of amusement from the slave trader camp, and groans from inside the bird enclosure. Eventually, both groups settled down. The night grew hushed with only the noises of night bugs and nocturnal creatures humming above the snoring of those asleep and the footfalls of a sentry.

In the dark, Jace listened and counted. At intervals, a thug walked around the pen then moved away before returning to complete a circuit. Where the sentry went for a count of five hundred, Jace had no idea. He just knew that when he broke out, he'd have a count of under five hundred to find his pack and get away. But for the moment, he counted footfalls and waited for the deep shadows that came with a moonrise.

***

After a change in guards, as Jace could tell by the different strides, the night grew darker. It was an illusion that preceded the appearance of the moon. At tree top level, the branches became less of a blob against the stars and more identifiable as creepy fingers.

The guard had moved off and where the night sounds should have dominated the evening, a new set of footsteps approached the enclosure.

"Bow maker. I hope you can use these," a voice whispered.

Two long objects slid through the mesh and touched the ground. Before the objects settled against the wall, the footsteps faded as the bringer of gifts ran off. In the dark, Jace collected a bow case and a quiver. Pulling them close, he smelled the distinct aroma of iron flakes.

A quick inspection of the bow case and the quiver told Jace the outcome of the morning. He would not be scurrying off into the night, trying to avoid the slave traders. Nor would he rush around desperate to locate his long pack and avoid Acestes' club. None of those were fated for the morning, because Galip, the metalworker had brought Jace his war bow, and his quiver of stiff spined arrows. In the hands of a Cretan archer, those weapons were designed for one thing and one thing only.

Jace Kasia settled back against the wall and closed his eyes. He'd rest for the moment. Then at twilight, because he had no choice, he would kill the slave traders.

Chapter 12 – Weapon Of Choice

At the false dawn, when most people had difficulty focusing and separating shadows from reality, Jace gently bent the bow over his knee. He flexed the wood, sinew, and horn back and forth until the war bow became pliable. He looped the end of a bowstring around one tip.

"Three hundred and forty-five."

Then he braced the strung end of the bow behind his ankle. After bending the bow across his right thigh, he looped the other end, completing the process of stringing the bow.

"What are you doing?" one prisoner asked.

"No matter what you hear or what happens," Jace warned, "stay in the coop until I'm finished."

"Where are you going?"

"To have a short talk with Lieutenant Acestes."

"A short talk about what?"

"His treatment of the recruits," Jace told the captive. Before walking to the entrance and kicking out the door, he counted. "Four hundred ninety-eight."

Timing the escape for when the sentry was on a return track, Jace emerged from the bird enclosure. To the guard, in the low light of morning, the archer was an indiscernible shadow. But to Jace, the sentry was a clear as a target on a range.

The stiff arrow rode the string to the side of Jace's chin. Then, with the power of the war bow behind it, the missile flew to the slaver's chest. The man yelped once before his heart stopped pumping. He fell to the ground. As the light went out in his eyes, Jace notched another arrow.

Jogging around the bird coop, he searched for Lieutenant Acestes' camp. Once he found the low fire, the empty wine skins littering the ground, the mule cart, and three reclining bodies, he released the arrow into the neck of another slaver. Without bothering to check his accuracy, Jace continued forward. Notching a third arrow he shot another one. The arrow traveled into the man's chest, through his heart, and stopped when it broke ribs in the man's back.

If the situation was different, Jace would shoot to wound and ask for surrender. But a war bow shot with so much power that, at a close distance, the stiff arrow could easily push through soft tissue, doing little damage. A puncture wound would leave an injured man mobile and still in the fight.

Jace had height and wide shoulders. But the teen's frame hadn't filled out yet. It forced him to kill rather than chance a hand-to-hand struggle with any of the slave traders.

Acestes came out of his bedroll snorting like a mad bull and waving his meaty arms around.

"Sorry, Lieutenant," Jace remarked.

The big slaver stopped and stared at the teen.

"Look here boy, I'm…"

The arrow leaped from the war bow, traveled in a snap, and snaked into the Lieutenant's eye socket. With the bronze arrowhead deep in his brain and the shaft sticking out of the eye hole, the slaver dropped to his knees before toppling over.

"What's it going to be, teamster?" Jace inquired of the mule handler who knelt near the cart. "Run or fight? The choice is yours."

In a flash, the man jumped up and in an all-out sprint left the campsite. He quickly vanished into the weak light of dawn.

"Can we come out?" one of the captives questioned.

"Yes," Jace replied as he dropped to the ground.

On his knees, he searched the slaver's food stores. After selecting six cuts of meat, he shoved them on sticks. Then he built up the fire, placed the meat over the flames, and went to secure his long pack.

***

Five of the former detainees sat around the camp eating and staring at the ground. They had gone to sleep with no hope and awakened to a fine breakfast. The change left them happy but shaken.

After reclaiming his arrows, Jace carried them back to the campfire.

"I heard you say sorry to Acestes," one mentioned. "What did you mean?"

"My war bow left me no choice," Jace replied. "I was and am sorry for not giving them a chance to surrender."

"You really think they would have given up?" another asked.

"Put enough arrows into anyone and they will," Jace assured the man. "It's preferable to murder."

"What you did wasn't murder," the man with the bruise on his wrist insisted. "It was retaliation for us being forced from our homes."

"From how far away?" Jace questioned.

"Four days ago, I stayed home when my brothers took our fishing boats out," the bruised man responded. "When Acestes and his animals came to my village, I greeted him."

"And he just took you?"

The man twisted around and pulled his shirt up. A series of deep bruises marked places on his back where the club impacted.

"Not without a fight," he bragged while pointing at the black and blue spots. "But I didn't have training or weapons. I owe you for freeing me. And Klaus always pays his debts. What do you want?"

"Us as well," the other detainees echoed the sentiment.

Having five strangers, all much older than him, profess their debt to the teen confused Jace. He didn't have a ready answer. Then he glanced around at the dead and thought of Galip, the metalworker, having to deal with corpses.

"We need to remove the bodies from the town," Jace tested to see if any of the captives would challenge the idea.

"We can load them onto the mule wagon and dump them in the sea," Klaus suggested. "If we time it to the outgoing tide, they'll wash away from the area."

"You can keep the mule and cart," another offered.

"They won't do me any good," Jace said while cleaning his skinning knife, "unless the mule can swim to Phalasarna."

"You need a ride to Phalasarna?" Klaus exclaimed. "That my young rescuer is easy. It'll take us a few days to sail the sixty-five miles. But we'll fish along the route. And when we arrive at the port city, I'll split the profits from selling the fish."

"What can we do for you?" the others begged.

Jace looked from one dirty face to the next.

"For me, nothing," he told them. "But there is a lady near the village of Zoniana who is dear to me. If you want, send something to Neysa Kasia at her farm. That will be payment enough."

"You're very generous for one so young," Klaus complimented him.

"Someday I hope to be recognized as a Cretan archer," Jace remarked. "Until then I'm trying to be as good an example as my teacher would want."

"I think he would be pleased," the fisherman stated. Then to the other detainees, he coached. "Now, let's get those bodies loaded before they begin to stink in death more than they reeked in life."

While Jace repacked his gear, the five former captives harnessed the mule and moved to recover Acestes.

Groaning as they began elevating the big Lieutenant, one remarked about the arrow hole in his eye, "that's a nasty way to die."

"No. That's a perfect shot," Klaus corrected. "Everybody, lift. We still have three more of these rats to collect."

***

On the trip westward, they dropped men off at intervals. The second claimed to be a poor farmer so the group gave him the mule and cart. Once all three left the shoreline to return home, Klaus glanced at Jace.

"It's odd, I know this stretch of shoreline," he marveled. "I've traveled it and sailed by it many times. Yet, I don't remember walking these rocks with the slavers."

"Physical intimidation does things to the memory," Jace informed him. "My teacher said if you aren't trained to recognize what's happening to you, your mind will blank out sections or even entire days."

"That explains my forgetfulness," Klaus agreed. "But why the cruelty? Why beat us when we did everything Acestes asked?"

"Part of control has to do with instilling responses," Jace recalled from his lessons with Zarek. "Every time you flinched from the club, your mind went blank, and you followed orders without question. The harsher the punishment, the quicker you followed orders. And, here's the key. The less you thought about what you were doing."

"I always think about what I'm doing," Klaus bragged.

"Of course, you do," Jace sympathized. Then he asked. "What were you thinking when you laid down on the bed of bird manure in the coop?"

Klaus continued for several strides before kicking a loose rock.

"I was thinking that my wrist hurt and how grateful I was to have a wall between Acestes and me," Klaus replied. "I didn't realize I was laying in bird droppings, because I was looking forward to the bread in the morning."

Jace didn't need to point out the blind obedience stated in the fisherman's description.

Farther down the shoreline, Klaus inquired, "How does an archer use that knowledge?

"There are different types of pain," Jace answered, "But basically there are two, physical and mental. We've been talking about abuse to the body. The second kind of agony is in your head. In combat, your mind will tempt you to move away from the noise and clash of the fighting. And just as you forgot about walking on this section of rocks after being clubbed, combat will make you go blank in the face of the brutality. But an archer's job is to ignore the danger, fight the response, and stay focused on winning the battle."

"And you can do that?"

"Fortune provided me with the best training," Jace stated. "And a teacher who instructed me in the art of being a Cretan archer. Only after walking the fated road and immersing myself in the tides of battle will I know the answer to that question."

Klaus accepted the teen's explanation and the two continued along the shoreline. They occasionally talked, but mostly the two travelers watched the birds fly over the waves.

***

Three days later, after stretches of beach and longer segments of rocky trail, they rounded a bend in the shoreline and came to a sandy sections.

"This is Damnoni, my home," Klaus announced.

Upside down fishing boats and fanned out nets occupied a section of the beach. Higher up the slope, fires bathed drying fish in smoke. And above the sand and gravel, huts sat on the edge of a tree line. Klaus whistled, and in a heartbeat, a gaggle of four children ran from the homes and attempted to tackle the former captive.

"Your children?" Jace asked.

"Not mine," Klaus declared while fending off the little arms. "These brats belong to my brothers. I want to grow them a little bigger before I turn them into fish bait."

"You are fish bait," a little girl exclaimed.

"No. You are fish bait," Klaus responded. He plucked her from the sand and put her on his shoulder. "Come, Jace Kasia. Let me introduce you to my family."

***

The fisherman's family consisted of his mother, three brothers, two with wives and four children between them. Klaus and his youngest brother were the only bachelors. But Jace noticed four women from the village who came to greet Klaus and stayed for the homecoming feast.

The afternoon was taken up by eating, drinking, and Klaus telling the guests about his captivity by evil men, and his release by the hero Jace Kasia. As soon as they cleared the table, Jace excused himself. On the beach, he sat looking out over the sea. Elek, Klaus' younger brother, dropped down beside him.

"My family has fished those waters for six generations," Elek offered.

"How did Klaus get taken by slavers?"

"Four years ago, our father and uncle went out in the family's fishing boat," Elek explained. "They never came back. Klaus started working on other vessels until he saved enough to buy our first. Then as my brothers got older, Klaus bought more fishing boats. As the head of our clan, his one rule is no two members of the family could go out together."

"Because of what happened to your father and uncle," Jace guessed, "I assume you took the boat that day and he stayed home."

"Yes," Elek confirmed. Then the brother grew quiet before gushing. "Teach me how to fight."

"What weapon did you have in mind?"

"The bow sounds impressive. After what Klaus said about your shooting, I'd like to defend my family like that."

"The bow is a difficult weapon to learn. At least well enough to use in a stressful situation," Jace told him. Elek's shoulders shrugged, and he hung his head. Seeing someone only a couple of years older than him sulk, he inquired. "What weapon do you use now?"

"We're fishermen," Elek replied. "We use our oars to fend off large predators and rocks for smaller ones. But no real weapons."

Jace made an exaggerated push on the sand with both fists, twisted at the waist, and gazed at the drying racks behind them.

"So, those fish in the smoke," he questioned, "they crawled ashore and climbed to a perch in the smoke by themselves?"

"Don't be silly," Elek scolded. "We net them, and row the baskets to the beach. Then we gut the fish in the surf before we put them on the drying racks."

"Tell me, which do you gut the fish with the oar or the rocks?"

Elek reached to his side and rested a hand on the hilt of a thin bladed knife.

"Neither, I use…" the brother stopped and smiled. Then he added. "My knife is a weapon."

"Show me how you use it to gut a fish."

Elek drew his knife with his right hand and held his left hand over it as if holding a fish on its side. He began making sawing motions.

"Good. Now roll your hand over and place your thumb on the blade."

With the blade flat, the fisherman swiped back and forth with the knife.

"You make that motion everyday as a fisherman," Jace pointed out. "I don't have to teach you the weapon, just the steps to move out of danger."

"But I wanted a devastating weapon," Elek protested.

Jace jumped to his feet and walked to a pile of wood. Selecting two lengths, he carried them to Elek.

"That wool scarf around your neck? Do you wear it every day?"

"I use it to keep the sun off my head and to wipe sea water and sweat from my eyes."

"Take it off and wrap it around your left wrist and hand," Jace instructed. As Elek wrapped material around his left hand, Jace folded a piece of cloth over his. Then after tossing one stick to the brother. "The cloth is your defense against minor cuts. The stick is your knife. Now, stab me."

Elek stepped forward and limply stabbed at the archer. With his protected hand, Jace pushed the knife hand down, took a half pace forward, and slammed the stick into the side of Elek's head. The fisherman stumbled away before dropping to his knees.

"I said to stab me, not tickle my ribs."

The younger brother came to his feet and rushed at the archer. Leading with the stick, he charged as if intending to drive it home by sheer momentum.

Jace shifted to the side, stuck out a foot, and tripped Elek. He added a shove to the fisherman's back, sending him sprawling face first into the sand.

"You're right," Elek said while rolling over and brushing sand from his forehead. "It takes a lot of training to learn weapons."

"Stand up. Slide your right foot back and separate your feet," Jace instructed. "A fight only happens when your enemy comes close. Your problem was you attacked blindly. Why? Let the enemy come at you. Then you can defend your ground and control the situation. Ready, stab me."

"Step over here," Elek challenged while swiping the stick across his front. "I can't reach you."

"Now you understand," Jace said.

Klaus, his mother, brothers, wives, the village women, and the children poured from the home. They ran to the two combatants.

"What's the problem?" Klaus pleaded. "Elek, why are you two fighting?"

"It's not a fight," his youngest brother assured him, "until Jace attacks me."

"Why would Jace attack you?"

"He won't. Because he's afraid of my defense."

Klaus squinted in confusion at his brother who had sand on his clothing and on his face. Then he spun on Jace.

"Elek isn't wrong," the archer told Klaus. "His stance is good, and he brandishes the weapon as if it's an extension of his arm."

"It's his knife, not a weapon," Klaus remarked. "We're fishermen. We use the tool every day."

"I've trained with knives and swords, both long and short ones," Jace described. "I'm practiced and proficient with the blades. But my primary melee weapon is the war hatchet. Can you guess why?"

"It has a longer handle?" Klaus ventured.

Jace smiled and indicated the knife on Klaus' hip.

"I favor the hatchet for the same reason the knife is Elek's best choice for a weapon," Jace informed him. "I've used one daily since I was a little boy. Cutting down trees, trimming trunks, splitting logs for firewood, or to plane them into boards. From carving bow parts to shaving arrows, I've held a hatchet longer and more often than any of my bows."

"You're teaching Elek to fight?" Klaus inquired.

"I'm showing him how to defend his life and his home," Jace clarified. "Fighting is a different mindset all together."

"We leave for Phalasarna at down," Klaus advised. "Don't hurt each other."

Elek laughed then mentioned, "That's the problem with my big brother, he's always worried I'll get hurt when I'm having fun."

With Elek chuckling and looking at Klaus, Jace stepped inside the fisherman's guard, hooked a leg behind his knee, and dumped Elek on the ground.

"When you're defending, never assume your foe is done as long as the blades are out," Jace warned while tapping the young fishermen on the forehead with the stick.

Klaus shook his head and mumbled as he strolled back to the house, "Give boys sticks and they'll beat on each other every time."

Jace was confused by the comment. For him, weapons training was serious.

Act 5

Chapter 13 – For Free Food

The fishing vessel skimmed across the water. Usually, the boat hauled heavy fishing nets, baskets for the fish, a crew of four, and the weight of the catch. Without the normal equipment and crew, the wide boat took advantage of the wind.

"I almost can't see the difference between the sea and the sky," Jace remarked.

"Sometimes, depending on the location of the sun, the sky and sea swap places," Klaus described. "The blue and green flip and you feel as if you're sailing across the sky with the water above you."

"I'm not sure how I feel about sailing upside down," Jace commented, "but, it is beautiful."

"If nature impresses you, wait until you see the majesty of Phalasarna," the fisherman said. "The harbor itself is a wonder."

A high peak just off the shoreline blocked the landscape ahead. Then, as the fishing boat progressed, it came abreast of the peak and a wide bay appeared. On the far side of the inlet, buildings stretched along the shoreline and from a wall facing the sea to the base of the hills rising over the city.

"What are those on top of the ridge?" Jace questioned.

"Phalasarna is a major port," Klaus answered. "The city guard keeps lookouts on the high ground in case of pirates or an invasion."

"Who would attack the home of the academy for Cretan archers?"

"The agoge is but a small part of city life. Beyond the archers and their school, the city is a hub for international trade."

From Zarek's description of the agoge, the teen expected the archers, the Herds, and the advanced students of the Troops to be everywhere. Yet, the sheer size of Phalasarna offered a different reality. The view forced Jace to question if his teacher had intentionally exaggerated or simply idealized the academy for archers.

"I thought the archer school would take up a big part of the city," Jace stated, trying to justify Zarek's description.

"The residents barely pay attention to Cretan archers," Klaus told him. "On any given day, there are more sailors, tradesmen, and warehouse workers than archers in the city."

As the boat approached the channel through the sea wall, Klaus ordered the sail rolled. Jace and the crewman manned side oars while Klaus worked a rear oar.

"Stroke, stroke," he called until the three were working together.

The boat passed the opening to the channel and Klaus steered it to where the defensive wall turned inland. A fleet of fishing boats crowded a beach outside the wall while on higher ground a market bustled with activity.

"Only major shippers and allied warships are allowed into the protected harbor," he explained as they rowed. "We'll beach and sell our catch."

"You didn't haul in much," Jace pointed out.

"I wanted to keep us moving. Besides, if we brought in too many fish, the city would tax us," Klaus said. "As it is, we look like fisherman on vacation come to spend coins in the city. Which we are."

"When will you leave?" Jace asked.

"Late tomorrow," the fisherman replied. "If you change your mind and want to go back to the farm or to become a fisherman, we'll give you a ride."

When the keel ground into the sand, Jace and the crewman jumped out.

"I'm not going back," he swore to Klaus while tugging the fishing boat up onto the beach. "I can't be a Cretan archer on a farm or as a fisherman."

"You're Latian," Klaus remarked. "Can you be a Cretan archer in Phalasarna?"

Jace reached into the boat, lifted out his long pack, and hooked his arms through the straps.

"That remains to be seen," he declared while walking away.

"Wait. What about your share of the catch?"

"Keep it. Put it towards buying Elek his own fishing boat," Jace shouted over his shoulder. "I've got coins enough."

Without thinking, he touched the purse on his left hip. While he spoke off handedly, two men lounging against a fishing boat heard his words distinctly. And with focused interest, they observed him touching the coin sack.

Out of habit, Jace touched the war hatchet on the other hip. Comforted by the presence of the weapon, the teen archer hiked from the edge of the water, by rows of boat, and approached the public market.

Unnoticed, the pair peeled away from the hull and followed the youth with the fat coin purse into the market. As he moved between the stalls, they strolled on the parallel aisle, keeping track of him. Up the steps and at the gates to the city, they held back until the teen cleared the portal. Then they rushed through the gate, maintaining their pace to get ahead of the youth.

***

Jace had been to Eleutherna, the city near Neysa's farm. For all his life, he considered it large. Local farmers and traveling vendors arrived to buy and sell goods, filling the streets on market days. But in the metropolis of Phalasarna, if he could put all the people who crowded the streets of Eleutherna into one section, they wouldn't even be noticed in the port city. Here were buildings reaching two, three, and even four stories above the street. And the volume of bodies so packed the roads that he couldn't keep from bumping into people.

"Excuse me," he uttered for the hundredth time. But when he moved aside, his shoulder or the pack, swinging sideways, brushed or nudged another passersby. "Pardon me. Sorry. Excuse me."

Yet, no matter how polite he tried to be the city people cursed his interference in their busy lives. After a block of him dodging and the pedestrians elbowing him, a man bumped directly into the teen's chest.

"Whoa, there young fellow," he said as he stumbled. Catching Jace by the elbows, he steadied himself. "You seem lost, and in a rush to get nowhere."

"My apologies, sir," Jace exclaimed. "I've never been to the city before. I'm looking for an inn."

"Oh, a farm boy?" spittle flew from his mouth as he spoke. A hint of wine on his breath informed Jace that the continuing presence of the man's hands on his elbows was for balance. "Take my advice and get off the main street. All these people have somewhere to be. And noon is approaching."

"What does noon…"

A second man plowed into the pair. The drunk tightened his grip on Jace, even as he scolded the second man.

"See here friend, you are intruding into a private conversation. Move around. Can't you see when gentlemen are conversing?"

"If I saw a gentleman, I would avoid him," the new arrival sneered. "All I see are a couple of deadbeats blocking my path."

"In some quarters, those words would get you stabbed," the drunk replied. His words seemed more slurred than earlier.

"I've got your 'stabbed' right here," the angry man threatened.

He pulled a knife and sliced upward. Seeing the blade, the intoxicated one spun Jace, putting the youth's back to the aggressive man.

"Let go of me," Jace screamed as he shook his arms to dislodge the man's hands.

Then in fear of getting knifed in the back, he twirled around. The angry man had disappeared into the crowd. When he turned to address the drunk, that man had also vanished.

Shaking off the encounter but remembering the advice, he found an alley and left the busy main street. When he reached the rear of the building, three men stepped from the shadows.

"There's a toll to use our alleyway," one stated. "Three bronze each."

Jace glanced around and remarked, "I don't see any signs."

"Can you even read Greek," another inquired.

"I don't think Latians, trespassing on other people's alleyways, know how to read at all," the third offered.

Jace smiled, reached to his right hip, and slid the war hatchet from the metal loop.

"Is it worth it?" he asked.

"Is what worth it?" the first robber inquired.

In an underhanded move, Jace flipped the hatchet behind his back. It flew up and over the teen's shoulder and, as if it had a mind of its own, the weapon dropped to waist level where the handle smacked into his outstretched hand.

"Losing fingers over a few coins?" Jace answered.

"He's carrying a long pack," one advised.

"But he's too young to be an archer," the second thief said.

"Let's not take a chance," the third suggested.

The three alley thieves turned tail and ran. Jace laughed, slipped the handle into the holding ring, and let the war hatchet settle. Then he patted his coin purse. Except, the bulge from a sack of coins wasn't there. Only lengths of frayed leather, where the purse had been cut, remained.

Racing back down the alley, he entered the main street and looked both ways. But neither the drunk nor the angry man were visible. One thing he learned early, running through the woods, hysterically looking for your prey, never worked. His coins were gone, for now.

***

A few questions asked of obviously poor folks, gave Jace directions to the Prowess, the public feeding area. Although coinless, Phalasarna offered the blessing of a noon and evening meal for the poor. Best yet, the downtrodden were attended to by the little Herds, the youngest members of the agoge. For several years, they would serve the poor, then eat with the lowest of the city's population. It taught the boys humility and served as a cautionary tale about hard work and earning a profit.

Jace traveled down the road, passed through the high city walls, and strolled halfway across the city until arriving at an intersection. He turned off the main road and entered a plaza. Stopping in the middle of the street, he gawked at the venue.

A few unfortunates coming to the plaza groused at him

"Look out." "You're blocking the way." "If you're not hungry, go somewhere else." "Don't impede the famished."

Jace ignored the complainers while absorbing the location. For years, Zarek had described the square, the buildings surrounding the open area, and the defensive wall just down the road. And as detailed in the lectures, the wide gate in the agoge wall where little boys, young teens, and older teens passed through season after season. They learned, were tested and finally, those who qualified left the compound as Cretan archers.

"You better hurry," a beggar in rags suggested. "Find a spot close to the pots. The boys will be here soon to serve. If you're too far out, you'll only get watery soup."

"But everyone is served equally," Jace stated. He remembered the lessons and lectures on humility during his training. "And the boys are fed last, so they understand want and hunger."

"What hole did you crawl out of?" the vagabond questioned. "With nonsense like that on your brain, you'll starve to death in this city."

Without another word, but a decidedly judgmental shake of his head, the beggar pushed his way into a crowd of men. They shuffled and pressed forward trying to get a spot near the cookfires and the steaming pots suspended over the flames.

Before Jace decided if he was hungry enough to join the horde, ten little boys holding small self-bows with recurved tips rushed from the portal. They lined up as if a color guard on either side of the opening. Shortly after, ten older teens jogged from the agoge and passed between the boys. In a file with matching steps, they moved snake like around the edge of the square. Jace rotated to watch the precision maneuvering.

He knew they represented a wealthy patron from the bronze covers on their small shields and the matching steel swords on their hips.

"Troop, halt," a teen acting as a file leader commanded. "Secure the road."

In pairs, the archery students moved to block the entrance to the square. When several men arrived for the Prowess, they were rudely turned away.

Jace placed his long pack against the wall of a building and worked his way through the crowd.

"Excuse me," he interrupted the file leader. "I understand your Troop is here to keep the peace and protect the youngsters. But aren't you overstepping your authority by denying food to the poor?"

The file leader was a year or so older than Jace. A good-looking youth with the broad shoulders of an archer, but like Jace, he lacked the thick muscles of a fully grown adult.

The leader replied, "Well, I'll tell you, Toxophilite…"

The statement rocked Jace. How did the file leader know he was a master archer?

But a sneer appeared on the leader's face that revealed the sarcastic meaning of the word. He waved a pair of older teens to his side for support and offered, "Perhaps after you eat the charity meal, you should takeover and set an example for the little Herd. But hey, why wait? Kostas! Bring a plate of food over here for our new Troop Leader."

"Right away, File Leader Inigo," a nine-year-old acknowledged.

He grabbed a bowl, and a cook ladled a serving into the container. Kostas marched over to Jace and held out the vessel.

"There you go Toxophilite," Inigo proclaimed, "a nice bowl of free food."

Jace reached for the container and started to say, "thank you."

But Inigo's hand slapped the bottom of the bowl launching it out of the boy's hands. Spinning in the air, the vessel flung stew against Jace's cheat and into his face.

"Kostas, what have you done to our Troop leader?" Inigo exclaimed.

"Sir, I didn't…you, you", the small boy stammered.

"Are you accusing me of something, little Herd?" Inigo demanded.

Seeing the fear on the boy's face, Jace wiped the broth and pieces of vegetables from his forehead. Then he licked his palm and declared, "For free food, the stew is delicious. I think I'll go and get another bowl."

Jace backed away from the three teens and the boy.

Satisfied with the results of bulling, Inigo instructed, "Kostas. Pick up that bowl and don't be so clumsy in the future. Now, don't you have serving duty?"

"I do, File Leader, sir," Kostas agreed.

"Then get about your business," Inigo ordered.

Four paces away, Jace stopped.

"I'll have your name, Cretan archer," he requested.

"I have yet to earn that title," Inigo protested. Then with an arrogant jerk of his chin, he bragged. "Not that it's any of your business, but I am Lynceus Inigo, fifth of my family to attend the agoge."

"Lynceus Inigo, I'll remember that name," Jace promised. "All the best to you on your trials. May you still your breath so your hands are steady, calm your heart so your eyes are clear, and have the strength to focus your mind on the task."

"What do you know about the testing for…?"

But Jace had turned and walked into the crowd, leaving Lynceus speaking to a plaza full of underprivileged men. With a huff, the acting file leader began pacing behind his Troop.

***

Halfway to his pack, a thin arms hooked Jace's.

"That's Lynceus. Don't get tangled up with him," a destitute man warned. "His brother is Lieutenant Hylas Inigo. It makes Lynceus untouchable."

"Lynceus is a Trooper of the agoge," Jace said. "He's only an archery student and no one to fear."

"It's your funeral," the beggar declared.

After leaving the man, Jace worked his way through the crowd to his long pack. There he found a little Herd standing next to the pack. Maybe ten-years-old, the boy held up a fresh bowl of stew.

"What's your name?" Jace inquired while taking the vessel.

"Anatol, sir," the boy replied. "Thank you for not taking the spill out on Kostas."

"Kostas did nothing wrong," Jace remarked.

"Most men who come to the Prowess assume we're here to take abuse," Anatol explained.

"That's nonsense," Jace said. "The purpose of serving and eating with the city's poor is to learn to be humble and weary of laziness. It's not to be punching bags for disgruntled losers."

"And yet, sir, we are," Anatol told him while backing away.

Jace sipped the broth and studied the area over the lip of the bowl. The Prowess, the Troop, and the Herd were nothing like Zarek described. Feeling depressed, he sank down beside his pack and ate while watching the boys of the little Herd serve the gathered poor.

Once done with the duty, they lined up, and shuffled by the cooks for their share of stew. Then in a loose file, they marched to where their small bows leaned against the wall. Not far from Jace, they dropped to the ground and buried their faces in the bowls.

Jace couldn't understand why they were eating like savages. According to Zarek, the little Herd relished the noon time duty. It gave them a full belly while they reflected on the conditions of their dining companions.

Not long after the undignified slop session began, Lynceus Inigo marched up. He strolled along the line of boys, grinning at each as if they were pets placed there for his amusement.

Chapter 14 - A Good Pack

Jace ignored the acting file leader and concentrated on his food. Based on his recent experience with Lynceus, expressing another opinion would not go well.

"You look like a litter of piglets," the file leader observed. "Stop eating when I'm talking to you."

Jace now understood why the little Herd rushed their noon meal.

"Jencir. Put down that bowl, you piglet, and show me your bow," Lynceus ordered.

A child around eight, shaking with nerves, placed his half-finished bowl of stew on the ground, pushed to his feet, and lifted his bow from where it rested against the wall.

Although light weight with an easy draw, the bow wasn't a toy.

"Brace your bow," Lynceus instructed. "Show me you can handle your weapon."

Several of the Troop drifted over to watch their file leader impose discipline while imparting knowledge to the little Herd.

For years, Zarek berated Jace in the same manner so he would learn to perform intricate tasks in the face of adversity. As uncomfortable as it was to watch a small boy berated by an older teen, in the end, it would harden Jencir and make him a better archer.

It was longer than the boy was tall, and he struggled bending the self-bow over his thigh. He might have had the strength, but he lacked the leverage to bend a cold weapon. Jencir had neglected to flex the bow and warm it up. Jace expected Lynceus to correct the oversight at any moment.

"You are weak and have no heart," Lynceus shouted at the little Herd member. He glanced at his Troop and returned their smiles at the distress of the boy. "Brace means string your bowstring, piglet. That means to ready your weapon for battle. Any archer who can't, should leave the agoge in shame."

Trembling from the exertion, Jencir managed to bend the bow and hook the bowstring to the other end. But it wasn't fast enough for the file leader. Lynceus caught the boy's stew container with the toe of his sandal and upended the bowl.

"Losers don't eat," he screamed. "You should go home to your mother's pigsty."

"My mother keeps a clean house," Jencir said in defense of his family.

It was a mistake. Lynceus leaned down and put his face a hand's width from the boy's.

"Piglets eat off the ground," he shrieked. Then while still looking at Jencir, he addressed the rest of little Herd. "I said piglets eat off the ground. Dump your bowls."

Nine more bowls were turned over and the unfinished stew fell, splashing onto the bricks of the square. And nine sad eyes followed the broth as it seeped between pavers.

"Make them lick it up," one of his Troop encouraged.

At the suggestion, Lynceus rotated his head and locked eyes with the teen.

"I've a better idea," he said. "Brace your bows."

In response, the rest of little Herd snatched up their bows. While eight quickly looped the bowstring over one end, Anatol put his knee on the belly and gently flexed the limbs to loosen up his bow. Seeing the more experienced boy following procedures, the others mirrored his example.

"I said to brace your bows," Lynceus said growing impatient with the delay.

While the acting file leader hassled the little Herd, the cooks began cleaning the empty pots and most of the poor vacated the square. Only a few vagrants remained to watch the show.

Faster than Jace would have expected, the boys affixed their bowstrings.

"Let me see your draws," Lynceus directed. "All the way back to the side of your chin. Remember, your left hand and shoulders must be in alignment."

Jace approved of the instructions. Finally, there was value in the file leader's methods. Although little Herd had no arrows, the stance and exercise of holding the string taught the proper feel to their young muscles.

"Now, on my word," Lynceus told them, "you will 'release' as a group. It's an effective way to test the power of your bows. Ready…"

Jace came off the ground and sprinted to Lynceus. Putting a shoulder into the teen's side, he shoved him away from the boys.

"Relax your draw," Jace commanded. "You never release without an arrow…"

***

Lynceus came in low and hit Jace in the hips. Lifting him, the file leader drove Jace towards the wall. But the uncertified archer got a foot up and kicked off. Both teens appeared to bounce off the stone. They flew back and sprawled on the ground.

"You are supposed to feed the hungry," a command voice projected, "not wrestle them for entertainment."

Jace and Lynceus jumped to their feet. They snapped into the position of attention in front of a Lieutenant. Around them all the members of the agoge popped to attention as well. But the Cretan officer didn't make eye contact with anyone. Rather, he fixed his gaze on something off to the side.

"What happened here?" he inquired.

"Well, sir," Lynceus began.

"Acting File Leader Inigo, if I wanted to talk to you, I would address you directly," the officer scolded. "Anatol, don't make me ask again. What happened here?"

The ten-year-old shuffled his feet and the bow in his hands shook. He didn't want to lie, but he didn't want to suffer the wrath of the older teen for telling the truth.

"Sir, File Leader Inigo was having us display our draw technique when the guest interfered," Anatol stated.

The little Herd member had chosen his words carefully. He left out the release part of the exercise, giving him a little wiggle room if confronted by the file leader later. Plus, he had said the stranger interfered in the lecture, which should account for something.

The officer made a ceremony of scanning the ground.

"I see spilled strew and bowls," he remarked. Turning, he peered over the near empty square. "But not a lot of waste anywhere else."

"Sir, let me explain," Lynceus offered.

As he spun back to Jace and the students, the Lieutenant stopped and gazed off to the side as if distracted.

"I'm not finished, Inigo," he growled.

When he returned to facing Jace, the Troop, and the little Herd, the officer pointed out, "Other than the food and containers, I don't see any arrows. Now, it's your turn, Mister Inigo. How do you run a release drill without arrows?"

"Lieutenant Gergely, there has been a misunderstanding of my instructions," Lynceus explained. "I was simply giving little Herd the benefit of my years of experience."

"I'm sure you were," Gergely remarked. "So, let's call the city guard and have the itinerant civilian arrested. You can explain all this to the Captain. I'm positive he'll grant you time off for the trial."

"Sir, there was no harm done," Lynceus stated. "I don't feel the need to get the city guard involved. Or to bother the Captain."

"Are you sure?" Gergely questioned. His eyes again shifted to the side. Then as if searching for someone, he peered around the square. After his visual probe, he studied the stranger. "What's your name?"

"Sir, I'm Jace Kasia," Jace told him. "And I, as well, don't see the need for the city guard to get involved."

"I wouldn't think you would. But indulge me. What is a Latian doing at the Prowess?"

"My plan is to catch a ship to the Roman Republic," Jace told him. He left out the part about him being coinless. "I came to the Prowess to have a noon meal and to watch little Herd from the agoge do their duty."

"That is surprisingly precise, Mister Kasia. Alright, we've had enough distraction," Gergely announced. "Troop, once the cooks remove the pots and bowls, you are dismissed. Little Herd, you have class. Get to it."

"Yes sir," the ten boys acknowledged.

They lined up in a file preparing to leave.

"Hold. Unbrace your bows," Lieutenant Gergely ordered. Then while looking at Jace, he added. "I don't think you'll be attacked between the square and the academy."

***

In short order, the boys unstrung their bows and marched away. Lynceus and his Troop gathered away from the officer, and Gergely strutted to the long pack.

"Has anybody seen who belongs to this equipment?" he inquired. "I've been watching it since I arrived in the plaza."

"Sir, that's mine," Jace volunteered.

“What is a Latian doing with a Cretan archer’s long pack?”

“I’m a bowyer, sir. Trained by a retired Cretan archer,” Jace answered. “He talked fondly of the agoge and his time here. Unfortunately, he was killed by Rhodians a few days ago.”

“How long was your apprenticeship?” Gergely asked. He didn’t expect the teen to have much experience.

“Twelve years, sir,” Jace replied. “As well as being a journeyman bow maker, I’m an expert archer.”

“The Goddess Tyche sure delivers her blessings of luck in mysterious ways,” Gergely stated. Spying another weapon hanging off the side of the pack, he inquired. “You didn’t mention an expertise with the war hatchet.”

“Hatchets, knifes, swords, and spears,” Jace listed. “Master Mikolas said…”

Gergely shuffled close to Jace, put a hand over his mouth, and whispered, “Just indicate with your head. Was your teacher Zarek Mikolas?”

Jace nodded an affirmative.

“Zarek Mikolas has many friends among the Cretan archer community,” Gergely advised. “But there are just as many who think ill of him and would gladly take it out on his student. Do you understand?”

After another nod, Gergely removed his hand and stepped back.

“My repairman/armor for the little and middle Herds retired,” he explained. “If you would grant me a few months until I find a replacement, I would be grateful.”

"What does it pay?" Jace asked.

"You were trained by a Cretan archer," Gergely ventured. "You'll eat with the quartermaster, the accountants, and the cooks. The pay is a silver coin a week if you teach classes on bow maintenance."

"I can teach," Jace assured him. "Who would I be working for, sir?"

"Me. I'm Acis Gergely."

"I'd like to say yes, Lieutenant. But in case you hadn't noticed, I've had a problem with Lynceus Inigo. I understand his brother is an officer at the agoge."

"You let me worry about the Inigo brothers," Acis said. "Just avoid Lynceus as much as you can. Well, do you want the job?"

Jace picked up his gear and slung it over his shoulders.

"Yes, sir, it'll be my honor to work at the agoge."

"You load a good pack," Gergely observed while studying the bulk and the items strapped to it. "I'm guessing one of those cases contains a hunting bow. What's in the other?"

"My war bow, sir," Jace said.

"You are full of surprises, Master Kasia. Follow me and I'll show you to the workshop and sleeping quarters for the armory."

The two left the square. Behind them, Lynceus Inigo scowled and remarked, "I wonder where Acis is taking the beggar."

***

Jace and Lieutenant Acis Gergely strolled through the gates. After all the talk with Zarek about the agoge, Jace never figured on actually seeing the facility.

Larger inside than it appeared from the street, the walls ran deep into the city, placing the back wall far away. Not surprisingly, no buildings were constructed against or even close to the defensive wall. Inside the compound, barracks were separated to keep the Herds in age groups, and the Troop barracks away so the seventeen and eighteen-year-olds could practice for their qualifying trials.

Behind the cook sheds, the headquarter offices, and supply buildings, an archery range began outside the doors of a long, squat building with two entrances.

"The range looks to be about five hundred feet deep," Jace observed.

The range offered the only unobstructed view to the far-off back wall.

"Three to five hundred feet is our kill zone," Acis Gergely explained. "Of course, the little Herd with their self-bows can't reach much farther than one hundred. And the middle Herd usually only hits their targets at three hundred. At least until they're big enough to handle a hunting bow."

"I can do a sequence of five at four hundred with my hunting bow," Jace informed the Lieutenant.

"That's impressive," Gergely allowed. "But for how long?"

"When Zarek put me through the trials. I shot two hundred arrows into the targets with a hunter," Jace mentioned. "That's with rotating and changing the bowstring after each sequence."

Acis Gergely halted and looked around to be sure no one else was close to them.

"Twelve years under a master Cretan archer," he whispered almost to himself. Then directly to Jace, he suggested. "You learned more than bow making from him, didn't you?"

"Yes, sir. When he presented me with the war bow, he said I was qualified as a Cretan archer," Jace told the Lieutenant. "Of course, I can't claim the title as I didn't attend the agoge."

"That's another thing you need to keep between us," Gergely told him. "But know this Jace Kasia. If you do a good job for me here, when I leave with a Company, you're coming with me."

"As a Cretan archer?" Jace asked.

"Not at first," Lieutenant Gergely promised. "But once we're away from Crete, you'll get the title at the first opportunity."

"Thank you, sir."

***

Echoes of Zarek Mikolas' voice rang in Jace's head.

"We are not beavers to leave our gnawed wood on the floor," the old archer would roar. "Nor are we livestock requiring shavings on the floor to protect our hoofs on cold winter nights. Clean up this mess."

"Yes, sir, I'm working on it," Jace muttered to the empty repair shop.

He scooped up another load, examined the shavings and splinters of wood. Most were hardwood, he tossed them into one basket. For scoops he couldn't categorize, he put those scraps and the sawdust into the softwood basket.

"Kasia," a man called as he stepped through the doorway.

"Over here," Jace replied from under a workbench.

"Where is over here?"

"Second bench back," Jace answered.

Scooting to keep from spilling a scoop full of wood shaving, Jace eased out from under the workbench and stood. As he raised his head, he found another archer officer almost in his face.

"When my brother warned me that Acis hired the boy who attacked an acting file leader," the officer boomed, "I told Lynceus, he must be mistaken. But sure enough, here you are. Don't get used to the accommodations, Latian, you won't be here long."

"Are you the archery officer, Lieutenant Inigo?" Jace inquired.

"No. I manage the physical training for the agoge. Why do you ask?"

"Because the archery targets are in disrepair, and need to be restuffed," Jace replied. "The next time you take the Troops and Herds for a run, have them bring back armloads of straw."

"I don't take orders from vagabonds," Hylas Inigo exclaimed.

"No sir, you don't," Jace confirmed. "But the Captain wants the range in top condition. If you like, I can send a note to the headquarters building. I can't imagine it'll be a problem having him issue you a written authorization to have the boys carry straw."

The muscles in Hylas' face rippled and the veins in his neck stood out against his skin. After a few quick breaths, the Lieutenant spun on his heels and marched out of the repair shop.

An old man stepped from a doorway that connected the Herds' shop from the Troops' bow shop.

"We just stuffed the targets last year," the bowyer mentioned. "Does the Captain think they need to be redone?"

"I have no idea what the Captain wants," Jace admitted while dumping the wood shavings. "But than again, neither does Lieutenant Inigo."

"That's obvious," the old master bow maker said. "The name's Leksi. If you need anything, I'll be next door. But the way you handled Inigo, I've a feeling that won't be necessary."

"This shop looks more than prepared for the maintenance of self-bows and a few hunters," Jace stated.

"I take it you haven't examined the weapons yet," Leksi teased.

Then he laughed. The sounds of his amusement drifted through the doorway long after the other bowyer left.

"No, I haven't," Jace conceded that he hadn't checked the self-bows or the old hunters, "but thanks for the head's up."

Chapter 15 – Publius Scipio's Son

The Legion transports and Republic warships rowed out of Marseille harbor. Publius watched his brother's fleet until it reached the northern horizon.

"Don't look so long in the face, Senior Tribune," Publius Scipio offered. "We'll catch him before he does too much damage."

"That's not what's bothering me, General," Rabanus said.

"What is bothering you, Senior Tribune Rabanus?" Tribune Urbicus inquired.

The question wasn't to make frivolous conversation. General Scipio's head of planning and strategies had good reasons for the inquiry.

"What bothers me," Rabanus explained, "we sailed for Iberia too late to catch him there. Then, when we land here and march out, he's gone over the Alps, and we're running back to Genoa."

"Do you think we should have chased him into those mountain passes?" Consul/General Scipio questioned.

The eyes that locked lesser men in place and mesmerized crowds in Rome bore into the Senior Tribune's.

"Our Legion didn't have the cold weather gear for those higher elevations. You did the right thing bringing us back here, sir," Rabanus assured the General. "It's just, he seems to be two steps ahead of us at every turn. No offense, Tribune Urbicus."

"No offense taken, Senior Tribune," the head of planning and strategies granted. "General Barca is moving faster than my intelligence reports."

"You've been awfully quiet, Pericles," Scipio noted. "What are your thoughts?"

Senior Centurion Pericles drove a fist into his open hand. The loud report of the hard punch caused the General's staff to jump.

"Hannibal Barca and his Punic barbarians might have evaded us before," the senior combat officer answered. "But now General, he's up in the mountains and his refuse will come oozing out of the chasms like merda. And we'll be there with our wash rags and butt sticks to clean up his mess."

"A little graphic," Consul Scipio allowed, "but accurate."

"We should move to the beach, sir," the Centurion of First Century advised. "The pier will be filled with dock workers soon. I'm worried about your safety."

"Pulcher, I imagine even if I was turning in for the night at my villa in Rome, you'd be worried about my safety."

"Yes, sir," Centurion Pulcher agreed. "Can we move now, sir?"

Consul/General Publius Scipio lifted an arm and indicated the end of the dock.

"Gentlemen, we are moving to the quinqueremes," he announced.

"First Century, form a tunnel to the General's five-bankers," Pulcher directed.

Following Scipio, the staff walked between the shields of First Century. Each protected by a battle-hardened heavy infantrymen.

Battle Commander Tortoris already occupied a section of the steering deck. Next to the Colonel was Cornelius Scipio, the Consul/General's sixteen-year-old son.

***

Three days after launching from the beach at Marseille, the two warships backstroked onto the sand at Genoa.

"Rabanus, get couriers out with orders to form the Northern Legion," Publius Scipio directed. "Let's make Piacenza the rally point. I know it's a little off center and some Centuries will have to force march to get there. But when they leave the mountains, the Carthaginians will follow the Ticinus river, and land right on our gladii."

The Senior Tribune called over a few scribes and dictated the commands. While they worked, the Consul/General and his staff walked the ramp to the beach.

"Urbicus, round up fifteen mounts and four wagons," the General instructed. "I don't want to stay in Genoa any longer than necessary. We have a welcoming party to organize."

"Yes, sir," the Tribune acknowledged. He saluted before jogging off in search of the stables.

A Consul of Rome did not travel light. Besides the business of war, he had to stay connected to commercial ventures and the politics of the Republic. Plus, there were the Gods to keep pacified. To help him, he traveled with aides from all four disciplines, their underlings, and their luggage.

"Colonel Tortoris, mount a squad from the First and head for Piacenza," Scipio ordered. "I want the facilities prepared for when the Legion arrives."

"General, sir, I'd like to accompany the Battle Commander," Cornelius requested.

"Junior Tribune Scipio, you will stay with me and help organize this circus," Publius told his son. When the teen deflated, the Consul made a promise. "For this campaign, wherever I ride, you'll ride with me."

"That would be grand... Ah, yes sir, General," the youth remarked.

The Battle Commander saluted and went to speak with Pulcher. Publius Scipio spoke with a few more of his entourage before addressing his son.

"Now, Junior Tribune, go talk to the First Principales of the ships and make arrangements for our baggage to be transported to town."

***

The baggage train and gaggle of riders, hikers, and marchers were on the road for three days. Eighty miles and two river crossings later, the weary travelers entered the new defensive walls of Piacenza. Just outside the city, a massive Legion Fort dominated the landscape.

"And here are the walls and shields that will break Hannibal's advance," Publius Scipio declared as he rode into the fort.

"General, welcome to Piacenza," a Senior Centurion of light infantry greeted the Consul. "You'll have all the room you need in the commander's villa."

"Where is the commander of the fort?"

"Sir, Proconsul Marcus Atilius Regulus arrived this summer, settled the Gauls, oversaw the construction of the fort and the city's defenses," the Centurion reported. "After installing a garrison, he marched his Legions back to Rome, sir."

"How many Velites are under your command?"

"Four thousand in this sector of the Po River Valley, General," the Senior Centurion replied. "But they're spread out in garrisons."

Consul/General Scipio huffed but maintain a neutral expression on his face. It wouldn't do to let the Velites see the frustration on the face of their commander. Hoofs sounding like thunder saved him from further discussion with the Senior Centurion.

Moments later, Battle Commander Tortoris galloped through a side gate leading columns of mounted spearmen.

"General Scipio, welcome to Piacenza," the Colonel greeted him. "I trust your journey was uneventful."

"The journey was fine," Scipio replied. "The fort is fine. But the lack of heavy infantry was not what I expected or needed. Give me your report."

"On the downside as you noted, we don't have any heavy infantry here," Tortoris related. "On the plus side, General, the walls are new, and we have a Legion's worth of light troops."

As they talked, the riders continued to stream into the fort.

"Who are they?" Scipio inquired.

"Those are two thousand mounted Gallic infantrymen," Tortoris replied. "They fit nicely with the thirty-six hundred cavalrymen garrisoned in the region. We are as mobile as any Legion in history."

"I wonder if Hannibal Barca would agree to only battle with mounted troops."

"Sir, we have more light infantrymen coming in," the Senior Centurion of Velites offered. "By weeks end, you'll have fifty centuries under your command."

"You are wrong, Battle Commander Tortoris," Scipio said as he slipped off his horse.

"How so, General?" the Colonel inquired.

"It's not one mobile Legion," he replied, "we have enough light forces to create two of the most mobile Legions in the history of the Republic."

***

Anywhere a co-Consul of the Republic set up shop, his place of residence became a hive of activity. Couriers and messengers dashed into and out of the fort's headquarters and the commander's villa. Much of the communications went to regional garrisons, urging them to send Centuries of heavy infantrymen. Others traveled to the Senate with almost the same message.

On day five of Publius Scipio's arrival, a scout, dusty and dirty from a hard ride, stomped into the headquarters building.

"General, we have sightings of Punic mercenaries pouring from the mountains," the Gallic courier reported.

"And in their vanguard is their commander, Hannibal Barca."

"How do you know it's the General?" Scipio demanded.

"A few of our companions took his coins in Iberia," the messenger informed General Scipio.

"General, do we know we can trust the sighting," an aide inquired.

"When your income depends on knowing who is paying, recognizing the commander becomes important," Publius pointed out. Then he turned to his senior staff officer.

"Senior Tribune Rabanus, when do we expect the heavy infantry?" Publius asked without taking his eyes from the junior staff officer.

"Two weeks or more, General," Rabanus answered.

"Too long. Call out the Legion."

"How many cavalry, mounted infantry, and skirmishers are we taking, sir?" Senior Centurion Pericles requested.

"All of them," Publius Scipio exclaimed. "Hannibal is coming right into our arms. Let's not give him a chance to veer off course."

While only one official message went out to alert the Senate, command orders flew throughout the fort and the town of Piacenza. Centuries packed and prepared for war.

And in every pub, house, and place of business, the residents boasted, "General Publius Scipio is marching out, ten thousand strong, to take the Carthage renegade Hannibal Barca into custody."

***

Thirty miles northwest of Piacenza, the forces of the Roman Republic constructed a marching camp south of the small village of Pavia. Publius Scipio sent out scouts to search for the Carthaginians while he discussed tactics with his Battle Commander and staff.

"We'll place the light infantry in front of the Legion cavalry," Tortoris described. "Then to keep the enemy off our center, we'll bracket the formation with the Gallic horsemen on the flanks."

"If I might make an observation, sir," Cornelius Scipio ventured.

"Go ahead," his father said acknowledging the teen.

Battle Commander Tortoris, senior staff officer Rabanus, Urbicus, the head of planning and strategies, and senior combat officer Pericles bristled and frowned at the intrusion by the boy. But, while they discounted Cornelius based on his youth, the Centurion of First Century admired the teen. Plus, the veteran combat officer viewed the interruption in a philosophical manner.

Centurion Pulcher leaned closer to hear the boy's comments, while thinking of Socrates.

"The mind is everything; what you think you become."

Each of the staff members spent their adult lives studying their field of expertise. The senior staff officer prioritized methods of command and control, the combat officer thought in terms of infantrymen holding a line, planning and strategies pondered objectives, and the Colonel visualized the distribution of a full Legion. They, as Socrates stated, had become what they thought.

"We don't have the shields of Legion heavy infantrymen to form the Maniples," Cornelius Scipio pointed out. "To replace them, shouldn't we build fortifications and fight the Punics from behind barricades?"

The staff politely nodded at the teen's opinion before Tortoris stated, "With our mobility, we can close with them fast. Before they have time to plan, we'll have them on their heels."

The tent flap flew open, and a Legionary from First Century ushered in a scout.

"Sir, we've located the Punic army," he announced. "And their General is isolated with the advance element."

"Gentlemen, the Gods have presented us with an opportunity. Right here, right now, we can end this incursion before it reaches the Republic," Publius Scipio proclaimed. "Organize the Legions. Today, we march for glory and honor."

***

The Legions moved only as fast as their slowest units. And because they were cupped around the Velites, the horsemen walked their mounts. Adding to the delay, Consul/General Scipio stopped to sacrifice to the Goddess Victoria. He wanted a bull to assure victory. But, in the rush to prepare for the march, the only livestock available was an old ewe.

"Forgive me for the humble offering, Goddess. Bless us in the battle we take to the barbarians," he prayed to Victoria. Then he cut the sheep's throat and handed the knife to a Priest. "Finish this while I finish Hannibal."

The forward elements angled northwest around the village. On the far left, the Ticinus River flowed with water that originated in the mountains to the north. The same mountains the Punic Army traversed in their quest to destroy the Republic.

Publius Scipio, his son Cornelius, Centurion Pulcher, and ten mounted Legionaries rode behind the light infantrymen. Way out front, Colonel Tortoris traveled with the scouts. He wanted to know the moment they sighted the enemy.

Meanwhile, Senior Tribune Rabanus and Senior Centurion Pericles were on the flanks introducing themselves to the Junior Tribunes, the Tribunes, and the Centurions.

In their rush to gather the Legions, they hadn't drilled maneuvers or established familiarity with the lower ranks.

"This better be a straightforward fight," Pericles uttered. "If it's any more complicated than that, Furor will take over."

"Don't go invoking the God of Insanity," Rabanus warned. "We need better intelligence, a few weeks for the Legions to develop unity, and a hundred Centuries of heavy infantry."

"You sound like young Cornelius," Pericles offered.

"I wasn't ready to listen before," Rabanus admitted. "But Junior Tribune Scipio is clever, and he wasn't wrong."

"He spends enough time asking questions and hanging out in the Centurion's mess," Pericles commented. "He's bound to have learned something."

They reined their horses around and started for the other side of the formation.

***

The first sign of trouble was Colonel Tortoris and the scouts galloping back to the formation. The second was the reason for their haste.

Ranks of heavily armored horses and rows of cavalry lances appeared across the open field.

If the Battle Commander had slowed to a dignified walk, the Punic horsemen might not have caused as much panic. But in his attempt to reach General Scipio, the Colonel, and the scouts, thundered through the tightly packed ranks of light infantrymen. Brushed aside by the horses' flanks, the ranks fell into disarray. Then, the sight of the Punic heavy cavalry approaching broke the center formation. Almost as if to return the rude behavior, the Velites turned around and ran through the ranks of the Legion cavalry. Horses reared up, danced aside, kicked, and nipped their neighbors. In the chaos, Consul Scipio, and Centurion Pulcher were separated from the General's security detail and his son.

While the center of the Legion formation buckled into a mob scene, on the flanks, the mounted Gallic infantry maintained their forward pace. Watching for the signal to envelope the Punic cavalry, they readied their lances and tightened their grips on the reins. Then, from outside both flanks of the Legion formation, piercing war cries announced the arrival of a different type of Carthaginian unit.

Breaking from a distance but converging quickly with the Gallic riders, the Punic light cavalry slashed into the outer ranks. Then pulling off quickly, they allowed a second wave of Numidian riders to slash and run. Caught between a center filled with heavy cavalrymen, and the flashing blades and thrown javelins attacking their sides, the mounted Gallic infantrymen chose to ride away.

***

Cornelius Scipio's mount spun in the confusion. Shouting men and panicked horses banged against his, sending the beast into a mindless rage. Only Cornelius' steady hand and solid knee pressure kept the animal in the same location.

Snapping his head as they turned, Junior Tribune Scipio searched for his father or any place he could be of use. For one so young, his head was clear and his thoughts concise.

In a rout, the best way to survive was to gather fighters around you and pick your escape path. Then…

Three of his father's veteran infantrymen pushed out of the dust and the crush of bodies.

"Tribune, come with us," one directed.

The three circled him, their spears creating a ring of steel. Cornelius understood their loyalty to his father was being extended to Publius Scipio's son. But the son wasn't ready to concede the field, just yet.

"Legionary. Where is the General?" he demanded.

"Sir, he and Centurion Pulcher were over there," the mounted Legionary pointed to the left. "But then the wave of heavy cavalry came between us, and we lost sight of them."

A First Century NCO broke into the island of calm

"Tribune, we need to go, right now," the Optio instructed. He pointed to the south and turned his horse in that direction. "We're in an undefendable spot."

"You are correct Optio," Cornelius agreed. He drew his cavalry spatha and leveled the blade to the left. "But you're facing the wrong way. We're riding to the General, not away."

Cornelius kicked his mount and savagely jerked the reins. In the harsh treatment, the stallion found something to take its mind off the horrors surrounding it. He settled and bunched his muscles in anticipation of his master's next command. And the veterans of First Century discovered that a teen with a vision and confidence could take command of a broken situation.

Screaming *"Nolite Timere"*, Cornelius Scipio nudged the braced horse. Released from the hold, the stallion shot into the heavy cavalry mounts while the teen slashed left and right with his spatha.

"You heard the Tribune," the Optio bellow. "No fear!"

The four mounted veterans formed a wedge and charged after Cornelius. Using the lane he created, they soon caught up to him. As if they were harvesting blades in a field of ripe grain, the five widened the lane until Legion cavalrymen recognized the route.

Cornelius searched the field of melee combat, looking for his father. Then through a gap that opened and closed, he saw Centurion Pulcher stabbing with one arm while holding Publius up with the other. Clueless to what followed him, Cornelius pulled his horse around and charged for his father and the Centurion.

A roar of *"Nolite Timere"* rolled from the Legion horsemen trailing behind the young Tribune. Oblivious to the river of Republic steel and Latin muscle in his wake, Cornelius Scipio broke through to the General and the Centurion.

***

Fighting and guarding his wounded General, Centurion Pulcher slashed with his gladius while holding Publius Scipio with his other arm. Although both were mounted, at any moment one could be unseated which would take them both to the ground.

Thinking to free Pulcher of caring for the wounded man, Cornelius rode to the other side of his father. As the teen reined in, he dropped an arm around the elder Scipio's shoulders, taking the weight. Then, Cornelius braced and prepared for the first and last battle of his young life.

But there were no Carthaginian blades or spears threatening him. Instead, a rotating line of Legion cavalrymen rode in an ever-increasing circle around him.

"Tribune Scipio, we should go," Centurion Pulcher suggested.

"What?" Cornelius asked. Some of the bravado had drained away and for a moment his was a confused teen.

"You led the cavalry charge in," the veteran combat officer replied. "You should lead us out, sir."

Cornelius relinquished his father to a pair of veterans, before racing the stallion around the circle.

"*Nolite Timere*. No fear," he cried as he rode. Then, Cornelius Scipio headed the horse southward while commanding. "Follow me."

Act 6

Chapter 16 – Terror at Dawn

Cornelius Scipio and the escaping riders expected to run all the way to their camp and maybe beyond. But first they had to break away from the Carthaginian heavy cavalry. Cutting a swatch became harder as the enemy horsemen clustered to the rear of the fighting.

In all of Cornelius' studies, he couldn't remember a military commander with the foresight to order a blocking force behind an enemy's defensive line. Yet, here, in this fluid situation, General Barca had a second front to the rear of the Legion's line. Before he could ponder the subject more, his stallion smashed into the heavy cavalry.

Part way into the mass of men and horses, Cornelius realized most of the enemy faced away from him. Then he broke through and discovered why.

Velites in a defensive square had created a barrier with their mid-sized shields. In the center of the Legion square, Senior Centurion Pericles strutted back and forth bellowing orders, encouragement, and pointing out targets.

Facing the sides of the square, Punic cavalrymen pranced, postured, and called insults in several languages. But wisely, they stayed a safe distance from the lethal javelins of the light infantrymen.

Cornelius rode into the square and reined in beside Pericles.

"What do you need, Senior Centurion?" he asked.

"Keep those Carthaginians off my backside and we'll walk this square all the way to our camp," Pericles told him. Then with a smile, he added. "Good to see you, Tribune Scipio."

"It's nice to be alive, Senior Centurion," Cornelius offered. He waved the Legion cavalrymen to the rear of the formation and instructed. "Keep the General here. The rest of you, open a back door. We're moving to our camp."

For the rest of the day, the Legion forces fought a fighting retreat. Just as they came abreast of Pavia, an attack by the Punic heavy cavalry cut a corner of the square. Pericles reformed the defensive formation, but hundreds of Velites were cut off and captured. The Senior Centurion roared his anger all the way to the Legion camp.

***

Sixty-three years before the engagement at the Ticinus river, King Pyrrhus invaded the Republic. After battling the Greek King's hordes of cavalry and war elephants all day, the Legionaries were frightened as night fell. To secure their bivouac, they built rudimentary fortifications. Over the ensuring decades, the Legions had formalized the construction of the defenses.

The surviving Legion cavalry, what was left of the mounted Gallic infantry, and the remaining Velites collapsed their formation and trooped across the bridge. Once within the walls of the Legion marching camp, they could eat in peace and tend to their wounded.

Outside the camp, Carthaginian horsemen circled but didn't dare approach. Beyond the sharpened stakes, leg breaking trench, and high walls, the skirmishers had javelins, and many took bows from the armory wagons and launched arrows at any enemy rider who ventured too close.

With the setting sun, the Punic cavalry pulled back and set up camps of their own. Tomorrow, they agreed, General Hannibal Barca would have his heavy infantry available. They would root out the Latians and their allies. The horsemen had done enough for the day.

A peculiar feature of a Legion marching camp, unrealized by the mercenaries, was the portable nature of the fortifications. Deep in the night, sections of the stockade wall were removed, laid over the trench, and the survivors of General Scipio's expedition escaped.

***

At dawn, the Piacenza garrison came to full alert. In the distance, men approaching the town marched or rode horses in a ragged manner. They were too far out to be recognizable, but the disorderly procession didn't appear to be Legion.

By mid-morning, the Legionaries who were left on garrison duty watched as the remnants of the Legion detachment trudged into the fort. The First Century veterans ran to take charge of the wounded General. Their Centurion, riding by his side, remained close to Consul Scipio, as did the General's son.

The day passed with tales of slaughter and bravery, especially the story of Cornelius Scipio's charge into the fray to rescue his father. Others told of broken defensive lines and failed assaults, leaving a cloud hanging over the fort as night fell.

In the morning, the mood remained dark but not from events of the day before. The dawn brought Punic heavy infantrymen to the field facing the Legion facility.

"Come out and fight, you cowardly Roman dogs," was the most used enticement. Others were cruder, but they were all challenges which Consul/General Scipio declined to entertain.

After a tense day, the Carthaginian forces withdrew to a camp five miles away. It was after dark when the sky to the north glowed with the reflection of thousands of campfires.

The night light did two things. It let the Legion know they faced a much larger army than a few thousand cavalrymen. And, it incited a blood bath.

***

The moon cast shadows around the fort. On the north wall, Centurion Appius Pulcher and Tribune Cornelius Scipio met on the observation platform.

"Can't sleep?" Scipio asked.

"It seems, I'm not the only one," Pulcher suggested.

"The enemy fires are so vast that there are no stars to the north," Scipio noted, "nor peace in my heart."

"Then unrest is rampant," Pulcher remarked. He pointed to the tents of the Velites on the far side of the fort. "See, even the skirmishers are restless."

"You don't suppose Pericles is rousting them this early?"

"Even our hard charging Senior Centurion isn't that cruel," Pulcher laughed.

Then he stopped, bent forward, and squinted as he peered into the darkness across the fort.

"What's wrong?" Cornelius asked.

"Listen," Appius ordered.

From the distant tents, the rising buzz of men awakening in confusion and asking about the situation drifted to them. Then a full-throated roar accompanied lines of riders racing for the main gate.

"Those are the mounted Gallic infantry," Cornelius pointed out. "I wonder where they're going?"

But Appius was ahead of the youth.

"They've murdered the guards and opened the gate," the Centurion said while drawing his gladius. At the top of his lungs, he screamed, "Guards, alert in the fort. Attack, attack."

He ran to the ladder and climbed down. Right behind him, Cornelius hit the ground and drew his spatha. The two officers ran to the open gate, but the Gallic riders were gone. The ready Century arrived and secured the portal.

"What was that about?" Cornelius asked.

"Deserters, I guess. At least we know they won't leave us in the middle of a battle," Appius remarked. "Come on, let's go see what mischief they were up to in the Velites area."

They had only gone several paces when the growls of angry voices reached them from among the tents. By the time they arrived, pairs of skirmishers were carrying headless bodies and stacking them on the lanes between the tents.

"I don't understand," Cornelius Scipio admitted. "Where are their heads?"

"The Gallic infantry wasn't simply deserting the Legion. They went to join the Punic invasion," Appius Pulcher answered. "And they took the heads of our Velites to demonstrate their new allegiance."

***

Winter crawled into the Po River Valley, bringing frigid nights, days only slightly warmer, and stalks of brown grass poking up through a dusting of snow. Consul Scipio's Legions and the citizens of Piacenza were resupplied by rafts coming up the Po River. And Barca's army and the Gallic tribesmen who joined him foraged, traded, or raided for their supplies. Long past the season for war, both camps settled down to wait for Spring.

Then in mid-December, the rattle and clang of infantry shields and armor, and the clomp of horses' hoofs on frozen ground announced the arrival of a new element. Co-Consul/General Tiberius Longus marched four Legions along with allied troops from the east coast of the Republic to Piacenza.

However, after scouts told him where the Carthaginians were camped, Longus ordered the Legion marching camps built south of the town and the fort. At that location, only five miles, numerous dry gullies, a flood plain of the Trebia river, wetlands, and the river proper separated the two armies. Enough so they stayed out of each other's way, but close enough to keep an eye on their adversary.

While Legionaries from four Legions dug the defensive trenches and built the stockade walls, Tiberius Longus rode to the fort to consult with his co-Consul, Publius Scipio.

***

"Publius, you look terrible," Tiberius declared when he walked into Scipio's quarters.

A servant handed him a glass of wine. Tiberius Longus sat next to the bed and raised the glass in salute.

"The wounds are taking longer to heal than I would like," Publius admitted.

"You should return to Rome for better care," Tiberius urged.

"And leave the victory to you? I have doctors, and I can recover here just fine," Publius countered. "I'll be well enough to crucify Hannibal Barca before our term as Consuls ends. On another subject, I didn't expect reinforcements until spring."

"I was training and conditioning the Legions for an invasion of Carthage when the Senate received your letter," Tiberius explained. "We loaded the Legionaries and sailed from Sicilia to the port at Rimini. Then I forced marched them one hundred and fifty miles, and here I am."

"Just where are you?"

"We're camped a few miles south of here," Tiberius boasted, "closer to the Punics."

"You'd be safer near the fort," Publius warned. "As much as I hate to admit it, General Barca is a clever commander. I've tasted the steel of his cavalry."

"He's a barbarian who got lucky," Tiberius scowled. "I've brought eleven thousand heavy infantrymen. They are the backbone of my four Legions, and they are the rock that'll break your General Barca. As you pointed out, we only have until March to earn glory before the new Consuls are installed."

"I can't argue with the timing," Publius commented. He shifted to a more comfortable position, picked up his glass, and tilted it at his fellow General. "All I can do is counsel caution."

***

The four large marching camps housed forty thousand warriors and supply men. Twenty thousand were a mixture of allied horsemen, spearmen, and javelin throwers. The rest were disciplined Legion cavalrymen, Velites, and heavy infantrymen. It was such a formidable force, that Consul/General Longus complained at staff meetings that they were wasting time waiting for spring.

"If the Punics didn't control the high ground," he proposed, "we'd march out and destroy them. But I'll not risk victory by walking uphill into his javelins and arrows."

His staff agreed, but the frequency of General Longus' enthusiasm for battle grew by the day. Two weeks after arriving, a scout galloped into camp and gave the Consul/General an opportunity to sate his desire.

"Gauls and other Carthaginian mercenaries are ravaging the landscape," the scout reported. "They've filled wagons and loaded pack animals with food and plunder."

"How many?" Tiberius demanded. He walked the scout to a table map and waved his hand over the parchment. "Show me where?"

"About three thousand," the scout answered. "They forded the Po river and are attacking village and towns to the north."

"They'll be weighed down when they cross back," Tiberius shouted. "We'll catch them on the flood plain. Our force has to be lightning quick. Mount the cavalry. Call out seven Centuries of Velites and another five hundred javelin throwers."

"Where do we send them, General Longus?" his Senior Tribune inquired.

Tiberius Longus moved a finger over the map before stabbing an area across the Trebia river. The spot put the Legion forces between the Carthaginian camp and the raiders.

"We'll catch them here and reduce their numbers."

***

Centurion of Horse Silvestris spread his cavalrymen across the plain. In the center, he positioned the light infantrymen and javelin throwers. The chance of them meeting the Punic raiders head-on was slim. But with his ground forces in the middle and clustered around fires, they at least had an opportunity to warm up. Wading through the chest high waters of the Trebia left them chilled to the bone. And the winter air had little drying effect on their soggy clothes.

"You know the General is watching, sir," his Optio told him.

On the far side of the Trebia river, Consul Longus and his staff sat on their mounts watching the maneuvers. Beside them, a signalman kept up a steady supply of instructions.

"I'm aware," Silvestris said. "Thankfully he's out of yelling range. Or I'd be getting verbal orders. As it is, the flags directing us to move left and then right are distracting enough."

"Sir, we have movement to our left," the NCO exclaimed.

Far beyond his last horsemen, a caravan of wagons and pack animals came through the trees and brush.

"We have our target," Silvestris acknowledged. "Get the infantry moving in that direction."

The Centurion pulled the reins and kicked his horse, heading west. Behind him, the Optio turned in the opposite direction and galloped to the center.

On the far riverbank, Consul/General Longus vibrated with anticipation. When the Gauls and their partners in crime dropped their spoils and raced for the Carthaginian camp, he screamed, "Cut them off."

***

Back across the river and flood plain, Silvestris and his fastest riders were attempting to catch the Gauls. But as they raced to intercept the escaping raiders, one of the cavalryman shouted, "They have horsemen going for our infantry."

The Centurion of Horse glanced back. His Velites and javelin throwers were strung out and running for the Punic caravan. And aiming for the unorganized line of light infantry were hundreds of Carthaginian horsemen.

"Take it around," Silvestris ordered while dragging his mount to the side.

Well trained and practiced, his entire detachment curved around and bore down on the Numidian light cavalry.

Across the river, General Longus bellowed, "Colonel, get reinforcements over there. This could turn into the battle we've been waiting for."

As soon as they were in ranks, the Battle Commander sent a thousand more Legion cavalrymen and another three thousand light infantrymen over to the flood plain.

To Tiberius Longus' delight, Carthaginian troops began flowing down from their elevated position. For moments, he was ready to send all his Legions into the fight.

Then, the Punic forces began pulling back. Under cover of flights of arrows, slugs from slingers, and javelins from the high ground, they retreated.

"Sir, they've withdrawn," the Colonel noted.

He expected complaints or criticism from the Consul/General. Instead, he heard a laugh.

"Did you see them run from our cavalry?" he gushed. "We had them in the open and they folded like a cheap piece of linen. Now I know if we get them out of their camp, we will carry the day."

The victory celebration ran late into the night. Feasting followed sacrifices to the Gods. And rounds of wine for the cavalrymen were poured from the Legion supplies. In the

Centurion's mess, Silvestris sat in the back avoiding the congratulations.

"What's wrong Centurion of Horse?" the Legion's senior combat officer asked. "Don't like being the hero of Trebia?"

"Senior Centurion, if I had done something heroic, I would be proud to step up and accept a medal," Silvestris replied. "But I didn't. That engagement was run by someone on the hill. Someone who knew what they were doing."

"Don't say that too loud," the senior combat officer warned. "You'll ruin the General's mood."

A crowd of Centurions gathered around the table and filled their glasses.

"To our hero," they exclaimed.

Gods forbid a Centurion of Horse would disappoint a General. So, Silvestris lifted his glass in salute and drank with them.

***

A wet snow began to fall in the dark hours before dawn. By sunrise, the Legionaries on the forward picket lines were shaking off snowflakes, shivering, and looking forward to being relieved.

In the four marching camps, the damp cold kept even the hardiest infantryman in his tent longer than usual.

"When I get off," one of the sentries announced, "I'm going to boil a sack of grain and eat it right from the pot. Scalded lips or not, I'm that cold."

His partner at the post adjusted his red cape to try and keep out the chill. Turning to look in the direction of the river, he stopped.

"Do we have any patrols out?" he asked.

"No. Everyone's been tucked in nice and comfortable all night."

"Then we may have a problem," the Legionary warned.

He grabbed his spear, slammed the shaft into the top of his shield, and dropped into a guard position. Not understanding, but trusting his fellow squad member, the other armed himself and tucked his shield in next to his mate's.

"What did you see?"

"I'm not sure. There were dark shapes on the far riverbank, I think. Then there weren't."

The snow had increased, dropping visibility to a wagon's length.

"Are you sure, you saw something?"

Dark forms burst from the gray dawn and approached quickly. Still wet from crossing the river, they spun, slinging icy water droplets at the Legionaries. Then in a blink of an eye, they were gone.

"What was that?"

"Snow ghosts," the other suggested.

"I don't think spirits splash water. Unless it's a drowned seaman haunting the valley."

"It could be…"

Four Numidian riders came out of the flurries. Dryer this time, there were no flying water droplets. But two thrown javelins buried themselves in the big infantry shields.

"Optio, attack. We are under attack," the Legionaries shouted while holding their ground.

One whined, "They have us targeted. The next time, we duck."

In a few heartbeats, although it seemed longer, four, then five more shields snapped into the line next to the original pair. As the squad formed, their Sergeant exchanged five spears for javelins. Once their ranged weapons were deployed, he stabbed more into the ground behind the line.

"Standby to throw," he said.

Calls of attack rang from Legion posts up and down the river.

"We've got us an attack for sure," the Duty NCO offered while yawning.

"Aren't you nervous, Optio Zythum?" one of the infantrymen asked.

"I'm standing behind ten of the best shields in the Legion," the NCO bragged. "How do I know? Listen to the other picket posts. They're just now sounding the alert and you are already in formation. Just don't get greedy."

"Greedy how, Sergeant?"

"By murdering all the mercenaries, yourselves," he responded. "Let's leave a few for the other squads."

Despite having an enemy lurking in the snow, and butterflies in their stomachs, the infantrymen laughed.

***

From horseback, Centurion Silvestris clearly saw the shadows of the riders in the snow. They dashed around in the soup like fish just beneath the surface. But slowly, the weak winter sun was pushing through the storm clouds, illuminating Numidian light cavalrymen.

"I've seen enough," Silvestris called to his troop. "Let's get them off our pickets. Lances."

"When we get back, I'm going to sacrifice a lamb," one cavalrymen remarked as he pulled his weapon from a holder.

"Fearing the Gods this morning?" the rider beside him inquired.

"No. I'm just that hungry," the Legion horseman replied. "And lamb sounds good. A blessing from the Gods will be an added benefit."

"Forward," Silvestris ordered.

The fifty mounted Legionaries trotted out of the marching camp. They planned to chase off the Carthaginian probe and then get back for breakfast. Unfortunately, none would get back for breakfast and fewer still would get back at all.

Chapter 17 – The Hand That Commands

The squads charged with picket duty felt the ground quake as their cavalry thundered by. Almost as if a chase response in a hunting dog, the infantrymen jogged after the horses. At the top of the embankment, they stopped as the cavalry splashed through the chest deep water. On the far bank, light cavalry from the Carthaginian army dashed in and out as if playing tag with the Legion horsemen.

"Optio, the Trebia has risen from the storm," the squad leader warned. "What do we do?"

"I guess we could sit here, sip fine vino, and leave the fighting to the boys-with-horses," Zythum mocked the question. "Or we could grow a pair, suck it up, and get wet. What do you think an infantry Century should do?"

Stomping feet announced the arrival of the other seventy Legionaries of the Sixth Century.

"Optio Zythum, the river is higher," their young Centurion noted. "What should we do?"

The picket squad tensed, waiting for their Sergeant to unload on the officer.

"Sir, move across and support the cavalry," Zythum replied. "The Numidian's light horses are quicker than our Republic mounts. We can set shield barriers to create defensive islands for sheltering our riders when they tire."

"Then let's go," the inexperienced combat officer acknowledged. After a pause, he realized the Century was waiting for his command. He raised his hand and shouted. "Form the Maniple ten paces from the far riverbank. Go."

The eighty men and their NCOs slung their capes around their necks, ran down, and yelped when they splashed into the freezing water of the Trebia. After struggling through the cold that came up to their armpits, they climbed the far bank with teeth chattering. While shivering in wet armor, they marched ten steps from the river.

As they moved, the Century split into three lines, locked their shields together, and leveled their spears.

"Forward," the Centurion instructed. He added for the benefit of the Legionaries. "It appears the Carthaginians are coming out to play. And we're right where we need to be."

"Rah, Centurion," came back to him.

Optio Zythum smiled at the enthusiasm. His Century had trained hard in Sicilia, learning the ways of the infantry. And the remark by his youthful Centurion informed him that the combat officer had learned his leadership role. Now it was time to get the inexperienced Sixth Century, Longus Legion South, bloodied.

***

Scipio Legion Scouts reported the probes to the Legion fort. Shortly after receiving the news of the Punic aggression, Tribune Cornelius Scipio and Senior Centurion Pericles led a thousand Scipio cavalrymen from the fort. At a trot, they moved swiftly through the dwindling flurries. When he had a view of the flood plain, Cornelius lifted his hand and waved the riders to a halt.

"Your opinion, Senior Centurion?" he inquired.

The senior combat officer for Scipio Legion East studied the skirmishing.

"Have you ever watched a bucket coming up from a well?" Pericles ventured. "It swings wide at first, but as the rope coils around the pole, it shortens. And as the bucket gets where you can reach it, the swings becomes less and less pronounced."

"Of course, especially on hot summer days at my father's country villa," Cornelius snapped. "What does water from a well have to do with making sure my father reaps some of the glory from this battle?"

"You are cold to the bone," Pericles guessed. "And I'd put coins on the fact that you didn't have breakfast."

"True on both counts, Senior Centurion, so what…," the teen stopped talking when he realized an experienced combat officer was offering insight. "My apologies for being rude. Please, explain your thoughts."

"The Numidians are riding close to our advancing cavalry. Then they race away before coming partially back. On each loop, they pull our cavalry further across the flood plain," Pericles described. "Almost as if drawing them, like a bucket, to within reach."

"I see that now," Cornelius remarked. "But into the reach of what?"

"That, Tribune, I don't know," the Senior Centurion admitted. "But it's the Carthaginians, and it can't be good."

To their left, the blare of rally horns sounded at all four marching camps.

"It seems General Longus believes the Punics are coming off their hill. Should we cross over and join the battle?"

"It's not a battle yet," Pericles pointed out. "Rather than riding over there and trying to figure out where we fit in, I'd recommend waiting for an opportunity. Let Longus' Legions handle it for now."

"How will we know when there's an opportunity?" Cornelius questioned.

"Either desperation or providence will guide us."

Down the riverbank, Legion cavalrymen, heavy infantrymen, and Velites ran from the stockades. They dropped into the river and waded across the chest deep channel. Then the Republic forces climbed to the flood plain, dripping frigid water from their arms, legs, and armor.

Over eleven thousand heavy infantrymen formed the Legion center. With three ranks of three Maniples, the lines of shields were long with a high degree of built-in redundancy.

Once the center was established, the Velites split and jogged to flank the heavy infantrymen. With them guarding the sides, no Punic javelin men, riders, slingers, or archers could come around and shoot or throw into the ranks.

Finally, the Legion cavalry trotted to positions outside the light infantry. They would keep the Carthaginian heavy cavalry, and the fast and agile Numidians, off the Velites.

"I've never seen Legions form up so fast," Pericles observed. "It's very impressive. I'd like to admire the General's staff, except for three issues."

"What three concerns?" Cornelius asked. "They look ready for battle."

"Grains, Gods, and Sicilia," Pericles replied. "They received the warning when we did. In order to wake the Legionaries and get them into the field quickly, like grouchy you, they skipped the morning meal. And command neglected to make a sacrifice to the Gods, asking for victory."

When the Senior Centurion stopped, Cornelius scanned the ranks of the Legions for details.

"They didn't take rations with them," he noted. "They'll have to fight hungry."

"And why is that a problem?" Pericles tested.

"Because up on the hill, the cookfires are roaring," the youth said. "The Punic forces will have full bellies and lots of energy."

"What else?"

"You said Sicilia," Cornelius pondered. He examined the ranks of armor with red under tunics showing from the arms of the Legionaries. Something about red stuck in his mind. Then the young Tribune threw both arms into the air in frustration. "They trained in Sicilia where it's warm."

"And so, taking their red wool capes into combat wasn't part of their drills," Pericles confirmed. "They are hungry, have no supplies, and no capes after wading a near freezing river."

Tribune Cornelius Scipio twisted around and examined the cavalrymen behind him.

"I see red capes," he reported. "Do they have rations with them?"

"I passed the word before we left. Each of your horseman has feed for his mount and food for himself."

"Get them dismounted and fed," Cornelius directed.

"So, all the lessons about caring for your men first are having an effect," Pericles bragged. "You are becoming a true commander of Legionaries."

"I like to think that's true," Cornelius said. "But mostly, I want us ready for that."

He pointed at the distant camp of the Carthaginians. From the top of the hill, giant war elephants lumbered down the slope. But that wasn't what concerned the young Tribune. And neither was the massive number of horsemen flowing around the large beasts. That ranked as a caution but didn't set off any alarm bells. What did turn the Tribune's guts were large groups of men matching in uniformed armor and carrying large shields and long spears.

"Hoplites, heavy infantrymen," Pericles whispered. "It's going to be a hard day's work in the center of our lines."

"Between the elephants and the phalanxes," Cornelius agreed, "it's going to be a very hard day."

***

"Not such a hard day," Zythum announced to his Legionaries. "We could be on the end and spend the battle chipping away at ivory tusks. Or be positioned in the center and have a day of dodging long spears and climbing walls of shields. For tonight, plan on a sacrifice to thank the God for being the Sixth Century. Can I get an affirmation?"

"Rah," eighty-one voices replied.

"Because we were the alert Century, we were already dressed," their Centurion advised. "Everyone have their wool cape?"

"Rah!"

Forming a triangle, the Centurion stood at the rear of the formation with Optio Zythum and the Tesserarius ahead and on either side. Before them the three lines of their Century faced an advancing enemy.

"First line draw and brace. Second and third lines two javelins."

The swish of twenty-six steel blades leaving leather sheaths, the crunch of infantrymen pushing spearheads into the dirt but within easy reach, and heavy breathing resulted from the order. They had been trained to listen not talk in the ranks.

"Stand by javelins," the Centurion commanded. He lifted his hand to match the other combat officers behind their lines. When the Legion's Senior Centurion dropped his, the combat officers slashed the air and bellowed. "Throw javelins."

A flight of seven thousand javelins arched into the sky and picked up speed on the way down. They zipped into the front line of Iberian infantrymen and Hoplites. Most javelins punched through shields, fouling the straight ranks. And some dropped heavy infantrymen to the dirt, where the wounded screamed in agony while trying to pull out the iron shafts.

The next flight of javelins found more flesh as the Iberian second rankers rushed forward to fill empty spots in the forward line.

"Spears and brace," the Centurions ordered.

Sixth Century of Longus Legion South had done their best to disrupt the forward momentum of the enemy. Now it was time, as Optio Zythum often said, "to earn your Republic coins."

The Iberian infantry came in hard, but they stopped dead as if meeting a brick wall. In essence, they had in the form of the Legionaries of the Sixth standing their ground. Now, shield to shield, both sides tried to eviscerate the other.

Once the fighting settled down to hacking and slashing, the Centurion called for the second rank to roll forward and the front rank to rotate off the combat line. Due to Optio Zythum's aggressive training, the Sixth Century quickly put fresh arms and legs into the fight. After furious battling along the line, the combat officer called for another. By the third rotation, the inexperienced Legionaries of the Sixth were bloodied and holding their combat line.

***

"Get them off the ground," Cornelius Scipio ordered. "I haven't seen an opportunity either from desperation or providence. I think we should get into this fight before it's too late."

"Think hard about your next order, Tribune," Pericles advised while lifting his chin towards the battle on the flood plain. "They have twice the number of horsemen. Our cavalry is being beaten back. And our light infantry is falling by the hundreds."

Cornelius scanned the battlefield then squinted into the distance. Despite being far away, he gasped at the wreckage on the Legion flanks. And although hemmed in at the front by war elephants, the tight formations of the phalanxes, plowing into and out of the ranks, and the steady pounding by the Iberians, the Legion center was holding. Lifting his face, the young Tribune peered over the fighting to a man sitting on a magnificent horse, dressed in fine furs, and wearing a silver helmet.

"I think that might be General Hannibal Barca," Cornelius mentioned. "He's waving with his left hand, making big circles with it."

"Look around him," Pericles suggested. "Can you locate any signalmen."

Scipio and Pericles tried to pick out the Punic signalmen from the noblemen gathered around Barca. It took long moments before one in the back and partially hidden, faced to the north and began waving flags.

"Who is he signaling?" Pericles questioned. "They don't have any soldiers over there."

"Providence," Cornelius Scipio exclaimed. "Mount up."

"Where are we going?" Pericles inquired.

"To warn General Longus."

"About what?" Pericles asked.

"About the second Carthaginian force coming from the north," Cornelius replied while vaulting onto his horse's back.

"I don't see anything to the north," Pericles remarked.

"Neither do I," Cornelius admitted while raising his hand to command the cavalry forward. "But drawing the Legion halfway across the flood plain and staging a second force to the north is a move worthy of a master strategist."

"One such as," Pericles said allowing his pride to ebb, "Hannibal Barca."

Cornelius dropped his hand and shouted, "Forward."

He nudged his mount and the beast sprinted down the embankment and into the river.

***

Centurion Silvestris took a stream of water. Then he looked around at the cavalrymen near him. He didn't recognize most of them. It wasn't the blood splatters, the dirt, the vacant eyes of beaten men, or the exhaustion and strain on their faces. He didn't recognize the riders because he had never met most of them.

A tattered collection of Legion cavalrymen from different Legions had somehow gravitated to the same spot. A section behind the heavy infantry where they could catch their breaths and rest their horses.

"We've lost the flanks, Centurion," a cavalryman spit out. "What more can we do? Die?"

"Not yet," Silvestris responded. He paused trying to think of a mission that wasn't suicidal. But death waited for any Legion rider who engaged against the terrible odds outside the zone. "We can't go directly against the Punic cavalry. Is there a spot where we can screen a section of the Legion and be of use?"

Giving them something to think about other than their losses, gave the men a little escape from the reality of the situation. Some of the fear seeped away while they pondered the question.

"Who are they?" one cavalryman asked while extending an arm wrapped in a bandage.

From the bank of the Trebia river to the north, a long string of riders stretched out behind a Tribune and a Senior Centurion. At a full gallop, they moved rapidly towards the battle.

"I don't know, and I don't care," Silvestris shouted. "Even if that Tribune is riding directly to Hades, I'm riding with him."

The Centurion of Horse kicked his mount and the weary beast responded. Behind Silvestris, the other cavalrymen paused for a heartbeat before they rode to the unknown Tribune who hastened towards the fight.

Chapter 18 – The Price of Luck

The General's staff for multiple Legions numbered over a hundred. Only a few were required to officiate over the battle. The rest were there to solicit favors from Consul Longus. Or, for bragging rights about the experience when they returned to Rome. Kept back by the First Century, the businessmen, priests, politicians, and money lenders, created a barrier around the command staff. Even Junior Tribunes, carrying reports from the four Battle Commanders, had difficulty getting through to the General.

"Respect your elders," a pompous politician scolded a young messenger. "Wait over there until…"

"Sir, I must see the General," the junior staff officer whined. He had tried to break through the civilians in two other places but had been rejected. He pleaded. "It's important."

"We all must see the General, and it's important to us all," the man blustered. "When I was your age…"

A cavalry horse shouldered aside the man's gentle riding mare. In response, the politician drew a dagger and lifted his arm to stab the cavalryman. But an arm locked around his neck and pulled him into a chest of hard muscles.

"I wouldn't do that, sir," Senior Centurion Pericles growled. "Tribune Scipio is young, but he is very good with his spatha. And should you manage to kill him, I would be obliged to avenge Cornelius."

The politician went limp and sputtered, "I didn't recognize Consul Scipio's son."

Pericles pushed him away and used his horse to cut the mare out of the group.

"Junior Tribune, what's your Legion?" Cornelius asked.

"Longus Legion South, sir," the boy replied. "I need to see the General."

"And why is that?"

"We have movement to the North," the boy said. "And no one believes me."

"Because you are with the South Legion positioned to the north and that confuses people?"

"Yes, Tribune and because I'm small for my age."

"I believe you," Cornelius announced while pulling his blade. "Everyone shut up or I'll begin clearing this circus. Now, where is the First Centurion? I need him before the Carthaginians get so close, you'll smell what they had for breakfast on their breath."

Handpicked by General Longus, the four Colonels of his Legions ran the battles and coordinated with each other. Consul Longus remained back and oversaw the fighting. As most Consuls, he had limited command experience and relied on his Battle Commanders for military matters. The system fit with the Latin ethos of a leader not bothering with the minutia of any situation. As such, Consul Tiberius Longus stayed above tactics and visualized how he would manage the acceptance of General Barca's surrender.

"General Longus, the Junior Tribune here has a message from Legion South," Cornelius advised.

"If it isn't young Scipio. Come to watch the Carthaginian defeat?"

"No, sir. I'm here to verify the Junior Tribune's message."

"What message?" Longus' Senior Tribune inquired.

"Sir, a message from Colonel Propertia, Battle Commander of Longus Legion South," the young staff officer announced. "Without delay, you are to order a total retreat and flee yourself."

"At the moment of my greatest victory?" Longus asked. He pointed ahead and insisted. "Our center is holding and even advancing in places."

"Sir, there's a second Punic army coming from the north," Cornelius informed him. "If you delay any longer, your head will adorn General Barca's dinner table this evening."

Tiberius Longus looked left across the vast number of combatants then to the right. Unlike Barca, Longus only had the height of his horse which limited his view to a few hundred feet. From the hill, the Punic commander saw the fighting along the entire two-mile front.

"Send runners to order a withdrawal," General Longus instructed.

While his young junior staff officers galloped to the four Legions to deliver the messages, Cornelius Scipio wheeled his horse around and rode north to Legion South.

***

Optio Zythum rested on the ground. All through training, he never sat or leaned or showed weakness. But the rotations to the combat line had cost him nine men, his officer, and his Tesserarius. Now the NCO sat in exhaustion.

Soon orders would arrive that would send him and his infantrymen forward for another trip to the meat market.

The legs of a mount appeared in front of the Sergeant.

"Is it our turn again?" he asked while looking up.

"Zythum, is this your flock?" his Battle Commander inquired.

"Sir, I thought you were a courier," Zythum explained while pushing to his feet.

"Your people are the only ones with capes," Colonel Propertia noted. "I need you to collect our walking wounded and the Junior Tribunes."

"Yes, sir. What am I supposed to do with them?"

"Escort the noblemen and injured across the river," Propertia instructed. "Then, set up a blocking force on the other bank. Your red capes will serve to mark the line of our retreat. Understand?"

"Yes, sir," Zythum acknowledged. Once the Battle Commander was away, the NCO called to his infantrymen. "Sixth Century, brush the dust off your capes and circle up. We have new orders."

***

Pericles studied Cornelius as they rode north. In half a mile, Longus Legion South came into view. Split, almost overwhelmed, and fighting both to the North and the southwest, the Legion was collapsing.

"Tribune Scipio, you need to leave," the Senior Centurion remarked.

"I'm not running out when there's fighting to be done," Cornelius shot back.

"I understand your feelings. But your family's name is already associated with one defeat. A reputation for bad luck will hurt your career," Pericles warned. As they approached their cavalrymen staged behind Legion West, he added. "Besides, the battle here is decided. The only question remaining is how many more will die."

They arrived at the rear of Longus Legion West. Among the detachment from Scipio's Legions, they found a gathering of scruffy survivors from Longus' Legions.

"Senior Centurion, I'm Centurion Silvestris," a cavalry officer greeted Pericles. "We're beat down but not out. Where do you want us?"

"We're just organizing," Pericles responded.

Cornelius held up his hand to signal wait. Twisting around, he studied the river and scrunched his face in thought.

"Centurion Silvestris, take half these riders and cross over the Trebia."

"No offense Tribune, but we want to stay and fight," Silvestris protested.

"You'll have your chance," Cornelius assured him. "You'll be screening the retreating Legions from attackers crossing the river. You've got three miles of march to protect. I suggest you get going."

***

Centurion Silvestris and his mixture of fresh and battle-weary cavalrymen trotted towards the river.

"Where to, sir?" a mounted Legionary asked.

The Tribune's words sounded simple. Patrol the eastern bank of the Trebia northward to the Legion fort at Piacenza and keep the Punics off the retreating Legions. But where was the crossing point?

As they rode, an Optio appeared on the far side of the river. He untied a red cape from around his neck and snapped the material out as if unfurling a flag. It billowed in the wind, identifying the NCO's location. Still climbing were injured Legionaries, groups of junior tribunes, and a Century of heavy infantrymen. Their red capes still wrapped around their necks as they scrambled up the far bank.

"There's the crossing," Silvestris pointed out. "From there to the fort, we let no Punic scum through. Rah?"

"Rah, sir," the riders near him responded. As his words were passed back, the 'Rah' became an echo until every Legion cavalryman shouted his enthusiasm.

Despite their zeal, it would be a long and sad day for the forces of the Republic.

***

By late evening, Cornelius Scipio sat with his father at Piacenza.

"It's done," he informed the elder Scipio. "Only about ten thousand escaped the flood plain. Most were heavy infantrymen who brought Consul Longus and his staff out with them."

"What in the name of the Gods happened?" his father demanded.

"General Barca lured us in and sprang a trap," Cornelius replied. "I watched it unfold, yet I couldn't think of any way to counter him."

"Don't let any Senators hear you say that," Publius warned. "Exalting the virtues of a Punic commander will get you exiled."

"I know when to be silent, father. Hannibal Barca is an enemy of the Republic. And I swear, I will be there when he falls."

Publius closed his eyes and hung his head. Cornelius couldn't tell if his boast sounded like breast beating by a teen and embarrassed his father, or if his father needed a break after receiving the bad news. Cornelius began to rise from the sofa.

"This defeat is worse than if we had given ground to Barca," Publius offered. Cornelius rested back in the chair and listened. "With his victory, every Gaul and disgruntled tribesman for a hundred miles around will rush to join the Carthaginian."

"We'll need to build more Legions," Cornelius suggested. "And maybe call in favors from client states."

Publius took a sip of watered wine and said, "I'm sending you to Rome with my report from the battle. We need to counter any lies by my co-Consul."

"But you weren't at the battle, father."

"That's alright, I'm not writing the report," Publius informed his son. "You are and I'm signing it. I trust that I'll be humble but heroic in the narrative."

"Absolutely, father," Cornelius assured him.

***

Between Consul Publius Scipio's letter and Consul Tiberius Longus', the reports of the two disasters in the Po River Valley were presented to the Senate in graphic detail. Some Senators lobbied to assign blame. But two Consuls in two separate battles spread the responsibility too thin to lay on any one General.

"We have a need, gentlemen," the Chairman of the Senate announced. "I am proposing that we send demands to our allies and request military troops."

"What kind of soldiers?" one Senator asked. "I don't like the idea of paying for mercenaries."

Across the chamber, another Senator jumped to his feet and countered, "And I don't like the idea of spilling the blood of our sons."

"Senators, please. Be seated and allow the role to be called," the Chairman scolded. "For your consideration is a request to obtain troops, by any means necessary, from our allies. Those in favor say, Aye."

Overwhelmingly the vote carried. Scribes were called into committee meetings. One of the groups drew Syracuse. By late in the day, a delegation left for Sicilia to speak with King Hiero.

***

Two weeks later, the selected Senator walked into the King's chamber.

"Greetings from the people and Senate of Rome," the delegate declared. "We are always honored to call on our greatest ally on Sicilia."

"Every time one of you shows up, it costs me," the old King complained. "What can Syracuse do for Rome? The latest in catapults, bolt throwers, or perhaps this is another request for the Iron Hand?"

"There is always interest in Archimedes' inventions," the legislator remarked. "I admit, up ending a warship by pulling a single rope fascinates us. Is the Iron Hand for sale?"

"No. But is your Senate willing to pay for anything else?" the King inquired.

"The Senate has sent out a call for troops," the Senator informed the King of Syracuse. "We trust that you will fulfill your part of our mutual aggression pact."

"Who is attacking Rome?" Hiero questioned.

"A rogue Punic General. He and a band of mercenaries have assaulted our northern border. And we need to build an army to push him back over the Alps."

"The Legions require help?" Hiero asked. He rested his chin in the palm of his hand and allowed a puzzled look to cross his face. "You Latians are always so sure of your military."

"We're holding our best in reserve," the Senator lied. "To conserve the Legions, we're depending on our friends to fill the ranks of an army."

"You'll have your tribute," King Hiero agreed. "Just as soon as I can raise the Companies."

Two days later, the Roman Senator and the delegation left the harbor of Syracuse and sailed west up the Messina

Strait. On the same tide, a messenger ship left the harbor heading east.

"Is it a good idea?" an advisor asked the King. "Rome is expecting Syracusan forces."

"Whether they get fifteen hundred men from Syracuse or fifteen from somewhere else, I've met my part of the treaty," Hiero explained. "And I've kept our army intact. Let the Roman's complain, and I'll withhold payment. We'll see how much they cry when the mercenaries go home."

"Very wise, King Hiero," the advisor confirmed.

Act 7

Chapter 19 – Awakened Loss

Jace Kasia ran through the gate, sprinted across the parade ground, slipped between the administration buildings, and raced the short length to the range. Sliding to a stop in the gravel, he bent over with his hands on his knees, taking deep breaths to recover from the ten-mile run.

"That hurt," he said while brushing the sweat off his face.

Then from the corner of his eye, he noted four tiny bodies. They were lined up on the porch of the armory, facing Jace, and looking lost.

"Who are you?" he demanded.

"Little Herd," one stammered. "Lieutenant Gergely said to get our bows."

"Oh, he did, did he?" Jace questioned while walking to the door. The four eight-year-olds separated to let him pass. Then they followed him into the building. Halfway across the workshop, Jace spun on them. "And just where do you think you're going?"

"To get our bows, Master Kasia," the four said together.

"Not until they're ready."

"When will they be ready?" one asked.

"When I say they are. All four of you get out and move to the range."

As the little boys scrambled out the door, Jace went to a rack and selected four short bows with light pulls. He took time stringing them because the little ones would need instructions and training to learn how to brace their bows. But that was for later. He took the bows outside and stopped on the porch.

Lynceus Inigo had the little Herd members on their faces in the gravel.

"What are you doing on my range?" the newly graduated Cretan archer sneered.

In his hand was the war bow presented to him for passing the trials. A quiver of arrows rode low on his hip. For a casual onlooker, he appeared to be an archer come to the range for practice. But Jace knew better.

"Archer Inigo, the little Herd is here for a lesson," Jace stated.

Ignoring the remark, Lynceus continued berating the boys, "You are a waste. You should run home to your mothers and apologize for wasting her time creating you."

"They need an introduction to their bows," Jace insisted.

In a slow threatening turn, Lynceus faced the porch.

"No one is talking to you, bow repairman," he said.

Jace held up the beginners bows and agreed, "I am sorry to disturb you, Cretan archer. But the next generation, the ones who will save you in battles years from now, need to start learning."

"Like an itinerant tradesman can teach them anything," he shot back. "Can you even hit a target with a bow?"

For five months, Jace had worked with the little and middle Herds to teach them bow repair and maintenance. During those months, he practiced archery only when no one was around to see. He ran early, and practiced hatchet and blade drills in the armory when no one was around. Per his agreement with Lieutenant Gergely, master archer Jace Kasia hid his skills and taught classes.

Then Lynceus put a foot on the neck of a little one. He bent over the tiny body.

"I am a Cretan archer, and I can snap your neck if I choose to," he told the small boy.

At the helpless squeal of the youth, Jace placed the bows down on the porch.

"How many arrows do you have in your quiver?" Jace asked.

Lynceus leaned back and tilted his chin up. His foot remained on the frail neck.

"Are you challenging me, woodworker?" he questioned. "With what bow? One of those toys?"

"How many arrows?" Jace pressed him on the count.

"Ten stiffed spined matching arrows. Enough for two rotations."

"Take your foot off the boy and warm up your bow," Jace told him. Then he instructed the little Herd. "You four get off the ground and report to Lieutenant Gergely. Tell him your bows aren't ready."

The archer removed his foot and the four boys jumped up and scrambled from the range.

"I'll be right back," Jace assured the antagonistic archer.

Inside the building, Jace went directly to the case containing his war bow. Openly challenging Lynceus might be his last act as a teacher at the agoge and end his chance of serving with a Company. But Jace was angry. It no longer mattered who learned that his skills came from a disgraced master archer.

Ever since the day at the noon Prowess, Lynceus Inigo had poked, teased, and humiliated Jace at every opportunity. Now, the mean-spirited archer stooped to mistreating members of the little Herd just to get a rise out of Jace. Well, this time it worked.

"I'm sorry Lieutenant Gergely," he apologized while drawing the powerful war bow from the case. "But Inigo needs to learn a graduate of the agoge isn't a better archer than one trained by Zarek Mikolas."

Jace held the bow and smiled at the memory of his mentor. Then he whipped around, fast walked to the door, and into the chest of Lieutenant Acis Gergely.

***

"Going somewhere, Master Kasia?" the Cretan officer inquired.

Over the Lieutenant's shoulder, Jace saw Lynceus Inigo sitting in the grass off to the side of the range. Standing in front of him, while he described the parts of a bow, were the four new members of the agoge.

"I guess nowhere, sir," Jace replied.

"Come back inside and let me explain somethings," Acis urged. As they crossed between the workbenches, he offered. "You're not Greek, and you haven't been through agoge training."

"I've worked harder than any student here to learn my craft," Jace countered. "My instructions began at twilight and ended at twilight. For eight years, I practiced harder and longer than the students at the agoge. And from what I hear, my trials were more difficult. Even if I can't be a Cretan archer, why not acknowledge my skills?"

"Because I can't have an unaffiliated master archer teaching at the agoge," the Lieutenant explained. "The good and honest Cretan families who send their sons to the academy would find you blasphemous. And the proud, self-assured graduates would be furious to have a student of the exiled Zarek Mikolas soiling their hallowed grounds. Especially, a Latian archer."

"But Lynceus keeps pressing me," Jace complained. "He abused the little Herd to get at me."

"All bright and shiny new archers are stupid and unbloodied," Acis declared. "If we were in Rome and you were a Legion archer, how would you view archer Inigo?"

"The same way, I suppose."

"No Jace, if we were among your people, the archer would be looked down on and treated like cattle," Acis informed him.

"I would never do that," Jace protested while touching the medallion he wore. "Besides, the only way I know Latin is from lessons by the academic teachers at the agoge. It's not even my native tongue."

Jace squeezed the bronze medallion and chain through his shirt. In his mind, he visualized the words, *Romiliia household with bravery and the fierceness of wolves*. And the image on the reverse side of a snarling she-wolf. It was the only connection he had to his past.

"You can challenge Lynceus and probably outshoot him," Acis stated. "But then you'd need to leave the agoge. And thusly ruin any chance of joining me in a Company when I get a contract."

Jace dropped his hand from the medallion and lowered his eyes. He really had nowhere to go. No family on Crete other than Neysa Kasia but she was a farmer and Jace wasn't.

"I will continue to be an obedient bow maker," he swore. "And no matter the insults from Archer Inigo, I will still my breath, so my hands are steady. Calm my heart, so my eyes are clear. And focus my mind on teaching bow maintenance."

"It's not an easy path," Lieutenant Gergely allowed. "But in politics and in war, we all play our part."

The archer officer left the building and marched to the four little Herd members. He took a position behind the boys. For the rest of the class, Acis kept a critical eye on archer Inigo to be sure the lesson was professional and informative.

Jace envied the little boys. They would grow and learn to be respected archers, while he would continue to be a nonentity. He inhaled the aromas of the shop, gripped the medallion, and went to file on a new bow.

Lieutenant Gergely had been right, Jace Kasia didn't belong at the agoge. In fact, he didn't belong anywhere.

***

Late in the afternoon, when the final class cleared the workshop, Jace strolled to the gate of the compound.

"Good evening, Master Kasia," the guard on duty acknowledged him.

His relationship with the sentries assigned to guarding the agoge consisted of a nod and a word when he left. And the same brief exchange usually accompanied his return.

While he had roamed the city a few times a week, mostly to get away from the boys of the Herds, Jace had not really hunted the men who took his coin purse. Now, with the realization that he had no future on Crete, Jace Kasia began a search starting near the fish market.

***

After touring the stalls, he strolled to the walled harbor. Resembling a wide canal, the facility protected warships, and large transports from the whims of winds and waves. Although there were groups of men at the piers, none were the drunk or the irate pedestrian who robbed him. After examining the harbor, Jace moved towards the agoge in loops that took him up and down parallel streets.

Two blocks from the academy, a large man leaned out of a doorway. His hands were scarred, big as hams, and hard. He extended a finger.

"Is that him, Lieutenant?" Papinia inquired.

"That's the one," the archer officer confirmed. "He needs to learn humility. And to respect his betters."

"I never had any education, so I'm not a person one would call a teacher. But I know how to put fear into a man," the thug boasted. With a fist, he tapped the stone wall. "To me, fear is as good as respect."

"That's acceptable," the Lieutenant agreed. He pressed a small coin purse into the brute's other hand. "You'll get the rest when the bowyer has difficulty eating, and a hard time standing erect."

"Two specialties of me and my boys," Papinia remarked. Pulling his head back from the street, he glanced behind him. The archer officer had vanished. But the hoodlum continued speaking despite the archer's absence. "It's more for me if you don't want to get your hands dirty. Simply give Papinia your coins and leave the job to me."

With the coins in his hand, Papinia went to find his associates and set up surveillance. The next time the bow maker left the compound, he'd enter a different type of school. One taught by survivors from the streets and back alleys of Phalasarna.

***

After staying up to study a map of the city, Jace got a late start on his morning run.

"Hey, it's Master Kasia," a little Herd member noticed him. "I didn't know teachers ran."

"Everyone at the agoge does physical training," another commented.

Jace lumbered forward and turned off on a side street. Memorizing the area as he passed, he looked for landmarks. Later that afternoon when people were out, he would return and search the new quarter of the city for the men who took his coins. A block over, a Troop of older teens spied the bowyer. Jace slowed.

"It's the middle Herd's bow maker," an advanced student teased. "Is he trying to keep up with the children?"

"Not at that pace," another declared.

Jace slowed more before peeling off onto an intersecting road. Four blocks later, he met another Troop. Again, he veered off to avoid revealing the length and speed of his run.

Although he was seen by the Herds and Troops, they only witnessed a segment of his route. Their opinions might have changed had they realized he was doing a fast-paced ten miles while performing a grid search. The students from the archery academy weren't the only ones thrown off by the racing bow maker.

The thug Papinia and his observers lost track of Jace as he moved off straightaways to find and memorize other backstreets of the city.

"I had the bow maker in sight and tracked him for several blocks," one minion explained to the gang leaders. "Then he rounded a corner. I was just behind him, but when I reach the road, he was gone. Vanished, I tell you."

Balasi, the second in command of the gang used his walking stick to shove the underling aside.

"He must have sprinted to the end and turned onto another street," Balasi suggested to Papinia. "Us trying to run him down isn't going to work. We'll get him when he comes out for an evening stroll."

“Let’s be sure to slow him down in the future,” Papinia remarked. “The Lieutenant didn’t say we couldn’t install a limp when we beat on the bow maker.”

While his stalkers discussed him, Jace jogged through the gates of the agoge.

“Good morning, Master Kasia,” the guard greeted him. “Cut your run short this morning?”

“I did,” Jace replied, even though he had completed the ten miles. By returning before the Herds and Troops, he gave the appearance of an abbreviated workout. “I’m just not feeling it today.”

“It’s a good thing you aren’t in the agoge,” the sentry mentioned, “those boys don’t have a choice.”

“Neither did I, when I trained to be an archer,” Jace whispered softly. His words went unheard by the sentry.

***

The day drifted by with Jace Kasia placing little hands on the backs of bows. Guiding them, he taught the youngest boys to plane and shave the wood smooth. The older boys had already mastered the skill of blending the limbs with the bellies. For them, their time in the shop consisted of combing sinew into strips, dipping the hair like fibers in hide glue, and carefully placing the lengths in layers on one side of the bow.

“For a Latian, you know a lot about bows,” one boy stated.

Rather than a compliment, Jace felt the sting of being an outsider. He had the training to be a master Cretan archer, but it would never be acknowledged on Crete.

More determined than he had been for the past five months, Jace finished the day and left the agoge. If he wanted to escape Crete, he had roads, lanes, and streets to patrol and coins to recover.

***

Eneas, a young gang member, picked up the bow maker and shadowed him. They headed north from of the compound. A few streets later, they passed the Throne of Poseidon. At over eight feet above the street, the seat of the stone throne, they said, allowed for a view of the water over the sea wall. But no one would desecrate the God of the Sea by climbing up to verify the information. Beyond the throne, the bow maker entered the acropolis.

On both sides of the gate, walls ran around the base of the high ground. While high ground it may be, little soil was visible. Tightly packed buildings hid the earth and created a maze worthy of King Minos' Labyrinth.

As Eneas trailed the bowyer into the narrow streets, he thought of the story.

Poseidon sent a snow-white bull to King Minos of Crete for a sacrifice. But Minos, upon seeing the magnificent beast, refused to sacrifice the animal. When the God of the Sea heard, he punished the King by making his daughter, Pasiphae, fall in love with the bull. When Pasiphae gave birth to a Minotaur, a human body with a bull's head, King Minos had the Labyrinth built to house the creature.

Eneas rocked his head from side-to-side trying to imagine what it would feel like to have the head of a bull. Besides making him a good enough fighter to challenge

Papinia, the sight wouldn't impress the ladies. He decided it was better to have a human head.

Unlike the morning when the bowyer outran the observers, in the afternoon, he was easy to follow. Except, the bow maker didn't stop to allow Eneas a chance to contact either Papinia or Balasi. Out of fear that he would lose the target in the city streets, Eneas maintained his surveillance.

Off to the left, a sloping trail led to the warehouses and the protected harbor at sea level. It was also the location of the market. From any of the high walls or stone steps, Eneas could keep his eyes on the bowyer. But the bow maker didn't venture down to the stalls or the anchorage. He continued around the fortified city to the northern side. When he stopped at an intersection of two wide boulevards, Eneas melted into a doorway to watch.

***

That morning, Jace had run through the intersection and recognized the street where the drunk held his elbows. And just off the main street, the alley he used to get out of the crowd. The same place he met the alley rats.

In a few strides, he entered the lane and fast walked to the end of the building. Even when he spotted the three muggers, he didn't cut his pace.

"Who is trespassing…?"

Jace's left foot swung up and the toe of his sandal dug into the man's side. Normally a swift kick to the ribs served only to shove an opponent out of the way. But the exact targeting as taught by Zarek and practiced by Jace, drove the toes under the ribs and into the man's liver.

Quivering, the thief collapsed to the ground, curled into a ball, and wept from the pain. Jace straddled the man's shoulders, pulled his knife, and placed the blade at his throat.

"I need some information," the archer calmly informed the other two denizens of the alley. "And I'm afraid I can't leave without it. No matter who gets hurt in the process."

"We could run," one suggested.

"And leave your friend to bleed to death?" Jace inquired.

"He's not cut," the other pointed out. "He's just really messed up."

"Before I hunt you down and make you suffer," Jace promised, "I'll gut him like a fat pig on feast day."

The two backed up a couple of steps, preparing to run.

"All I want is information," Jace insisted. "I'm looking for two men who work in tandem. One appears drunk and approaches a stranger to Phalasarna. The other starts a fight and in the shuffle, he cuts the stranger's purse. I want them, not you."

"What about him?" one asked about the thief on the ground.

"He'll be sore for a day," Jace assured him. "But by tomorrow, you three will be back collecting tolls from people taking a shortcut."

"It sounds like the work of Kasmy and Theon," one announced.

"And where do I find Kasmy and Theon?"

"They hang out at the city market."

"I've looked there," Jace said.

"Not in the market, on the other side of the fishing boats," one robber corrected. "From there, they watch for gullible new arrivals."

"Gullible is right," Jace said as he headed for the mouth of the alley.

A flash of cloth vanishing around the corner didn't register as dangerous in Jace's brain.

Chapter 20 – Humbled or Restrained

Jace circled the city until he came to the steps leading down to the harbor. As he descended, the archer scanned the booths and stalls. This late in the day, many were closing, but that didn't bother Jace Kasia. He had no interest in buying anything. Halfway down the steps, he found what he needed.

Kasmy and Theon, as described by the alley rats, lounged next to one of the overturned fishing boats. The pair of cutpurses surveyed the arriving boats, most likely seeking a new victim. To Jace's benefit, they didn't watch the stairs. Even if they had, there was no reason to associate the seventeen-year-old in the short instructor's robe with the youth in traveling clothes they robbed several months ago.

Jace purchased a meat pie with his meager funds. The stipends from the agoge as the bow maker for the little and middle Herds was paltry. But the position fed him, gave him access to knowledge, and a place to sleep. Munching on the pie, Jace roamed through the market.

When the sun hung low over the western wall, the last of the merchants packed up. Before the final stall shut down, Kasmy and Theon headed for the stairway. Keeping a unintrusive distance, Jace fell in behind them. And while Kasmy and Theon had no idea they were being followed, neither did Jace Kasia.

***

"Forget being a Cretan archer," Jace said in exasperation. "I should take up crime."

A few people passing by gave him suspicious looks. He wasn't sure if it was the criminal part or the part where a Latian suggested he could be a Cretan archer. In any case, the very nice apartments across from where he stood attested to the profits available for relieving people of their possessions. Plus, the pedestrians on the street were better dressed than in other parts of the city.

Two city guardsmen stopped in front of Jace.

"We've had complaints about you loitering in the district," one said.

While their spears were held upright in a nonthreatening manner, their shields were forward. Mid-sized, the peltas covered from shoulder to knees. One had a cutout at the top while the second shield had side indentions, creating crescent shaped openings. Although light from the wicker construction and the animal skin covering, the cutouts further reduced the weight of the shields. Even though they were relaxed, the positioning of the peltas protected the guards from an attack.

"As you can see by my robe, I'm an instructor at the agoge," Jace explained. "I just stopped to admire the architecture of the apartment building."

"Well, you're making the residences and shop owners nervous," the other guardsman told him. "Move along."

Jace ran his eyes over the three-story structure once more. Pausing for a moment to focus on the top floor balcony, where he'd seen Kasmy and Theon, he memorized its location below the flat roof. Then Jace bowed to the guardsmen.

"I'll be moving along."

"Good idea," they acknowledged.

Jace was a block away when he laughed out loud. Criminals who could afford to live in an area where they had protection from the city guardsmen struck him as a grand joke being played on honest citizens.

In a few days, the security of the cutpurses would be rattled. Of that, Jace was confident. He could climb from the roof to the balcony and easily enter Kasmy and Theon's apartment. Chuckling, he skipped a few steps as he made his way down towards the exit from the acropolis.

***

With a nod to Poseidon and his enormous throne, Jace strutted by the stone monument. In a day or so, he would recover his coins and be able to buy passage to…

A child's crying drifted to his ears. Looking around, Jace didn't see the little one. Clearly in destress, the wailing appeared to be outside and not from any of the surrounding buildings. Jace rotated his head, listened, and slowed. The source seemed to be ahead on the left and just off the street. He rushed to the mouth of a narrow lane and cupped a hand behind his ear. Before his eyes could adjust to the deep shadows, his ears detected the child.

"Where are your parents?" he inquired. "Hush now. We'll find…"

The walking stick flexed across Jace's face. His eyebrow split sending blood into his left eye, his nose exploded in a gush of more blood, and his jaw swelled almost immediately. But the superbly conditioned archer didn't drop. Rather he stumbled back, trying to collect his wits.

The punch to the side of his head by the big meaty fist is what dropped him. A kick to his ribs rolled Jace onto his back. He moaned and covered up by crossing his arms in front of his face

"Now we aren't here to rob you," a big man assured Jace. "We're like you. Teachers. And while you instruct children in the agoge, we teach adults to respect their betters, and to be humbler in their everyday lives."

"Well said, Master Papinia," Eneas complimented the large man's speech.

"Shut up," the man holding the walking stick ordered. "No names when we're working."

"Sorry, Balasi…I meant, ah..."

Papinia punched the underling into the wall. When the youth rebounded, the gang leader stepped aside and allowed Eneas to slam into the ground.

"Now where was I?" Papinia asked, addressing Jace. "That's right, you will keep your opinions and restrict your ego..."

Jace attempted to sit up to get the pool of blood out of his eye. With a loud smack, the walking stick slashed him across his stomach. Doubled up in pain, Jace attempted to roll over on his side.

"No, my young friend," Balasi warned. "Remain on your back or we will have to stomp you to be sure you stay down."

To emphasize the command, Balasi pushed on Jack's chest with the tip of his walking stick. Gentle but firm, the stick urged Jace to lay flat. Then with a thrust, Balasi poked with the stick. Instead of a gasp of pain from the victim, the wood clinked against something metallic.

"What have we here?" Balasi inquired while reaching down and grabbing the front of Jace's shirt. "A medallion. Does our contract allow for robbery?"

"The Lieutenant didn't say anything about robbery," Papinia answered. "I'd say take the medal, if you want it."

With his only connection to his history in peril, Jace wrapped his hands around the robber's hand to protect the medallion. But a ham sized fist came in low, skirted the ground, and hammered into the side of Jace's head. Dazed and confused, he released his grip. The chain slipped over his head and the weight of the medallion lifted from his chest.

During the one-sided fight, Jace had remained silent while waiting for an opening to counterattack or at least a chance to defend himself. But the loss of the family medal hit him, and he screamed in anger.

"That won't do you any good," Papinia scolded. "Now listen…"

Then from the street, four voices shouted a challenge.

"Run," Balasi snarled. "We'll get him later."

He sprinted with the lumbering Papinia. A short distance back, young Eneas eluded the clutches of a man before bolting after the leaders of the gang.

"What have we here?" another man inquired.

He helped Jace off the ground and walked him into the fading light.

"Master Kasia?" he questioned. "What happened?"

Jace peered at four master archers. Older than the boys at the agoge, these were experienced, and battle-hardened Cretan bowmen.

"She was pretty and called to me from the alley," Jace lied.

"Oh, a honey trap," one archer offered.

"Come on, Master Kasia," the fourth said. "We'll escort you to the armory."

"That's not necessary," Jace said, trying to brush off the arm.

He staggered and another archer took hold of his upper arm.

"Jace Kasia, the other day I held a class on using the shield. The little Herd, before they would gather around, found a safe place to store their bows," the archer informed him. "When I asked why, they said they had just applied new layers of sinew. And they didn't want to scuff the layers."

"That's pride in their weapons and in their work," another archer added. He clamped onto the other arm. "You taught them that, Master Kasia. So, we're going to make sure you get home safe. No matter how cute the next girl calling to you from an alley may be."

Jace hurt, bled, and leaned on the archers for support. But somewhere in the back of his battered brain, a nugget of pride glowed. And somehow, in the wake of the brutal attack, he learned that his work at the agoge was appreciated. It didn't make him a master Cretan archer, but it eased the pain of the beating, a little.

***

The diagonal bruising, swelling, and scabbing made it appear as if Jace had run into a fence post - bent forward, in full stride, face first, and with great enthusiasm. He hurt. But the middle Herd was due in the morning and Jace had hurt before.

"Pain is never an excuse to avoid the duties of the day," Zarek Mikolas preached often. Especially after a particularly rough day of training.

Blinding light aggravated the headache, but Jace squinted and staggered to the range. Through slits in his eyelids, he examined the targets.

"Ah, not today," he whined.

After shuffling to the mid-range targets, he began extracting arrows. Everybody knew to retrieve their arrows after practice. Yet, someone hadn't.

Jace grabbed a shaft, yanked it out, and clasped it in one hand. It wasn't until he wrapped his fingers around a second arrow that he realized the thickness of the spines. Only a graduated archer with a powerful war bow could shoot fat staffs. Even then, most archers had no use for poles in their quivers.

Puzzled by the unique shafts and the rude behavior of a Cretan archer, Jace reached for a third arrow.

Zip-Thwack

A new shaft quivered in the target less than a hands width from Jace's fist. Not daring to move, he waited and counted.

Zip-Thwack

Zip-Thwack

Zip-Thwack

Zip-Thwack

Only when the shafts of five arrows from a cycle protruded from the target did he turn to see the archer. Although he suspected, Jace wanted to verify.

"Good morning, Archer Inigo," Jace greeted him.

"You look a mess, Kasia," Lynceus stated. "I heard your people like to drink and carouse. But I never imagined such damage from 'bad' behavior. Be a good Latian boy and pull my shafts. Then bring them to me."

"Yes, sir, right away," Jace agreed.

Quickly, in case Lynceus decided to shoot another cycle of five, Jace rushed to remove the arrows. Then, stooped in a subservient posture, he shambled to the archer and held out the shafts.

"A few have loose arrowheads," Jace noted. "If you leave them with me, I'll reglue the attachments and do new ties."

Lynceus Inigo leaned forward and studied the wounds on the bowyer's face. At least, that's what he appeared to do. But what he was searching for was a sign of defiance.

"Nothing to say?" Lynceus questioned.

"No archer. Except your shooting this morning was brilliant."

"I should have killed you when you were downrange."

Hanging his head as if he didn't have the right to look the archer in the eyes, Jace remarked, "Your display of mercy is much appreciated."

Frustrated at not getting a reaction from the bow maker, archer Inigo about faced and marched from the range. Replacing the bully, a gaggle of short legs and out of time footsteps came from around a building.

"And who are you?" Jace inquired, still looking at the arrows in his hands.

"We are little Herd, Master Kasia," they replied.

"The last time I checked, there were no bows to be filed, glue to apply, or sinew to comb at the range," Jace stated. He looked up and the boys saw the damage to his face. "But I have it on good authority, all of those supplies, and more are in the shop. So, go."

They hesitated while soaking in the rawness of the wounds. Several jerked while envisioning the pain, and others touched their eyebrow, nose and jawline, tracing Jace's injuries.

"We have bows that require your attention," he instructed. "Get inside."

They bunched up and shuffled in chaos before running for the workshop. Jace followed, clutching the handful of Lynceus Inigo's arrows.

***

The next day, Lieutenant Acis Gergely marched into the workshop. It was between classes and Jace was alone. The officer crossed to where the bow maker was bent over a project.

"What's going on between you and Lynceus Inigo?" he demanded.

Jace remained focused on fitting an arrowhead onto the nub of a shaft.

"Absolutely nothing, sir," he replied. "Did he complain about me? If he did, please explain and I'll try harder to avoid the offensive action."

"What is wrong with you?" Acis asked. "At the mention of archer Inigo, you usually have a lot to say."

Jace lifted his head from the project and peered at the Lieutenant.

"Perhaps, I've learned to humble myself before my betters," he remarked.

Acis Gergely lifted a hand as if to touch or to treat the black and blue bruises that surrounded the scabs and open wounds.

"Lynceus is going around bragging that he beat you," Gergely stated. "Did he do that to you."

"With respect, Lieutenant, archer Inigo couldn't on his best day."

"Then who did that to your face?"

"A confederation that's very good at delivering someone else's message," Jace said.

"Whose message?"

"I haven't the slightest idea, Lieutenant. No clue at all."

Acis Gergely spun to the door and fast walked to the frame.

"You really don't know who ordered you roughed up?" he inquired.

"No, Lieutenant," Jace assured him.

Gergely left and Jace went back to trying to affix an arrowhead to a fat shaft. But as he learned, since yesterday's abuse, focusing on anything brought on a disabling headache.

***

That night, when the compound had settled for the evening, Jace staggered around the inside of the walls. When the headache blinded him, he used both hands to feel his way around. Other times, he bumped the stone with his shoulder, so he kept in contact with the wall. He used every trick and sense to keep moving.

At the gates, he stopped and asked the sentries vague questions about the gangs of Phalasarna. It became a nightly ritual. By the end of the week, he was running and pondering a quandary.

Jace Kasia knew the names Papinia and Balasi, the gang's territory, and their gathering location. There was a debt of honor due from them. And he knew where Kasmy and Theon lived. They represented an economic debt due him. Collecting what was owed wasn't in question. His problem was the two subjects of interest were on opposite ends of the city.

Once bodies started falling from the first collection, the city guard would double or triple their patrols. With that much scrutiny, it would be hard for an armed archer to cross the city without being challenged. Hence, Jace continued to run and think for another week. By then, he knew the sequence of events and how to defeat the distance.

Chapter 21 – Hounded and Hunted

With a grunt, Jace swung from one arm while reaching overhead for the next fingertip hold. As part of his training, he climbed rocky cliffs in the mountains. It strengthened his hands, arms, and shoulders for archery. A secondary benefit of the ascents, he became an expert climber. With a final surge, Jace kicked a leg up to the roof of the apartment building. Following closely behind was the other leg. Then a roll onto his right hip helped him gain the flat surface.

The moonless night supplied cover for the archer. No one had seen him when he dropped over the wall of the acropolis or slipped through the back alleys to reach the building. From the ground, he climbed in the dark unseen.

Getting in wasn't his main worry nor was escaping from the apartment. His fear concerned keeping this part of the operation undetected until he finished the night's work.

Once positioned over the balcony, he rested his bow case and quiver on the roof. Next, he strapped the small shield to his left arm, pulled the hood of his jerkin over his head, and drew the war hatchet. After taking a deep breath, he stepped off the edge.

***

Kasmy, or maybe it was Theon, jerked away from the hooded man who appeared out of nowhere.

"What do you want?" he blathered.

"What every cutpurse wants," Jace answered, "coins."

"You can't come into a man's home and..."

A thin layer of bronze covered the small archer's shield. Although the metallic sheet wouldn't stop the strike of a sword, the metal would hold the strips of oak together under the stress. Extending from Jace's knuckles to just above his elbow, it acted more as armor than a shield. And while the size limited its use against javelins, lead pellets from slingers, and arrows, the archer's shield excelled during hand-to-hand combat. Small enough not to interfere with the archer's shooting, the circle could block a blade, or...

The man fell away from the tap on his hands. Following the smash, Jace rushed forward and bashed him again with the shield. A third hit with his armored forearm left the man in a puddle of pain and confusion.

"You can frighten a stranger on the street with a knife and harsh words," Jace offered while lashing the thief's hands together, "but you have no fight in you after a few slaps."

A rush of sandaled feet on tiles came from inside the apartment.

"Theon isn't much of a fighter," the other cutpurse told Jace when he reached the doorway. He held a curved sica sword with the blade dipping slightly below waist level.

"That would make you who, Kasmy?" Jace questioned.

"I am, and you are an intruder in my home."

"That's where you're wrong," Jace told him. "I'm a debt collector. And this is a courtesy call."

"Most businessmen come through the front door."

Kasmy shifted onto the balcony and shuffled until he stood between Jace and Theon. While the short sword posed a danger, Jace no longer worried about the outcome of a fight. As an inanimate object, the blade could only go where it was carried and strike where the swordsman willed it. By moving to protect his partner, Kasmy revealed his weakness and the limits of his fighting space.

"I never said I was good at the job," Jace explained. "I'll just take a purse of bronze and silver and be on my way."

"You what? You drop onto my balcony, and I'm supposed to reward you with my gold?"

"Have you ever seen a war hatchet thrown?" Jace asked. He snapped his wrist and the handle rotated as if flying forward. Kasmy dipped at the knees, trying to protect his partner. Jace caught the handle and apprised Kasmy. "You can't fight me and guard Theon. Pick your battle strategy. Or pay me."

"We don't have much gold," Kasmy begged. "We're just a couple of fish traders and, lately, the catch has been poor."

"Let's go with that lie," Jace suggested. "Put the sword on the ground and turn around."

"And let you stab me in the back?"

"Had I wanted bloodshed, my second move on Theon would have been with my right hand," Jace explained. He stepped forward, parried the sica with the shield, and tapped Kasmy's forehead with the side of the hatchet. "After splitting his skull, I'd have kicked his brain across the balcony. Turn around."

Kasmy spun, placed his hands behind his back, and crossed them at the wrists.

"There's a box inside," the thief told Jace as his hands were tied together. "In it are coins. Take them all."

Jace went into the apartment, found the coin chest, and took out an amount equivalent to what had been taken from him. Beyond the coins, he grabbed several pieces of cloth.

"I'm going to leave you tied and gagged," Jace told Kasmy and Theon. "The sica is here. I'm sure with a little effort, you can cut the ties and free yourselves. However, be forewarned, if the city guard begins searching for me, I'll come back tomorrow night. And you don't want that. Understand?"

Kasmy and Theon nodded their acknowledgment.

Jace put a foot on the top rail of the terrace, hopped up, and kicked off. Soaring upward, he grabbed the edge of the roof. Moments later, the archer reached the other side of the flat surface and began the climb down.

On the balcony, Theon blindly held the short sword as Kasmy sawed his bindings on the blade. When free, they pulled the cloth from over their mouths.

"We could call the city guardsmen," Theon ventured.

"Did you see his face?" Kasmy inquired.

"No," Theon replied.

"Neither did I," Kasmy said. "But I saw how he handled the shield and the hatchet. We don't want trouble with a Cretan archer."

Theon reached for a pitcher and inquired, "Wine?"

By the time the cutpurses had taken their first sip, Jace was dashing through backstreets, heading for the harbor.

***

The easiest place to slip through undetected was a crowded venue. Calmly so as not to call attention to himself, Jace strolled by the men dozing at the piers and on the merchant ships. After circling the protected harbor, the archer crossed the empty marketplace. On the beach with the fishing boats, a few campfires glowed in the dark. Jace used them as beacons to avoid the sleeping fishermen.

Zarek Mikolas taught that night wasn't the absence of light. Most nights, the stars supplied plenty. The difference in the dark had to do with the lack of tints. Stripping away the archer's dependence on colors to separate shapes, he drilled Jace by having him practice archery at twilight. Shooting for the center of a shape, always worked.

Away from the sleeping fishermen and their fires, Jace felt around until he discovered the dark outline of a small fishing boat.

With the oars in his hands, he ducked down, and he came up inside the hull. Then, in small steps, he moved the boat to the water. When the sea reached the upside-down gunwales, Jace tipped it off his head and righted the craft.

Once the pair of oars were set in the oarlocks, he slid over the side, and made an initial stroke. No one sounded an alarm and Jace continued to row.

This was the first phase in defeating the distance factor. Even if Kasmy and Theon called the guardsmen, they would search the acropolis and the gates for the assailant, not the ocean.

***

Five hundred strokes later, and without seeing the beach, Jace Kasia angled for shore. If his count proved wrong, he would end up on the rocks. If right, the small boat would ground onto sand and gravel, a half mile from the harbor's entrance. When the keel grated on the beach, Jace leaped into the water and hauled the boat to shore.

Before flipping it over, he opened the quiver, pulled out a couple of thick spined arrows, and shoved them under the seat. Once done, he flipped the boat over and glanced around to be sure he was unobserved. Then he faced in the direction of his next objective and sprinted away.

Jace had over a mile to go before reentering the city, far to the south of the acropolis and the agoge.

***

One advantage of hunting denizens of the night, they were out prowling while the shadows were black and honest citizens slept. Although prowling might be giving something extra to the big man sitting outside the single-story building.

Papinia hardly moved from his throne sized chair. Next to him, Balasi, the man with the walking stick, sat at a workshop table. The sum of their activity consisted of greeting underlings who brought the crime bosses coins, packages, and shiny items.

Unlike Kasmy and Theon, Jace didn't want coins from the thugs. All he wanted as payment, and why he came, was their pain and his medallion. Creeping down a lane one street over from the gangsters, he slipped across a road, and moved through the shadows to the rear of the single-story building. It took less climbing to scale the wall then the apartment building. Once on the roof, he strolled to the front of the building.

Lost in the dark, but backlit for anyone who happened to look up, the archer stood against the stars. Below him, the muggers for hire went about their business, unaware that vengeance lurked just over their heads.

If Papinia and Balasi had listened carefully, they might have heard a soft whisper drifting on the night breeze.

"Still your breath so your hands are steady. Calm your heart so your eyes are clear. Focus your mind on the task."

Zip-Thwack. The first fat arrow entered Papinia's left thigh, pinning the big man to his chair. *Zip-Thwack.* A second shaft split the bones in Balasi's right hand. The arrowhead shredded the small bones and anchored the criminal to the tabletop.

"Attack," Papinia bellowed. "We're under attack. Find him."

"Gods, my hand," Balasi screamed in pain.

Intending to help his bosses, one of the gang's enforcers ran towards the chair and table.

Zip-Thwack. The arrow shattered his right hip. Crying for his mother, he crawled away to avoid another arrow.

Zip-Thwack. An underling far down the street screamed in pain.

Everyone around the one-story building sprinted away. In a heartbeat, the street cleared of gang members and customers for the illicit goods.

Zip-Thwack. Balasi shrieked again. A shaft through his shoulder held him against the tabletop, and he began whimpering into the wood.

Zip-Thwack. Papinia felt the shaft glide along the side of his head and down his face before it entered the top of his chest.

"You missed," he roared into the night. "I'm still here."

Jace rested a hand on the roof and jumped. Using his arm to break the fall, he landed softly. In three strides, he reached Balasi.

A quick touch to the back of Balasi's neck showed the gangster didn't wear the silver chain or the medallion. Knowing he didn't have much time, Jace pulled the hatchet and slashed the criminal's coin purse. Gold, silver, and copper coins clinked as they fell to the ground. Then came a solid thud as the bronze medallion and silver chain dropped onto the pile.

***

The screaming and shouting of panic and pain drew a patrol of city guardsmen. When they entered the street, they saw black pools of blood, bodies, and arrow shafts.

"Papinia, you are a mess," the Sergeant of the Guard remarked. "You should know better than to offend an archer."

Between groans, Papinia bragged, "He wasn't that good an archer. He missed with the last arrow. Come here and pull it out."

"I'm not sure about your opinion. Your ear is gone," the Sergeant informed him, "and there's a deep cut down the side of your face. Brace yourself while I pull out the arrow."

The big gang leader closed his eyes against the pain. But the expected agony of having an arrowhead drawn from a wound didn't come. Instead, he heard a desperate oath from the Sergeant.

"Oh, Gods," the guard NCO said. "The shaft came free. But the arrowhead is lodged behind your ribs, near your heart."

***

Jace woke late. Feeling good, and if not wealthy, he at least was a man of means. Sometime in the next few days, after the troubles from last night settled, he'd inform Lieutenant Gergely of his resignation.

While preparing for the day's classes, a commotion arose from the porch.

"Master Kasia, your presence is requested outside," Lieutenant Hylas Inigo directed.

Jace went to the porch and found a small crowd waiting there.

"Lieutenant Inigo, good morning," he greeted the officer. "What can I do for you?"

With the archery officer stood his younger brother Lynceus, a Captain of the City Guard, and three guardsmen. One held a basket. The notches and fletching of several fat arrows protruded over the edge of the wicker container.

"You can explain these to the Captain," Hylas answered. He snatched a couple of arrows from the basket and waved them around as if no one could see the thick shafts. "They were used in a crime last night."

"Robbery with a single bow is rare," Jace offered. "For that many to be used, I suspect you have a team of archery bandits on the loose."

"Are you being smart with me?" Hylas demanded.

"No, sir," Jace replied. "You brought arrows to me and told me they were used in a crime. I thought you wanted my opinion."

"What I want, Kasia, is your confession," the Lieutenant snapped.

"To what, sir?"

"To the assault of…"

The Guard Captain pushed Hylas aside.

"My name is Cepheus," the Captain introduced himself. "Early this morning, men were assaulted on the street of my city by an archer. He used these arrows."

"Yes sir. I assumed they were evidence from the, what did the Lieutenant call it? Ah, the crime."

Hylas elbowed the Captain aside and put his face a hand's distance from Jace's still swollen nose.

"You know what you did," he shouted. "These arrows prove it."

While keeping his head in the same spot, Jace reached down and took the arrows from the Lieutenant's hand. Then he stepped back and examined the notches, fletching, shafts, and the connections on the ones where arrowheads were attached.

"There's the problem," Jace stated as if giving a lecture to a Herd of boys. "A thick shaft puts pressure on the arrowhead when it hits the target. You can see where the cracks in the fork have been reglued and new twine wrapped around the old. Most archers don't care for shafts this thick."

"Aha, there, you've just proven your guilt," Hylas Inigo exclaimed while stepping back and throwing his arms in the air. "These are your arrows, admit it."

"Why would I have thick shafts?" Jace protested. "I don't shoot with them."

"Because the other day after target practice, you took them from me," Lynceus Inigo sneered, "allegedly to work on securing the arrowheads. But your error was to use them for your crime."

"I think we've heard enough," the archery officer ordered. "Captain Cepheus, arrest him."

Jace blinked in confusion. Not because he wasn't guilty, for the arrow attack and the unreported robbery, he was absolutely responsible. And having the act traced to him fit into the strategy. However, he hadn't planned on Lieutenant Inigo overseeing the investigation and the hurried decision to arrest him.

"If I could only explain," Jace pleaded.

"Save it for the magistrate," Captain Cepheus advised while stepping forward.

"You can't go around putting arrows in citizens," Hylas scolded. "Both Papinia and Balasi are in bad shape. And Papinia is in constant pain."

Cepheus stopped and slowly turned to face the Lieutenant of archers.

"How did you know the names of the victims and what shape they're in?" the Guard officer questioned.

"Well, you told me."

"No. I only mentioned that I was looking for archers who used these shafts," the Captain corrected.

"Well, I might know them," Hylas admitted. "But that proves nothing."

"For an officer of Cretan archers, I expect honor and honesty," Cepheus reprimanded the Lieutenant. "With that in mind, let me ask you, what were your dealings with the Papinia's gang?"

"I was on duty last night," Hylas professed while dodging the question. "I couldn't have done the shooting."

Cepheus took several arrows from the basket. He held them up and studied the length.

"Your brother uses thick shafts. He admitted it," the Guard officer remarked. "You could have sent him to settle a debt with Papinia and Balasi."

"No, no," Hylas insisted, "Jace Kasia had the arrows."

"I still have the arrows," Jace informed the group. Then he added, "You're a sorry excuse for a Cretan archer, and a miserable officer, Hylas."

"What did you say to me?" Hylas Inigo thundered.

"I'm not one of your Herd or your Troop, so save your outrage," Jace whispered. "But understand this, someday I will repay you in kind."

"Repay what?" Acis Gergely asked. He marched from the corner of the armory and instructed. "The Captain asked that I take over the investigation. There's a representative from Syracuse in his office and he wants Lieutenant Inigo to sit in on the negotiations."

"If I may be allowed," Jace said changing his tone and the subject, "I have archer Inigo's arrows in the shop. They are repaired and ready to be added to the other thick shafts in his quiver."

He handed the arrows from the attack to Lieutenant Gergely and walked into the shop.

"Captain Cepheus, fill me in," Gergely requested. "What did I miss?"

Cepheus took the arrows and deposited them in the basket.

"Quite a lot," the Guard officer replied. "But it seems, so did I. We're taking this inquiry back to the beginning. I have questions for both archer Inigo and Lieutenant Inigo about his dealings with a known street gang."

***

The late afternoon sunlight streamed into the workshop. Jace passed between the rays as he moved around scrubbing spots where Herd members had missed stains of hide glue and strings of wet sinew. He didn't mind cleaning up. Young boys were terrible at details.

"Jace. Are you in there?" Acis Gergely questioned as he came through the doorway.

"Back here, Lieutenant."

Acis squinted through the particles of dust floating in the beams of light.

Inhaling, he offered, "The aroma in this shop brings back memories of my time in the Herds. Things were simpler then. I do miss the place."

"Are they that complicated now, sir," Jace inquired.

"I imagine you'll miss this building," Acis stated. "But all things must change. Master Kasia, pack your bags."

After the morning, Jace expected to be dismissed. But it disappointed him. He really wanted the opportunity to quit on his own terms.

"It was my outburst at Lieutenant Inigo, wasn't it?" he asked.

"Can we not talk about the Lieutenant?" Acis requested. "After the Guard Captain talked to our Captain, both Inigos were pulled from the contract with the King of Syracuse."

"Sir, what contract?" Jace asked.

"King Hiero needs five hundred Cretan archers to satisfy a military agreement with Rome," Acis Gergely told him. "I'm going as the commander of the left files. And you're coming as my bowyer. At least for the time being."

"Where are we going, Lieutenant?" Jace inquired.

"The Roman Republic. The Legions are having a problem on their border and require professional help," Acis answered. He turned and looked around the shop and said again. "I do miss this place. I imagine you will as well. Be packed by daybreak. You'll move to the staging area near the harbor. I need every war bow carried by a recruit to be checked. No one comes with us who isn't prepared for battle."

"You can count on me, sir," Jace assured him. Then he added while hiding a grin. "It's a shame about Lieutenant Inigo."

"The command of the advanced two hundred archers should have been his slot," Acis mentioned. "But somehow and for an unknown reason, he associated with gangsters. Let that be a lesson for you Kasia. People will judge you by the company you keep."

"Sir, I associate with the little and middle Herds," Jace offered. "What does that say about me?"

Lieutenant Gergely didn't answer directly. Although he was laughing when he left the bow shop.

Act 8

Chapter 22 – A King's Hire

Consul Gaius Flaminius strolled down the steps to applause and cheers. The popular politician grasped hands with staff officers along his route. Others, out of arm's reach, he greeted with waves and a select few were acknowledged by pointing a finger at the Tribunes. When he reached the center of the courtyard, Gaius raised his arms and signaled for silence.

"Gentlemen, look around you. What you see are sixty-eight Legion staff officers. The pride of our Republic. And without reservation, I say, I am proud to be your leader." Cheers burst from the attendees and Gaius nodded, accepting the adoration. Rotating so he faced the tables in each quadrant of the courtyard, Consul/General Flaminius continued. "We have gathered eight Legions and you command four of them. The other four are from our neighbors. And while we value our allies, it is you who will stop the rogue Punic general. If he's foolish enough to cross the Apennines."

A roar of approval erupted at the General's vote of confidence in his corps of staff officers. When it faded, the Consul/General told the gathering.

"To the east our brothers under the command of my co-Consul, Servilius Geminus, have Hannibal Barca's ragtag army pinned to the center and the west. Fortunately for us, that puts Geminus' Legions out of position to block the Punics. So, if this Hannibal character dares pass through the Apennine mountains, like he did the Alps, we will meet him. And mark my words Tribunes, at that moment, Barca and the murderous Gauls with him will meet their demise on the gladii of your Centuries."

Shouts of 'Rah' rang through the crowd. Gaius waited for the approval to die down.

"I want to remind you that tomorrow is the first day our Legions will train together. Go easy on the vino, gentlemen," he warned. Laughter ripped through the staff officers. Gaius chuckled along with them for a moment. "Now, before you are served the feast and I go and give a speech to our Centurions at the combat officer's feast, are there any comments."

Ever the politician, Gaius' question was a courtesy. He didn't expect a response. However, at a table near the edge of the courtyard, a young Tribune shook off the hand of his table mate.

"Cornelius don't do it," Appius Pulcher begged. "It's neither the time nor the place."

"Then when is the proper time and place to deliver unwelcome news?" Cornelius Scipio asked. "I've heeded your advice since you were the Centurion of my father's First Century. But in this case, the information must be said aloud."

"Go ahead, you've always been hardheaded," Pulcher complained. He picked up his glass of wine and saluted the stubborn staff officer.

Gaius, watching the exchange, assumed the raised glass ended the private dispute.

"You're Publius Scipio's son," Gaius guessed. "How fares your father?"

"He's still recovering from his battle wounds, sir," Cornelius answered. "Thank you for asking."

"A friend, a worthy political opponent, but a so-so General," Gaius declared, making a joke. Seeing Cornelius bristle at the remark about his father, Flaminius informed him. "Boy, I've dueled on the floor of the Senate against the sharp wit of your father many times. We've tangled enough that I can jest and not think less of him."

"Yes, sir," Cornelius allowed. "About General Hannibal Barca. I fear Consul that you are taking him too lightly. He has twice..."

Consul/General Flaminius snapped his fingers. At the sound, Cornelius ended his prepared remarks.

"Young man, you hold your position out of homage to your father," Gaius scolded. "Don't think you're speaking to an inexperienced man. I've dodged daggers and walked over deep ravines to get land grants for our Legion veterans from the first war with the Punics. And don't you think for a moment that it was a stroll in the park to wrestle the land away from landowners to build Circus Flaminius. Those were battles that went on for months."

"Yes, sir," Cornelius choked out. Wishing he hadn't said anything about Barca, he pleaded. "I would like to withdraw my statement."

"Actually, I find the topic of his Punic magic interesting, but all together impractical. Look around you at our professional staff officers," Gaius suggested. "They a strong, committed, and proud to be Roman citizens. think any of them would be an advocate for a Cartha

"Consul, I wasn't attempting to further his cause or excuse him in anyway," Cornelius protested.

"You sounded like you were," Gaius barked. "Yesterday I received mercenaries hired by King Hiero of Syracuse. Because you are a foreigner enthusiast, I'm assigning them to your Maniple. And I'm withdrawing your Velites. Let the Cretan archers cover your left flank. I'll send our great, Legion light infantrymen to a Tribune who values them."

Gaius Flaminius saluted the men in the courtyard and made his way up the steps. Robust cheering followed him from the venue.

As the General marched away, Cornelius Scipio dropped to his seat.

"What have I done?" he whined. "And what are Cretan archers?"

"I've heard they're good bowmen but weak skirmishers," another Tribune offered. "It has something to do with the teeny, tiny shields they wear like jewelry on their left forearms."

All but two of the staff officers at the table laughed at the description. Cornelius Scipio, Tribune for the Second Maniple left side Flaminius Legion North, hung his head. And Appius Pulcher, the Tribune for the left side Third Maniple of the same Legion, frowned into his glass of wine. Neither joined in the laugher because the substitution of skirmishers weakened both of their left flanks.

"Small shields? What have I done?" Cornelius repeated. "Appius, remind me to make a sacrifice in the morning."

"Sure. To what God?" the experienced officer inquired.

"Muta," Cornelius answered. "I need to learn to embrace the Goddess of Silence and keep my mouth shut."

"I think I'll be joining you for the offering," Appius proposed.

***

In the morning, after the sacrifice of a sacred chicken to the Goddess Muta, Cornelius Scipio mounted his horse and rode out of the corral. At the end of the lane, a mob of Legionaries blocked the street.

"It was here last night when I was walking my post," an infantryman explained to his Optio.

"Well, it's gone now, Legionary," the NCO informed him. "Were you sleeping on duty?"

"No Sergeant, I was awake the entire time."

Cornelius reined in his mount and inquired, "What seems to be the problem, Optio?"

Seeing the Tribune, the NCO motioned for his Century to open a lane before replying.

"Sir, we had three pigs last night," the Sergeant told him. "This morning we have two. I was trying to find out what happened to the third swine."

"Did someone sell it?" Cornelius asked.

"That would entail removing it from the pen, sir," the NCO pointed out. "But removing one, should have disturbed the other two. Yet no one heard anything."

"Good luck with your investigation," Cornelius said while easing the horse through the crowd.

On another straight road of the organized Legion stockade, he noticed a large gathering of two opposing Centuries. A combat officer stood between them.

"Centurion, what's the problem?" Cornelius questioned.

"When my Thirty-First Century went to bed, they had a stack of firewood as high as my chest," the officer related. "This morning, the pile is down to below the level of my waist. Someone stole our firewood."

"And you think it's the other Century?"

"That's what I'm trying to figure out, Tribune."

"Pair up the Sergeants and Corporals from each Century and have them search both the immediate and the surrounding areas," Cornelius directed.

Having offered a solution, he rode to an intersecting street, and headed for the gate. Before he reached the exit to the marching camp, the staff officer spied a handful of Optios crowded around the entrance to a tent. He would have ignored the group except for the raised voices.

"No, my infantrymen did not," one Sergeant insisted.

"Absolutely not," another NCO declared.

"Well, someone did," a supply Optio remarked. "If not your Century, then who?"

After the first two instances of theft, Cornelius guided his horse to the tent.

"What's the trouble here?" he asked.

"Missing baskets of turnips and carrots, sir," the supply NCO answered. "They were stored inside the tent waiting for distribution this morning. But now I have to delay delivery until I refigure the allotment to the Centuries."

"If you're not part of the supply team, get back to your areas," Cornelius ordered. "You'll be notified when the supplies are available."

The Optios separated leaving the supply NCO scratching his head and examining the tent for signs of the break in. Having helped, Cornelius turned his horse and made his way to the gate.

***

From the neatly laid out streets and purposefully designated zones of the Legion camp, Tribune Cornelius Scipio rode into a disorganized cluster of camping pods. Some tents were for ten men, others for double occupancy, while the rest fell somewhere between. And unlike the square design of the Legion camp, the Cretan archers' bivouac consisted of campsites placed in rings creating a large circular footprint. And around each campfire were wood shaving, pieces of sharp steel, and pots with gooey substances on the lips. The area appeared to be a disgusting mess. After many turns to follow a zig-zag road, he reached the command area.

Spying a Latin youth sitting on a short wagon and shaving a stick, the Tribune eased his horse alongside of the mule drawn cart.

"You, servant boy, I'm Tribune Scipio. Where can I find the commander of the archers?"

Jace Kasia lifted his eyes briefly then returned to shaping the arrow shaft. But he didn't respond to the Legion officer.

"Stop playing with that stick. When I speak, I demand respect and your attention," Cornelius scolded. Although they were the same age, the Roman officer felt older and superior to the youth in the woolen tunic.

"Let me see," Jace said. "Lieutenant Gergely should be over with the Sixth Stichos. Some of their bows got wet on the passage."

"Now that wasn't too hard, was it?" Cornelius tugged on the reins, intending to leave. "Where is the Sixth whatever you called them?"

"File, Stichos is a file of archers," Jace told him. Then he peered around. "You know, the Lieutenant may be with…no not there either."

"Maybe I should ask someone else," Cornelius suggested. "You don't seem to know much."

"I know I'm not lost," Jace reminded the Legion officer. "I think you'll find Lieutenant Gergely at the range."

Cornelius Scipio fumed at the disrespect in the teen's language. If he wasn't in a hurry to speak to the Lieutenant, coordinate the training schedule, and get away from the Cretan archers, he would ride to the Legion camp and bring back several Legionaries to arrest the Latin boy. Or he could draw his spatha and split the teen's head open. But that also would extend the time he spent in the Cretan pigsty.

"If I can get a direct answer, where is the range? I need to get back to my half Maniple."

"What's a Maniple?" Jace inquired.

"If you must know, it's a line," Cornelius said. "Now where is the range?"

"You mean a file or a row?"

"It's a line that faces the enemy. Range?"

"Oh, the range is off to your right over those low hills," Jace told him. "Just follow the smoke."

"Is there a fire?" Cornelius asked.

"Nope. The archers are cooking a deer and a pig, I believe, for tonight."

"What, no turnups and carrots?" Cornelius grumbled as he brought his horse around.

"They have plenty of those," Jace commented.

After Tribune Scipio trotted off, an NCO of archers came from a tent and stopped by the cart.

"You knew perfectly well where the Lieutenant was," the Lochias mentioned.

"I did, Sergeant Phylo, but he was too prissy on his big horse with the shiny armor and great plume on his helmet. And him, being no older than I am," Jace stated. "I figured he could dance for a while before dashing off to impose his presence on Lieutenant Gergely."

"He may be our employer. And it's never good to sour our benefactor with words," the Lochias suggested. Then Phylo admitted. "I'm afraid the deeds of our archers will do that soon enough."

"Speaking of deeds or rather misdeeds, I've finished repairs on the last war bow."

"We appreciate that," Phylo told him. "In a fight, those four are good men. Without your help, the Lieutenant wouldn't have brought them with us."

"Let's be sure they grease up their bow cases and close the tops when the bows are stored. Especially when it rains."

"You, Master Kasia, can be assured of it."

***

Over the hill, Cornelius located Acis Gergely. After a short intense conversation, the Lieutenant folded.

"I've brought two hundred archers and two Lochoi," Acis Gergely told the Tribune. "My Sergeants are battletested as are most of the bowmen. But, if all you need is for us to screen your left flank, no problem, we'll do it."

"Light infantry is what I need," Cornelius confirmed. "The Legion will march out and do a Second Maniple maneuver at noon. Be in the field north of here."

"Yes, sir," Gergely agreed.

Cornelius Scipio trotted away and Acis hand signaled for the Cretan archers to gather around him.

***

When the sun reached the top of the sky, nine hundred and sixty heavy infantrymen marched from the stockade. Along with the Legionaries came five Junior Tribunes, Cornelius and the right-side Tribune, and the Legion's Senior Tribune and Senior Centurion. Also marching from the camp were one hundred light infantrymen. They would practice guarding the Maniple's right flank.

Absent was the inexperienced First Maniple and the veterans of the Third Maniple. The Battle Commander and

Consul/General Gaius Flaminius weren't scheduled to attend the day's exercise.

The double line of infantrymen topped the hill. As the Legionaries came over the rise, two hundred Cretan archers stood up, brushed the dirt off their rears, and began meandering alongside the columns.

Cornelius rode up and warned, "You'll need to spread your archers out. When the Legionaries move into the maniple, they'll trample on your men."

Acis Gergely nodded, swung both arms to the left. In response, the two hundred archers jogged away from the column. When they reached a good distance, he waved again. The bowmen returned to strolling as they descended to the flatland.

The instant reaction to the Cretan Lieutenant's command surprised Cornelius Scipio. From slouching and rolling like a grazing herd to rapid deployment gave him a little confidence. But for him, the small shields on the left arm would only be good for a knife fight and not a spear and sword battle. Plus, none had a spear, only a short sword or a hatchet. But each carried a long leather case with quivers strapped to their backs.

They're good bowmen but weak skirmishers. Something to do with the teeny, tiny shields they wear like jewelry on their left forearms.

When the Junior Tribune galloped from the Senior Tribune's position, Cornelius rode close to the column.

"Tribune Scipio, deploy your Maniple," the junior staff officer declared.

"Inform the Senior Tribune that we are moving into formation," Cornelius responded. Then he shouted to his six combat officers. "Centurions, form the Maniple."

His command echoed up and down the columns. Fourteenth Century jogged from the trail and at the count of one hundred paces, the eighty men stacked up in three lines. Beside them the Fifteenth Century fell in tight, then the Sixteenth, and the others all the way back to the trail where the Nineteenth Century linked up with the Twentieth Century of the right-side of the Second Maniple. Tribune Scipio rode to Centuries where the movement lacked snap. Or where his infantrymen, NCOs, and officers lingered waiting for the slowest to catch up. Once satisfied with their urgency, he glanced at the Cretan archers.

Instead of chaos, the two hundred archers had already formed twelve files, sixteen lines across. The formation created a press of bodies that protected the end of his heavy infantry formation. While Cornelius Scipio would have liked to see bigger shields and spears, he'd take the quick reaction of the archers. He had to, thanks to his big mouth, he didn't have a choice.

***

The diagonal marches, surges forward, and backward moved the Centuries around as if they were blocks on a map. In essence, they were as the Legions top staff and top combat officers thought up situations and responses to an imaginary enemy.

When the sun evenly divided the sky between noon and dusk, the Maniple stood down. Mules arrived from the camp with water and weak wine.

"Lieutenant Gergely, if your people need water, they can help themselves to…" Cornelius caught a motion on the top of the slope. Seeing the Latin and the mule cart come into view, he changed his offer. "I see you have your own provisions. Give your men a rest and wet them down."

"That isn't water, Tribune Scipio," Gergely informed him. "That cart has our resupply of arrows. And Jace is late."

"But you haven't fired any arrows," Cornelius mentioned.

"In a battle, we would have," the Lieutenant remarked.

Hoofs pounding on the soil drew their attention to a rider. Despite having the reins hauled way back, the small Junior Tribune's mount overshot Scipio and Gergely. They watched in amusement while the boy turned the horse and trotted back to the officers.

"Tribune Scipio, get your half Maniple up and move them over the hill to the west."

"I thought the drill was limited to this flatland and confined to our Maniple," Scipio described. Being mid-afternoon, he didn't relish putting his infantrymen through a night march to get back to their camp. "Are there any details to rationalize the change of training venue?"

Cornelius didn't expect a junior staff officer to have an opinion, least of all an answer to his question. Unfortunately, the Junior Tribune did.

"Sir, the Punic army is passing to our west," he stated, his lips quivering from fear. "We're to engage their flanks. And if possible, disrupt their line of march until the Legions form."

"Do the scouts have an estimate of how many men oppose up?" Gergely inquired.

"More than twenty thousand," the young staff officer said. Then he added. "Hopefully, most of the barbarians have already gone by us."

While Lieutenant Cornelius rode to talk to his Centurions, Acis Gergely spun his finger in the air to gather his Sergeants and to wave Jace down from the slope.

"What's doing, sir?" Lochias Phylo inquired.

"I have a question for you," Acis Gergely asked instead of answering. "Why would a superior army bypass a relatively weak force. And, leave that enemy force in the rear to disrupt their supply lines?"

"Lieutenant, I don't know," the other Lochias said. "Why would they?"

"Unfortunately, Sergeant," Gergely admitted, "I have no idea."

Chapter 23 – Perhaps A Wounded Wolf

The concept of simply running field drills for a day ended when two hundred and fifty Legion cavalrymen galloped from the camps outside Arezzo. And as they marched over the hills, the Centuries of the Second Maniple glanced longingly back towards their stockade. Their tents, stock of javelins, cloaks, extra rations, cooking utensils, and other necessities were there, safe, but out of reach.

On the far side of the hills, the trail of dust from horses rushing southward confirmed that the infantrymen were going to war sooner than expected. Gossip held that against the odds, Punic General Barca had found an unguarded pass and brought his army south. For once, the rumor mill had it right.

Acis Gergely dropped to the rear of his archers.

"Jace, why the delay?" he inquired.

The young bow maker reached into the bed of the cart and tossed back a leather cover.

"When the word came through the rear about the Carthaginian army being sighted, I loaded up the pig and deer," Jace said while pointing to the meat. "If we're heading out, at least we'll have a good meal tonight."

Acis inhaled the aromas of pork and venison before inquiring, "What do you think of this situation?"

"I think, Lieutenant, a wolf who allows you to track him is either wounded and too weak to evade you," Jace replied. He pulled the cover back over the meat and finished, "or the animal is leading you to his pack."

"That's what I'm afraid of," Gergely stated. "It's late in the day and we're moving towards the unknown."

From the columns of Legionaries, a stirring Rah erupted. Then the infantrymen, loaded down with armor, metal helmets, spears, gladii, and big shields broke their march step and began to jog.

"I wonder if, as you said, we're rushing towards a pack of wolves?" Acis Gergely questioned. Then he yelled. "Sergeants, get us moving."

In several heartbeats, the Cretan archers were keeping pace with the Legionaries. Both following the trail of the Legion horsemen who had quickly outpaced the infantry.

***

When the sun floated over the western horizon, a squadron of cavalrymen returned from the south. Their Centurion rode directly to the Senior Tribune and Senior Centurion. After a brief conference, the Legion's senior officers sent for the Tribunes of the Second Maniple and called a halt to the jog. While the Legionaries dropped to the ground for a rest, Cornelius and his right-side counterpart rode to the command position.

"Gentlemen, we have news," the Senior Tribune announced. "I'll let the Centurion of Horse tell you."

The officer took a stream of water. By the blood and dirt on his face and the lather on his horse, they could tell he had been in a fight.

"We caught up with their rear element," the cavalry officer described, "and a group twice our numbers wheeled around and charged us. In a fierce skirmish near Cortona, we chased off their horsemen and their rear guard of infantrymen. If we hadn't arrived when we did, I fear the garrison and Cortona would have been destroyed."

"The garrison is behind solid walls and deep trenches," the senior combat officer pointed out. "Surely you're exaggerating about their destruction."

"No, sir," the Centurion insisted. "Every farmhouse, barn, villa, and structure in the path of the Punic army has been demolished or burned. I can only guess that they expected a day to overrun the fort before setting fire to

Cortona. We can thank the God Occasio for his blessing of luck and the opportunity to drive them away."

"Do you think they're running from us?" the Senior Tribune inquired.

"Yes, sir. They fought just enough for their infantry to get away," the cavalry officer answered. "In my opinion, I think they want to get away from our Legions. According to several prisoners, their general has been able to recruit from the Gauls based on his wins up north. We suspect he plans to gather followers from the Samnites and Greeks on the east coast as he scorches his way across the Republic."

"Then gentlemen, we need to stop him," the Senior Tribune exclaimed. "Second Maniple, we'll push on until we see the lights of his campfires."

"What then, sir?" Cornelius asked.

"We'll be a blocking force to pin the Carthaginians to the south, so they don't double back on Cortona. I and a few other Tribunes have villas there," the Senior Centurion informed him. "And we'll provide security for the rest of the Legions when they arrive."

"Who is going to provide security for the Second Maniple?" the Tribune from the right side asked.

"We'll remain alert," the senior combat officer told him. "The Second will be fine until General Flaminius arrives with the Legions. It'll be dark when we settle in, and no major force does night maneuvers. It's too easy for units to get lost or even stumble into enemy positions."

"Yet, we'll march in the dark," Cornelius mentioned.

"Indeed, you will," the Senior Centurion agreed. "And for that observation, your Centuries will be our pathfinders."

"Was the sacrifice not enough, Muta?" Cornelius uttered.

"Did you say something, Tribune Scipio?" the Senior Tribune inquired.

"No, sir, just organizing my thoughts on how to present the plan to my Centurions and the Cretan archers."

"Are those the light infantrymen with giant pieces of bronze jewelry on their wrists?" the Centurion of Horse asked.

The remark brought chuckles from everyone in the command position, except Scipio.

"If you'll excuse me, sirs," Cornelius requested, "I'll go arrange the order of march."

"You're excused," the Senior Tribune said between snickers.

***

Not long after the meeting with the Legion commanders, the nineteenth Century led off and Cornelius rode to the Centurion of Horse.

"What can I do for you, Tribune Scipio?" the cavalry officer asked.

"You can clear all the Legion cavalry from in front of us."

"We're ranging far afield. I don't think we're in danger from your forward screen."

"Normally I would agree," Cornelius told him. "But my Lieutenant of archers warned that his bowmen shoot first in the dark and ask questions later."

"A Legion archer does not release arrows in the dark," the Centurion suggested.

"But the Cretan archers do and now you've been warned," Cornelius insisted. Then he softened the message. "Before it gets ugly, clear your horsemen from the path of my Centuries. I don't know what they have planned, but the Cretan bowman have taken extra arrows and strung their bows."

"May Salus the Goddess of Safety grant us protection," the officer prayed. "If they're shooting at shadows in the night, men on horseback make big targets. I'll leave a few horsemen here as couriers and take the rest to Cortona."

The sun settled and, for a while, appeared as half a blazing ball on the horizon. Horses dashed away and the infantrymen continued to march southward.

"The Legion horsemen are pulling their pickets," Cornelius informed Gergely. "I hope you know what you're doing."

The Lieutenant and a ring of archers walked beside the mule cart.

"Tribune, care for a slab of venison or a pull of pork?" the young Latin bow maker asked.

"Venison sounds good," Cornelius replied.

An archer popped up in the back of the cart holding a knife in one hand and a fist sized piece of deer in the other. He leaned over the side and handed the venison to Cornelius.

"Lochias Phylo, I want a fan two miles deep to our front," Lieutenant Gergely informed the Sergeant. "I'll be around to check on it after dark."

"Yes, sir," the Cretan NCO acknowledged.

In the blink of an eye, the ring of archers around the cart vanished, as did the officer.

"Where did everyone go?" Cornelius questioned.

"They blended into the deep shadows," Jace told him. "They want to move into position unobserved by the Punics watching from the tall grass."

"Do you think there are really spies out there?"

"It's reasonable to believe so," Jace assured him. "The Cretan archers would do it to keep an eye on the movement of an enemy."

Cornelius scanned the grasslands but couldn't see anything in the shadows of early evening.

"I don't believe even the Carthaginians are that sneaky," Cornelius said brushing aside the idea.

Jace released the mule and walked to the side of the cart. He reached in and pulled his war bow from its case. After gently bending it over his knee a few times, he strung the bow. With an arrow in the fingers of his left hand and another notched on the bowstring, he searched the surrounding fields.

"That group of bushes," he said pointing far out. "I'm going to put an arrow in there. If anyone runs, tell me left, right, or straight back. But say it quickly."

"Is this silly exercise a jest?" Cornelius complained.

Even though he disbelieved the Latin archer, he fixed his eyes on the bushes. With the setting of the sun, the bushes faded into a gray shape against a gray background.

"Watch," Jace coached, "and spot me."

A long object flashed from the bow. The arrow arched slightly in its flight before vanishing into the gray. At the foliage, a man leaped up and ran.

"Left," Cornelius reported even though he felt ridiculous playing the game.

A second arrow flashed across the distance.

"He tripped," Cornelius scoffed. "He must have."

"We'll know later," Jace said while unstringing his bow. "An archer will find him and bring back my arrow."

"You're a very good bowman," Cornelius complimented Jace. "Tell me how a Latin came to travel with a unit of Cretan archers?"

"My name is Jace Kasia," he replied while putting his bow away. "I ended up on Crete after a storm sank the ship I was traveling on. At least that's what I was told. How I became an archer is a longer story."

"Master Kasia," a voice called from the dark. "I've one of your arrows. But the arrowhead stayed in the body when I pulled the shaft."

"Bring it in," Jace said.

It was then Cornelius noticed the small shield on Jace's left arm and a war hatchet in his other hand. An archer stepped out of the dark. Half turned to avoid the Tribune he went directly to Jace.

"Nice shot, Master Kasia," he said while handing the shaft to Jace.

Without another word, the archer, who was walking the flank screen, blended back into the dark.

"My name is Cornelius Scipio," the Roman nobleman introduced himself. Then he noted. "Other than your Lieutenant, none of the archers will even look at me."

"That, Tribune Scipio, is because you might be the client," Jace told him. "And nobody wants to take a chance on offending the client."

"That explains why the Lieutenant talks to me," Cornelius pointed out. "But you don't seem to have a problem looking at me or even giving me a hard time."

"That's because, Tribune Scipio, I'm a free thinker and say what I feel."

"Jace Kasia, that makes two of us," Cornelius remarked before nudging the horse. As it walked away from the cart, he inquired. "Where did the Cretan archers get the pig?"

"I'd like to say they hunted it," Jace responded. "But I won't."

Cornelius chewed on the venison and on the thought that Cretan archers were master thieves as well as marksmen. It was something to keep in mind while setting the guard rotation for his Centuries.

***

Deep into the night, the infantrymen stacked up as if firewood stood on their ends. Before the word passed back that the forward Century had stopped, one hundred and sixty Legionaries were bunched up and whining about the sudden halt to the march.

"What's the hold up?" Cornelius demanded.

A hand gripped the bridle of his horse.

"Look ahead and to the left, Tribune," Lieutenant Gergely directed.

Following the instructions, Tribune Scipio scanned before his eyes settled on a field of campfires. Beyond the closely spaced fires, he saw a reflection of the flickering flames blended with the likeness of the moon.

"That's the bank of Lake Trasimene," he declared.

"And where the Punic army is camped," Gergely confirmed. "But there is a problem Tribune."

"I'm almost afraid to add to the situation. What's the problem?"

"We shouldn't have reached this point," the Cretan officer replied. "It's been too easy."

A pair of horses walked up, and the Senior Tribune asked, "What's the hold up, Scipio?"

"The Punic army is down there on the banks of the lake," Cornelius answered. "But there is a problem."

"What's a problem?" The Senior Centurion demanded.

"We haven't encountered any resistance," Cornelius ventured. "We're like hunters tracking a wolf. We don't know if it's wounded and fleeing. Or if the wolf is bringing us home as dinner."

A laugh came from ahead of Cornelius' mount.

"Is something funny?" the senior staff officer inquired.

"No sir," Acis Gergely assured him. "It's just that Tribune Scipio reminds me of someone."

"If he's not germane to this conversation, keep your comments to yourself," the Senior Tribune advised.

"Sir."

"Tribune Scipio, set your half Maniple in defensive positions and prepare to resist attack," the senior combat officer ordered. "We'll place the other half of the Second behind your Centuries."

"Absolutely, Senior Centurion."

In the dark, the infantrymen placed shields in loose stacks then put sentries near the shields. Those not on guard duty stretched out on the damp grass and shivered in the chill of the evening.

Without warning, campfires in a half ring stretching around the Legionaries formation blazed to life.

"What the Hades are those," the Senior Centurion yelled. "Douse those fires. We don't want to give our position away to the enemy."

Feet shuffling in the dark approached the senior combat officer. When they got close, he made out four men in hooded leather jerkins. Three approached, shrugged something off their shoulder, and dumped what appeared to be sacks of grain at the Centurion's feet.

"They know we're here," the last one said as he dumped a body on top of the other corpses.

The four archers melted back into the night. After probing the bodies with the toe of his hobnailed boot, the senior combat officer put his fists on his hips.

"Fires are authorized," he bellowed. "And why not? It's cold. And we could be dead by morning. Might as well be toasty warm tonight."

Chapter 24 – Lead Us Not Into

Dawn brought a herd of light infantrymen to the forward position of the Second Maniple, Flaminius Legion North. Spanning across the plain, they marched ahead of the Legions. Some were Legion Velites while others were light infantrymen from allies of the Republic. Almost six thousand strong, the skirmishers filled the horizon to the north.

"If the Carthaginians didn't know we were here last night," Cornelius remarked to his six combat officers, "They do now."

"When do we attack?" a Centurion inquired.

"Certainly not until General Flaminius arrives," Cornelius told him. Then to his officers, he instructed. "Watch for the Legion North supply wagons. Pass out javelins and get our men fed quickly in case the General wants to step off immediately."

"Yes, Tribune," they said.

The group of Centurions broke up and shortly afterward, Lieutenant Gergely strolled to Cornelius from across an open field.

"I've barely seen you all night, Lieutenant," Cornelius commented.

"I was checking on my archers," Acis Gergely replied.

"The campfires almost set the Senior Centurion off, but your men calmed him down with the bodies," Cornelius described. "But lighting your positions wasn't a good idea. In fact, it was dangerous."

"Tribune, we weren't at the fires," Gergely explained. "They were lit to attract Punic raiders. And, like moths to a flame, they came to the campfires. And we intercepted them before they could reach your positions."

"I just assumed archers liked being comfortable."

"We do enjoy relaxing, sir, but not when we're hunting. My archers will have the day to sleep, eat, and warm up."

"Maybe not," Cornelius cautioned by pointing at the thousands of light infantrymen, "the Legions are arriving."

"Tribune Scipio, my flankers tell me there is no sign of the heavy infantry or the baggage train behind them," Gergely informed Cornelius. "Maybe there will be a battle tomorrow or the day after. But not today."

***

As the Cretan officer said, no heavy infantrymen followed the skirmishers. The first units to arrive were teams of surveyors to lay out areas for each Legion. Then came the cavalry. By early afternoon, the infantry and supply wagons arrived. Sometime later in the day, Consul/General Gaius Flaminius and his entourage reached the forward line. After seeing the Carthaginian camp by the lake, Flaminius went to his tent for an early dinner.

His presence at first sent the almost twenty-five thousand men under his command into a frenzy of activity. When he retired, the four reinforced Legions settled down to cook their evening meals.

"I don't think we'll need your archers this evening," Cornelius said when he found Lieutenant Gergely late in the day. "Units of light infantrymen are taking the forward positions."

"All the better for my archers. We'll get some sleep before the battle."

"Now you're sure there will be a battle tomorrow?"

"Yes, sir. Because the Punic army is still camped by the bank," Gergely said while pointing to the lake. "They seemed trapped between the water, the hills, and the narrowing bank around the lake."

"Which means what?" Cornelius asked.

"It's too tempting a situation for your General to ignore. I'll have the archers on your flank before dawn."

***

In the dark before sunrise, Junior Tribunes awakened Tribunes and the staff officers alerted their Centurions. In turn, the combat officers got the NCOs up. Then the Sergeants and Corporals kicked the infantrymen to their feet. While the Legions dressed in their armor, the senior officers rode to the front and watched for activity from the Punic camp.

"We have them," Gaius Flaminius declared. "Caught Hannibal Barca napping. This day, gentlemen, will go down in history."

"How many Centuries should we keep in reserve, General?" a Battle Commander asked.

"Colonel, I want the entire front sealed off," Flaminius described, "from the edge of the water to the hills. For that, we'll need every man in the assault. Our Legions will sweep through their camp and catch half of them lost in dreams and still wrapped in the arms of Morpheus."

"Say the word, General," another Colonel offered, "and we'll march to Hades for you."

"When the sky turns pink, I want the ground red with the blood of those murderous Gauls and the Punic horde," Flaminius bellowed. "Victory, gentlemen! Nothing short of total victory will please me."

"To victory," the four Battle Commanders shouted.

Hearing their commanders' enthusiasm, a roar of 'Rah' ripped through the Legions.

"So much for surprise," Flaminius admitted. "I'll let Legion North lead us in."

"Thank you, General," the Colonel for Flaminius North said. Then to his staff officer he ordered. "Senior Tribune, move to the attack."

***

As rapidly as the commanders envisioned a mass movement, the actual act required time. While waiting for the orders to step off, Tribune Cornelius Scipio and Tribune Appius Pulcher chatted.

"It may be the Cretan officer getting to me," Cornelius commented, "but I don't see much activity in the Carthaginian camp. I find it suspicious."

"Just because a bunch of warriors gather in the same place, doesn't make them an army," Appius advised. "They were probably drunk last night and are sleeping it off this morning."

"I don't know," Cornelius admitted. "Barca has proven to be a strategist and an able commander."

"Don't start that again," Appius warned, "As much as I admire competency, I won't say it out loud. And neither should you."

Horns sounded in the gray dawn and voices called for the light infantry to step off.

"Be careful today," Cornelius suggested.

"It's not me who likes to charge into a fight," Appius countered.

They gripped hands then parted. Appius Pulcher rode to his veterans in the Third Maniple and Cornelius trotted to the experienced Legionaries of the Second.

"First Maniple, forward," the Tribunes for the inexperienced infantrymen shouted. "Left, stomp, left, stomp…"

His orders were repeated by the Centurions, Optios, and Tesserarii.

"Second Maniple, forward," Cornelius and his counterpart called to their Centurions. "Left, stomp, left, stomp…"

Behind them, Appius and the other Tribune called the march, "Left, stomp, left, stomp…"

Warm air rolled in with the rising sun. It caressed the chilly water of Lake Trasimene creating a layer of fog. Then, as Legion North moved, the blanket of white blew off the lake. Climbing the embankment, the fog spread over the land, hiding the Punic tents. Soon the camp vanished, and Legion North marched blindly into the thick mist.

***

The assault positioned the Maniples in a single line. As they entered the cloud, visibility dropped to three shields wide on either side of an infantryman with a shadowy glimpse of the Maniple to the front.

"Tribune Scipio, we have movement in the hills to our left," Lieutenant Gergely warned. "You need to be in your combat lines."

"What is it Gergely? Can you tell?"

"No more than I can see you in this broth," the Cretan officer responded.

Other than the men to the left and right, each Legionary walked through a personal fog. They and their officers were unaware of what was transpiring outside their bubbles.

"Sir, we need to form our combat lines," a Centurion called from Cornelius' right.

Shortening his assault line to three stacked rows would be the best defensive move. But the shift would leave the archers and the right side of the Maniple out of touch with his Centuries.

With that in mind, Cornelius instructed, "Maintain your pace and distance."

A horse charged out of the wall of white and the Senior Centurion reined in.

"What Maniple is this?" he demanded.

"Second, left-side," Cornelius answered.

"Mercury, bless me," the senior combat officer mentioned the God of Travelers. He looked around until he recognized Cornelius and his mount. "I overshot the command post. Tribune Scipio, maintain your pace and keep your distance."

"Yes, sir," Cornelius acknowledged.

The Senior Centurion didn't reply. He rode into the fog and was gone.

"Tribune Scipio, we have more movement to our left," Lieutenant Gergely alerted him. "You need to be in a combat…"

Screams and cries of archers fighting drowned out the Cretan officer's voice.

Realizing the battle had come to him, Cornelius began to issue directions but was cut short, "Left side. Form your…"

A wedge of riders came from Cornelius' left. They cut his line of Legionaries in half and caused his horse to dance away. The Punic cavalry thundered through, leaving a gap of dead and wounded Legionaries.

"Close into the center and form up," he shouted. "Form up."

But more clashes and grunts from the Cretan archers drew his attention. This time, it was a triple column of Gauls running diagonally through the damage caused by the cavalry. As if drawing the number ten, the light infantry slashed into the Legion line forming an 'X' and leaving more dead and wounded on the ground.

"Archers, come to my voice," Jace yelled.

Following the sound of the Latin archer, Cornelius rode to the cart and found the bow maker standing in the bed.

"Archers need a rally point," Jace told the Tribune. "Archers of Crete, come to the sound of my voice. One. Select a shaft, and-a-two notch your arrow…"

Cornelius Scipio assumed Jace Kasia had lost his mind under stress. Yet, no matter the state of the Latin archer's sanity, his idea of a gathering point made sense.

"Centurions, Optios, on me," Cornelius shouted.

His call was picked up by the combat officers and their NCOs. In moments Legionaries rushed to their Tribune and began setting up a defensive square.

And from deep in the fog, voices joined Jace in the count.

"And-a-three, pick your target. And-a-four, draw. And-a-five, release, and-a-six, and-a-seven, and-an-eight, and-a-nine."

By the time Jace started at 'One. Select a shaft' again, multiple voices followed the count out of the fog. Cornelius saw about fifty bloodied and bruised archers stumble from the wet soup.

"The Lieutenant and the Sergeants were shoved away," one bowman told Jace, "when the riders separated us."

"Stay here and I'll see what the Tribune wants to do," Jace told the archer. "In the meanwhile, get a drink and fill your quivers. We're going to need your bow."

After a beating, warriors looked for leadership. Someone who seemed in control and could help gather the collective wits of a broken unit. For the Cretan files, the sight of Jace Kasia on the cart, welcoming them from the Hades of being isolated and fighting an enemy who appeared from the fog and then vanished, filled the need.

"Anything you say, Master Kasia," another archer acknowledged Jace's command.

"Tribune Scipio. Which way do you want to go?" Jace asked the Legion officer. "We'll punch a hole for you."

With Jace on the cart and Cornelius on horseback, the two were elevated above the heads of their men. They locked eyes, each looking to the other for guidance. Then Cornelius mouthed, 'I don't know.'

"Right you are," Jace announced. "Archers. Face to the rear and form up on the back of the cart."

Once the battered Cretans moved away, Cornelius eased his horse to the side of the cart.

"What are we doing facing backwards?" he inquired.

"Until you decide on a plan, I think we'll open a breach to the rear," Jace answered. "It's where your veterans are. If any unit can hold together in this mess, it's them."

A breeze touched their faces before it reached to the ground and blew away the fog. For a moment, Cornelius wished the mist would return.

***

Jace Kasia had been right, the veterans of the Third Maniple had stacked in back-to-back rows and were killing Gauls and Iberians. But they fought two hundred feet away. A river of Punic warriors divided the Left-Side Second and Third Maniples.

A voice brought Cornelius back to his fighting square.

"Are you ready to bring them to us?" Jace asked.

"What? How can we bring them to us?" Cornelius inquired. "I've maybe three hundred infantrymen. And they are doing everything possible to hold our square. There's no way we can wade into the melee and survive."

"Archers, give me ten files," Jace called to the fifty survivors. He used knife hands to indicate the direction. While the archers formed ten lines five deep, Jace instructed Cornelius. "When you're ready Tribune, remove ten infantrymen from your line and leave a gap."

"That's crazy, the Iberians will come flooding in," Cornelius protested.

"Three feet," Jace declared. Seeing confusion on the Tribune's face, he promised. "None of the Iberians will make it more than three feet into your formation."

"I have wood, muscles, and steel holding them back," Cornelius boasted. "And you expect me to believe you can do that with lengths of sticks?"

Jace nodded as if agreeing.

"First rank, face shots on the front rank," Jace ordered. "Now."

The flight of ten arrows released at the same time gave the impression of a group of birds flushed from a bush. Except, these feathers zipped between the heads of Legionaries, flashed over the top of infantry shields, and stuck in the faces of warriors. Across the combat line, ten Gauls jerked back with shafts in the cheeks, mouths, or eyes.

"And a six," Jace ordered.

Another flight, as straight and true as the last one swept away another ten Gauls.

"Step-up," Jace said before turning his attention to Cornelius. At the step-up command, the front rank peeled back, and the next row of archers took their place. "Tribune Scipio we can do this all day. But it's highly ineffective. You have Cretan archers in a Cretan archer formation. It's yours to command. But, sir, command you must."

The young Tribune swallowed and studied the battlefield. Off to his right, General Flaminius, his command staff, and the First Century battled a closing ring of Iberian heavy infantrymen. To the rear, he watched Legion cavalrymen fall to spears from more riders than he ever imagined existed. Twisting around, he saw a glimpse of hope. A hundred yards away, the First Maniple had formed a circle and were holding off multiple ranks of warriors.

"Centurion. Give me a gate at the rear. Ten shields wide."

"Is that wise, Tribune?" the combat officer questioned.

"No more than marching four Legions into a fog to get ambushed by an entire Punic army," Cornelius growled. "Do I need an officer who follows orders?"

"No, sir, one gate coming up," the Centurion confirmed.

As the Legion officer jogged away to carry out the mad orders, Cornelius saluted Jace.

"Lieutenant Kasia, the next step is yours."

"Cretan archers, One. Select a shaft," Jace sang out.

In response, the fifty archers picked up the chant, "And-a-two, notch your arrow. And-a-three, pick your target. And-a-four, draw. And-a-five, release, and-a-six, and-a-seven, and-an-eight, and-a-nine. Step-up."

Cornelius Scipio wasn't sure what to expect. But on each count after four, a flight of ten arrows went into the exposed bellies, arms, legs, necks, faces, and upper chests of Gauls, Iberians, and any Punic mercenary in the way. No arrow drifted astray. Every shaft buried its arrowhead in a victim.

In five quick breaths, fifty arrows had gone down range. Before the Tribune could admire the marksmanship, another volley of fifty arrows poured iron and steel arrowheads and shaft into a rapidly forming channel.

At the rear of the Cretan formation, archers checked their bowstrings, took a drink of water, and selected five more arrows. Then they stood in line waiting to deliver another fifty arrows into the Punic ranks.

A thousand arrows later, Jace called to Cornelius, "There's your escape alley."

Just as the Latin archer spoke, a wall of Legion shields entered the cleared lane. As if a dam had ruptured, veteran Legionaries fought to hold the sides back while their wounded limped or were carried to the Second Maniple and the archer's cart.

"Get off. We're taking the cart for our wounded," a newly escaped combat officer ordered Jace.

"Stand down, Centurion," Cornelius said while putting his horse between the Centurion and the Latin bow maker. "We still need arrows for the archers to get us out of this trap."

"But sir," he said as if pleading. Then the combat officer grabbed Cornelius' leg and yanked the young Tribune off his horse. "I don't need a nobleman's brat to tell me what to do."

He kicked Cornelius in the ribs before sneering at Jace.

"I said…"

The arrow impacted his helmet and ricocheted off the metal. The arrowhead split the horsehair comb before the shaft fluttered off to land harmlessly on the ground. Dazed by the impact, the Centurion sank to his knees.

"File Leader Kasia, I thought we were shooting the Punic mercenaries?" an archer remarked.

"That was an accident," Jace declared.

"An excellent accident, worthy of a Cretan archer," another stated.

Cornelius pushed to his feet, touched the sore spot on his ribs, then kneed the combat officer in the face.

"Who belongs to this animal?" he called to the arriving infantrymen.

"He's my Centurion, sir," an Optio volunteered.

"When we get out of this, he's going on the punishment post," Cornelius swore. "Then I want him digging latrines until I get sick of the smell."

"Yes, sir," the NCO said accepting the punishment. "Can we use the cart for our wounded."

"Not until we reach the First Maniple."

Act 9

Chapter 25 – For the Fallen

At a signal from Cornelius, Jace jumped to the ground and walked the mule in a half circle.

"Again, Cretan archers," Jace directed from the front of the cart. He showed them the other direction with his hands. "One. Select a shaft."

"One. Select a shaft," the archers repeated.

The fifty bowmen jogged to the back of the cart. Each picked an arrow. After examining the shaft, they searched the available arrows to find four more that matched the shaft. With five arrows that would draw and fly along the same path, they fell into the ten-file formation.

"Tribune Scipio. The Cretan archers are formed," Jace announced, "and waiting for your command."

With the addition of the veteran Legionaries, the defensive square solidified. Although they held out against constant attacks, the infantrymen on the shield walls would eventually falter.

"Centurions. We need to get to First Maniple," Cornelius instructed two combat officers.

"We'll lose more Legionaries than we'll get through," one grumbled. "It's best if we…"

Cornelius slid off his horse and stuck his nose in the Centurion's face.

"If I needed your permission to save your sorry behind, I would take a vote," he yelled. "As it is, it's up to me to save as many Legionaries as I can. Do you mind if I get on with saving lives?"

"Rah," the veteran combat officer responded.

With a leap, Cornelius remounted then pointed towards where the First Maniple battled for their lives.

"Pivot a ten-shield opening in our wall," he ordered. "And tell them to move fast or they'll get an arrow in the back."

The two Centurions raced to the shield wall. A quick argument with an NCO began, but it ended quickly when the disgruntled Centurion cuffed the Optio. Both officers looked back, waiting for the crazy Tribune to order them to open the gate and end their lives.

"Lieutenant Kasia, stand by your archers," Cornelius roared.

"Ready, sir," Jace answered.

"Open the wall," he shouted to the Centurions. With his arms, Tribune Scipio made a parting motion.

Before the Legionaries had a chance to step back, Jace sang out, "and-a-five release. And hold."

Zip-Thwack

If the Legionaries doubted the wisdom of opening a hole during a hard fight, the flash of arrows zipping by their ears got their attention. And the shafts appearing in the faces of the warriors over their shields, helped convince them. The infantrymen drew back and to the sides.

"And-a-six, and-a-seven, and-an-eight, and-a-nine," Jace chanted. Twenty, thirty, forty, fifty arrows flashed downrange. Shot from the powerful war bows, each arrowhead and shaft dropped a Punic mercenary. "Step up!"

A new row of ten archers took the first position and in breaths, they dropped fifty more. "Step-up."

The arrows cut the warriors down as if they were shafts of wheat during the harvest. In five rotations, a channel of withering or dead men carpeted the ground.

"...and-an-eight, and-a-nine. Step-up and hold," Jace commanded. "Tribune Scipio, any closer and we'll be taking down Legionaries."

Cornelius chopped with both hands as if guiding the infantrymen along the lane.

"Centurions, extend our walls to the First Maniple," he directed.

As if a fist, a face of shields pushed outward, and the Legionaries flooded the path to the First Maniple. From fighting back-to-back, the young infantrymen found themselves reinforced with experienced men from the Second and Third Maniples. Infused with hope, they helped push the Punic warriors back to form a new fighting square.

In the center of the new formation, Lieutenant Acis Gergely sat among other wounded archers. Healthy bowmen ringed them while using the last of their arrows to aid the Legionaries.

***

As the new zone expanded, the original defensive box shrunk. In order to manage an orderly withdrawal, Cornelius rode to the rear of the formation.

"Nice work incorporating the archers into the assault," a familiar voice complimented him.

Looking down, he spied a group of wounded Legionaries. Leaning on each other and moving like an uncoordinated centipede, the five struggled towards the escape channel.

"Tribune Pulcher. Would you like to take command?" Cornelius asked when he recognized Appius.

"I'm afraid, at this moment," Pulcher replied while nodding at his companions, "this lot is the extent of my command capabilities."

Cornelius signaled to Jace and pointed at the wounded staff officer. While a file of archers headed his way to help, Tribune Scipio rode the shield walls, instructing the infantrymen to collapse the formation slowly.

***

Jace glanced over the fray and peered at the position of the sun.

"Wishing you were back on Crete?" an archer inquired.

"When I was at the agoge, I felt as if I was in exile," Jace told him. "I just didn't know where I came from. And although it's been a strange journey, I feel like I'm home."

The bowman scrunched his face in confusion, scratched his head, and looked around at the infantrymen grunting, bleeding, and fending off blades.

"No offense, File Leader Kasia," he noted, "but your home is somewhere in the fourth level of Hades."

"No, I meant the land and the Latians," Jace remarked.

He dropped his eyes to the archer and saw the smile on the man's face.

"This Jace, this madness, is home for a Cretan archer. It's what we train for," the bowman informed him. "Orders, sir?"

"Should we ask Lieutenant Gergely?"

"He's in no shape to issue orders," the archer reminded Jace. "Orders?"

"The sun is only halfway to midday," Jace commented. "I'd like us out of the melee before noon. It'll take the last of our spare arrows. But let's set up for another push."

The Cretan ran to alert the other archers. They had picked up another ten survivors along with the injured Acis Gergely when they reached the First Maniple.

Jace aligned the rear of the cart and once he climbed onto the bed, he shouted, "Tribune Scipio. We can't stay here."

From across the new fighting square, Cornelius shot the Latin archer a hard look.

"Where can we go?" he demanded. "If we punch through, we'll die on the banks of Lake Trasimene."

"Same result if we stay here," Jace countered. He pointed at a split in the hills. The gap sat at the top of a long, steep grade. "It's a tough climb, but it's out of the Punic killing field."

"Can you open another path?"

In response, Jace called out, "Cretan archers. One. Select a shaft."

Chapter 26 – They Don't Like Us

Far below, the Legions fought and died. Out of the fighting but struggling, archers and Legionaries crawled upward towards the gap.

Jace had one of Acis Gergely's arms and an archer pulled on the Lieutenant's other wrist. While he could hobble across level ground, the Cretan officer couldn't manage the hands and knee clawing needed to climb the slope.

"This is embarrassing," Acis complained. Towed along on his back, his butt and legs scraped the ground while his shoulders and head were suspended by his arms. "You should leave me."

"Maybe at the top," Jace said between deep breaths.

"It's like the archer test," the bowman on the other side offered.

"Nope," Jace gasped between breaths. "The test was much worse and a lot colder."

The archer and the Lieutenant exchange puzzled looks. For the officer, he wasn't sure if he was ready for Jace to admit to being a tested archer. For the bowmen, he couldn't imagine the bow maker going through the trials.

***

The Cretans weren't the only ones who refused to leave wounded friends or commanders behind.

"Let me take him for a spell, sir," an Optio said as he reached and took Appius Pulcher's arm.

Cornelius released the arm and scrambled out of the way. As men clawed at the ground, scaling the steep grade, Scipio pushed to his feet. Balanced on the slope, the young Tribune gazed down on the battlefield.

Far to his right, riderless mounts bucked and circled dead and wounded Legion cavalrymen. Racing through the carnage, Punic light horsemen and heavy chargers crossed, lancing any Latin or allied horseman who moved.

Farther along the bank of the lake, a line of Iberian heavy infantrymen stutter stepped their assault line through piles of broken and bleeding Legionaries and client state infantrymen.

How they got behind Flaminius' four Legions, the young Tribune could only guess. Perhaps, General Barca sent his army into the foothills in the dead of night. And somehow, beyond all reason, they came down behind and to the flank of the Legions. While the tactic was a guess, Cornelius understood one fact. Hannibal Barca had outwitted the best Generals the Republic had to offer on three separate occasions.

Cornelius swore, "Never again."

After searching and finding the wreckage of Gaius Flaminius, his First Century, and the command staff for the Legions, he turned and dropped to his hands and knees. Once close to the ground, Tribune Scipio joined the survivors as they clawed their way up the steep grade.

***

Jace reached the top and sent his sixty archers across a mountain plain. When a Centurion reached the top, Jace approached him.

"I've stationed archers out there as early…"

"Don't talk to me. Don't come near me," the combat officer spit out. "Don't even breathe the same air as a true son of Rome. Go back to your lazy, thieving archers. Imagine, a Latin living with Cretans. There's nothing lower."

The hostility rocked Jace, and he froze. To reinforce his statements, the Centurion punched Jace in the chest.

Under the force, the bronze medallion pressed into Jace's breastbone. Folded over with pain, the Latin archer stumbled away.

"Form a defensive line," the Centurion bellowed. He grabbed Legionaries as they came off the slope and shoved them into position. They had a Century or more on guard when the officer reached out to help Cornelius onto the flatland. "We're in luck Tribune Scipio, there are none of those Punic mercenaries up here."

"Get the wounded on shields and ready to travel," Cornelius ordered. "Have you seen the archers?"

"Them? I saw those Cretans running away as soon as they reached the crest," the Centurion answered. "You know how they are, sir. As soon as it gets tough, archers run away."

Cornelius was too busy counting Legionaries and the injured to pay attention.

"Alright Centurion," he declared. "Get a couple of squads out front. We're moving."

"Where to, sir?"

"If I remember from the map, the town of Niccone and the Tevere River Valley are fourteen miles northeast of here. That's where we're going. I wonder where the archers went. I'd like to have them as our froward screen."

"Don't you worry about them rascals, sir. We'll secure our own front."

"I suppose we must," Cornelius remarked. "Move us out."

***

The honor of a Cretan archer hung on doing his best on every task and earning a profit. Jace held his head high and ignored the throbbing in his chest. As an unrecognized Cretan archer, he had done the best he could. Jace knelt beside Lieutenant Gergely.

"You were correct, sir," he told him. "The Romans don't like us."

"I won't ask what happened," Acis stated. "But we've satisfied our contract to Gaius Flaminius."

"Lieutenant, I believe General Flaminius is dead."

"Then the contract is definitely closed. We need to get to Rimini and link up with Captain Zoltar and the company."

"Which way? Jace asked.

"The Adriatic Sea is east of here," Acis Gergely said. An archer handed him a freshly trimmed pole. "I have a walking stick. We have sixty archers to get out of harm's way. So let me ask you, which route do we take Archer Kasia?"

"I'm a Cretan archer?" Jace asked.

"After today, I know sixty bowmen who will fight anyone who challenges your right to the title."

The honor of a Cretan archer started when he earned the title. Jace Kasia reached up and touched the bow case on his back.

'Thank you, Master Archer Mikolas,' he whispered an homage to his mentor.

Then Archer Kasia stood, reached down, and helped Lieutenant Gergely to his feet.

"Move us out," the officer instructed.

"We've a long way to go," Jace announced. He walked towards a high pass directly east of the mountain plain. "But we're Cretan archers. Still your breath so your hands are steady. Calm your heart so your eyes are clear. Focus your mind on the task. And follow me."

In the lines that trailed behind Jace, one of the archers complained, "Oh Gods, Kasia is going to be one of them."

"One what?"

"An officer. I can here it in his voice."

"He did get us out of that mess down there."

"I didn't say it was a bad thing. I only said he was going to be an officer."

"It didn't sound that way."

"All I meant was he's motivational."

The sixty-one Cretan archers and their officer reached the bottom of the slope and began to climb.

Chapter 27 – The Practical Type

The infantryman sliced another purse off a bloated body. Spilling the content in his palm, he used the tip of his knife to flick the copper coins from the pile.

"Last week, we were complaining about our pay," remarked a younger infantryman. "Today, we can't carry all the booty."

"As the General said, it's our reward for winning," the infantryman commented before taking a drink from a confiscated wineskin. "I'm thinking of dumping some silver and melting the gold into lumps. It'll be easier to carry than coins."

"You always were the practical type. Hold on. I've got a live one."

A hand coated in dirt and gore reached from a mound of corpses and gripped the young infantryman's ankle.

"Yup, he's a live one," the youth acknowledged. "Is he a Latian? Or do we need to treat his injuries."

Reaching down, the older soldier drew his blade across the man's neck. Gurgling, the Legionary released the ankle and collapsed with bubbles coming from his throat.

"He's Latian."

The pause to decide on the required course of action gave them a moment to look around. Displayed in front of the two was a double circle of bodies.

"I wonder who they were?"

Muscular bodies ringed a big pile of thin and fat men. After inspecting the scene, the infantrymen gripped several pieces of armor and unstacked an opening. Wading in, they tossed the skinny and fat ones aside.

"Oh my, that is pretty armor," the young infantryman exclaimed.

Buried under the mass of dead men, a gold chest piece caught the sunlight of the afternoon and glistened.

"Too heavy to carry," the older infantryman observed. "And think, there's not enough gold to melt down."

"It's tempting," the younger one remarked. "But you've always been the practical type, so I'll leave it."

They didn't take the armor. But they did cut the strings on Roman General Gaius Flaminius' fat purse. Then they worked their way outward, searching his bodyguards for gold. Because by then, their reward for winning the battle was an overabundance of riches. Just as General Hannibal Barca had promised.

The End

A sample of book #2 in *A Legion Archer* series:

Pity the Rebellious

Aleph! Aleph!

Larinum 217 B.C.

Dictator Fabius Verrucosus mounted his horse. With bared teeth, he silently expressed a challenge to his second in command.

"Marcus, I expect the camp to be intact when I get back from Rome," he instructed. "While I'm away, the only thing you're to disrupt are Hannibal Barca's supply lines."

"As we've been doing, per your plan, for most of the fall," Marcus Minucius responded.

Fabius missed the dissatisfied undertone of the comment. Or maybe he just ignored it. After the tragedy at Lake Trasimene, the Senate appointed Fabius Verrucosus as Dictator of Rome. With the power of the Senate vested in one man, Rome intended to see the Carthaginian General crushed. But Fabius surprised the Senate. Not only had he not forged a plan to bring Hannibal to battle. The entirety of his strategy called for doggedly following the Punic army. Attacking small detachments where possible and disrupting the enemy's supply lines constituted the bulk of Fabius' approach.

Another wonder, rather than selecting his second in command from his own party of supporters, Fabius Verrucosus picked Marcus Minucius as his Master of Horse.

A vocal opponent and a man holding distain for the Dictator's guerrilla tactics, Marcus had opposed the restraints ever since being chosen.

Swinging his horse towards the gate, Fabius Verrucosus and one hundred Legion cavalrymen trotted from the marching camp. Once the Dictator vanished down the hill and around the first bend, Marcus Minucius waved a young staff office to the steps of the headquarters tent.

"Tribune Scipio, what can you tell me about the enemy camp?" he inquired.

"Sir, I have Cretan archers ferrying reports twice a day," Cornelius informed him. "As of this morning, the Punics remain behind the trenches and palisades around Geronium."

"If anything changes, I want to know right away," Marcus responded. Disregarding the fact that a young Tribune stood in front of him, the Master of Horse swore. "This Fabian Doctrine is causing unrest. Not only in the Legions, but with the people of Rome and the Senate. Do you know what they're calling our illustrious Dictator?"

"No, sir," Cornelius replied, before cautioning. "Are you sure you want to say it publicly?"

"No. Yet I have an urge to live dangerously, unlike our leader," Marcus sneered. "They call him a paedagogus for Hannibal."

At a time when the Senate had consolidated power in one man, disparaging the Dictator could get the offender exiled or crucified. And, referring to Fabius Verrucosus as a slave who walked behind a Roman child carrying his books to school, qualified Minucius for corporal punishment.

Despite the seriousness of the slander, Cornelius chuckled.

"See even my staff officers understand it," Marcus Minucius observed. Before turning to go back to his office, he reiterated. "Any change at all in the Carthaginian deployment, I want to hear about. In short Tribune Scipio, find me a reason."

"A reason for what, sir?"

But the Master of Horse, the second most powerful man in the Republic, had already gone into the headquarters building.

***

Fifteen miles northeast of Larinum, four frustrated horsemen held back their mounts. It wasn't the trail in the narrow valley forcing them to bridle the high-strung horses or causing the energetic riders to fidget. Behind them, a slow, stolen mule plodded along, pulling a wagon of confiscated grain. To the rear and completing the mini caravan, four Iberian light infantrymen easily kept pace with the wagon. With their round shields on their backs and their spears on their shoulders, they had no complaints about the lack of haste.

"Jugurtha, I think we should patrol ahead," one of the riders suggested to the Numidian NCO.

"We're still miles from Geronium," Jugurtha scolded. "The grain is more important than you, joyriding around the countryside."

"It's more like mountainside," another complained. He scanned the trees and high hills surrounding the valley and announced. "I hate this land."

"Miss the warm climate of home?" the fourth teased. "Well, join the party. We all miss the plains, rolling hills, and the warmth of Numidia."

"What's that?" one asked.

"Where did he come from?" another questioned.

Jugurtha studied the trail ahead. In the middle of the path and strolling directly at them was a Latian teen with a crate balanced on his head. With standing orders from General Barca to slay any Latians, the NCOs next command gave a nod to their duty while providing a distraction for his light cavalrymen.

"Kill him," Jugurtha shouted.

Hearing the command and seeing four horsemen surge forward, the young Latian tossed the crate, spun around, and ran.

***

Jace Kasia pitched the package into the path of the cavalrymen, pivoted, and sprinted back down the trail. The sounds of hoofs on the hard packed dirt let him know the crate did nothing to slow the riders. However, their presence just behind him confirmed the success of the Cretan archer's plan. Considering the thunder coming closer and closer, maybe too successfully. Glancing over his shoulder would slow him, so he bent forward, pumped his arms and legs, and raced ahead of the horses.

The voices of the riders grew louder and more excited. They shouted, "Aleph! Aleph!"

Jace's shoulders tightened, imagining a javelin burying itself in his back.

"Aleph! Aleph!"

Just as the hot breath of the horses seemed to claw at the back of his neck, Jace pivoted to the left, planted a foot, and vaulted over a row of thorn bushes.

***

The four riders reined in and turned to face the thorns.

"Anybody want to go in there and flush him out?" Jugurtha inquired.

Getting negatives from his three men, the NCO wheeled his horse and…Zip-Thwack

Jugurtha tumbled from his horse with an arrow shaft in his chest.

Zip-Thwack, Zip-Thwack, Zip-Thwack… The other three horsemen followed him to the ground in quick order.

***

Jace dashed around the bushes. His small shield already strapped on his left arm and the war hatchet gripped in his right hand. At the bodies, he nudged each with the toe of his foot. None of the cavalrymen moved.

"Good clean shots," he declared to the three archers who scrambled from the tree line. "Search the bodies for coins. You've earned the profit."

"Where are you going, File Leader?" one asked.

"To be sure the mule, wagon, and grain are secured," he replied.

"Take a horse," one of the archers suggested. "We've got four."

Cretan archers trained in the peaks and valleys of the Island of Crete. Years of speeding up and down slopes made them fleet of foot and gave them stamina beyond most light infantrymen.

"The beasts take too long to gain momentum," Jace said before sprinting away.

***

The sun rested just above the horizon when the sentries at the gate called for the duty Optio.

"Sergeant of the Guard, they look suspicious," one Legionary stated.

The NCO took a moment to examine the wagon, mule, and four riderless horses. Six men walked in the procession. None of them rode.

"Cretan archers," he explained. "I don't think any of them can ride a horse."

"Barbarians," one infantryman commented.

"Thieving barbarians," the second sentry added.

Despite their opinions of the archers, the Legionaries stepped aside. And the Cretans, horses, and the wagon entered the Legion marching camp unmolested.

With day-to-day operations confined to drills and little else, word passed quickly about a wagon full of grain and the horses. Cornelius rushed to the Cretan area.

"Tribune Scipio, one of these horses is your profit," Jace said while handing him the reins.

"It's not common to distribute spoils from raids," Cornelius offered.

"Maybe not in the Republic. But on Crete, it is."

Before the Tribune could voice an opinion about the traditions of Cretan archers, Marcus Minucius boomed from the end of the street, "On Crete, it is what?"

"Customary for everyone involved to make a profit," Jace replied. To reinforce the idea, he handed Marcus the reins of a second horse. "The last two mounts are for Lieutenant Acis and Captain Zoltar."

"No movement by the Punics?" Marcus questioned.

"No sir," Jace answered. "They're still hold up in the hill town."

Noise from the back of the wagon drew their attention. Four round shields crashed to the ground when an archer pulled several spears and javelins from the bed.

"How many Carthaginians were there?" Cornelius inquired.

"Only nine," Jace said. "None got away, if that's your worry."

"I was thinking six against nine is not good odds," Cornelius observed.

"Nine mercenaries from the Punic camp," Marcus stated. "Is that rare?"

"Oh, no sir," Jace assured him. "They have hundreds of foraging parties out searching for food."

"There it is, my reason," Marcus exclaimed. "Our mission is to cut off their supplies. Is it not, Tribune Scipio?"

"Yes, sir," Cornelius agreed. "What is the reason?"

"To move our camp closer and end their scavenging," the Master of Horse said. "And maybe, to bring Hannibal out from behind his stockade."

He strutted away quickly with the horse prancing happily at the end of the reins.

"Tell me, Tribune Scipio," Jace inquired, "what does the expression aleph-aleph mean?"

"In Punic, Aleph means ox," Cornelius replied. "I would assume Aleph-Aleph would be a call used to herd oxen. Why?"

"Just something I heard recently," Jace Kasia commented, "nothing important."

End of the sample from *Pity the Rebellious*, book #2 in *A Legion Archer* series.

A note from J. Clifton Slater

Thank you for reading *Journey from Exile*. Hopefully, you're intrigued enough to come back for the next book in *A Legion Archer* series, *Pity the Rebellious*. Now, let me submit a few historical things for your consideration.

Why Cretans were more than average bowmen

Sparta was famous for their agoge where young boys were trained to be Spartan soldiers. Famed for their cruelty and the challenges thrown at the youths, the process created men who could withstand starvation, harsh conditions, and battle with shields and spears from dawn to dusk. But why am I writing about Spartans when the book revolves around Cretan archers?

The Dorians, one of four founding ethnic groups of the Hellenes/Greeks, influenced both Lacedaemon and Cretan cultures. Because of this, the Cretans also had a harsh training school for boys. Although mastering the bow required individual skills and the Spartans needed men to hold their shield line, both schools created military professionals.

The 'Troops' of Cretan archers were organized by age and progressed through the training together through the years from Herds to Troops. Dining together, the Troops and Herds ate on the ground with the poor of the city to keep the students humble and motivated.

Training from a young age provided the Cretan archers with superior talent with their bows and arrows, martial skills, and fieldcraft. However, unlike Lacedaemon citizens, the children of Crete weren't required to attend the agoge. Only those suitable and able to endure the regiment attended. For those who entered and survived the rigors, they became elite Cretan archers.

Aelian, a Greek writer in 106 A.D. wrote, "Of countermarches, there are two forms: one by companies and one by ranks. And for each of them there are three types. For one is called the Macedonian, another the Lakonian, and another the Rustic, which is also called *The Cretan* or the Persian drill."

Seeing as warriors from Crete were acknowledged as archers, the heavy infantry phalanx maneuver named *The Cretan* must have come from observing the bowmen's movement. This leads to the assumption that the archers used fluid formations during battle.

Strabo, a Greek historian from 50 B.C., reported on the Agoge of Crete, "…and in order that courage, and not cowardice, might prevail, he commanded that from boyhood they should grow up accustomed to arms and toils, so as to scorn heat, cold, marches over rugged and steep roads, and blows received in gymnasiums or regular battles; and that they should practice, not only archery, but also the war-dance…"

Polybius a Greek historian noted, "…the ancient Cretans and Spartans...introduced the pipe and rhythmic movement in war…"

By keeping a steady rhythm with a chant or a song, the archers would remain in good order during their war-dance/battlefield maneuvers. Therefore, the mercenaries from Crete were more than a cluster of bowmen for hire. They were military specialists and highly trained marksmen. One source I read called *the Cretan* formation the machinegun of the ancient worlds.

The Color of Carrots

As an edible tuber, wild carrots were either white or pale yellow. Around 2,000 B.C., the root crops were domesticated, and the color changed to purple and yellow. Since then, selective breeding created the orange carrot with high beta carotene that we recognize today. And although purple, calling carrots a royal crop, as Dryas Kasia did in the story, would have been an outlandish claim.

Archery Overview

For expediency, I have simplified the archery terms used in *Journey from Exile*. This doesn't mean I skipped on reading and researching the bow and arrows in the era around 220 B.C.

There are three type of Mediterranean bows mentioned in *A Legion Archer* series - Self Bow, Hunting Bow, and War Bow. A Self Bow was made of a single piece of wood and was used for defense and hunting small animals. On the other hand, the Hunting Bow was constructed of a composite of three pieces. But was shorter than the War Bow, had less sinew coating, and weaker horn backing so it didn't have as heavy a draw. War Bows were built with multiple layers of sinew and thicker bone backing on two limbs attached to a center belly. The thick sinew coating on front, and the bone in the back created a sturdy bow with a weighty draw that delivered arrows with penetrating power.

Cretan archers wore a small shield on their left forearm while in battle. Because of this obstacle, they would have placed the arrows on the right side of the bow and rested the shaft on their thumbs. Most people don't care about this detail, but fans of archery will want to know why I decided on the right side. Also, my research leaned toward the Pinch draw instead of the Mediterranean draw with three fingers. Early Crete was influenced by bowman from the east and pinching the bowstring between the thumb and forefingers to draw it back was their norm. Today we discount the Pinch pull as requiring too much thumb and finger strength. But Cretan archers were trained from an early age to handle their bows.

Any study of archery will bring up the paradox. The archer's paradox is the change in perspective between an arrow resting on a bowstring and a fully drawn arrow. When resting, the arrowhead at the end of the shaft points far to the side because of the body of the bow. Only when drawn back does the arrowhead point at the target. If things remained constant, releasing the arrow should return it to the off-target position where it started. But the physics of a bending shaft moves the arrow around the bow and sends it downrange to the target as it was at full draw. The logic of a starting position and a different ending flight path is the paradox, not the bending of the arrow.

The paradox does lead us to spine strength, or the flexibility of an arrow. A bow with a strong draw will overpower a weak spine, bending it too much around the bow and sending the light arrow off target. Conversely, an arrow with a spine too stiff for the bow will send the arrow off to the side. In this case, the arrow will not be released with enough force to bend it around the bow.

Adjusting the draw to compensate for different spine strengths is the reason archers pre-selected arrows before a battle or a competition. Using uniformed spines allowed the bowman to get the same result from their arrows without altering their draw and aim during a session of shooting.

Alexander the Great

Arrian of Nicomedia wrote a history of the campaigns of Alexander the Great in the *Anabasis of Alexander*. Thanks to his writings, we know the history from Alexander's campaign for the city of Thebes. The King, along with a unit of Cretan archers, and light infantrymen from Agrianes (what is now Western Bulgaria) attacked an advancing force of Thebans. During the fighting, Eurybotas, the Cretan commander, and seventy of his archers were killed.

After he captured the city state of Thebes, Alexander the Great would move on to conquer the known world. Famous for using only the best warriors, during the remainder of his campaigns, Alexander kept a unit of Cretan Archers in his army.

The Lyttian War on Crete

Cnossus and Gortys, two dominant cities, had forced every city on Crete to swear allegiance to them. The Spartan colony of Lyttos refused. In 220 B.C., the two cities decided to attack Lyttos. To aid them, they enlisted Polemocles, an Admiral from the Island of Rhodes. He arrived with six ships and began visiting the cities on Crete.

On a tour of Eleutherna (the largest city near where Zarek and Jace were raised in *Journey from Exile*) the Admiral was accused of assassinating a citizen named Timarchus. This caused Eleutherna to declare war on Rhodes creating a crack in the alliance. When Cnossus and Gortys did attacked Lyttos, other cities broke their agreement and sided with the Spartans.

The events started a civil war on Crete that lasted four years. I took slices of that history and added a few elements to create a story around the murder of Timarchus.

The 2nd Punic War

There were conflicting reports about who started the 2nd Punic War. It began when Carthaginian forces attacked and ravished the pro-Roman city of Saguntum in Iberia. But who ordered the assault? Was it the idea of General Hannibal Barca, or was he acting on orders from Carthage?

Carthage had an ongoing problem. Their Generals in far off regions of their trading empire sometimes declared themselves as Kings. The issue was so prevalent that one of the two rulers of the empire was designated as the Military Suffete. He guided the military arm of the government. Part of his duties included punishing Generals who exceeded their authority. There are no reports of Hannibal being called before the Suffete, but there are no records left from Carthage. The other Suffete handled domestic affairs.

In either case, the Roman Senate responded to the attack on Saguntum by declaring war on Carthage in 218 B.C. They dispatched Consul Publius Scipio to Iberia with orders to apprehend Hannibal. But on the way, Publius learned that Hannibal had left Iberia. The Consul landed his Legions at Marseille, intending to find and capture Hannibal. However, by the time he began marching inland, the Carthaginian General had started his march into the Alps. Unable to engage Hannibal, Publius marched his army back to the Roman fleet.

After sending the Legions to Iberia under the command of Proconsul Gnaeus Scipio, Publius' brother, Consul/General Scipio sailed to the northern border of the Republic and took command of the available forces. And that was where *Journey from Exile* picked up the story.

In November 218 B.C., Publius Scipio finally met Hannibal at the Battle of Ticinus. Wounded during the fighting, Publius' sixteen-year-old son, Cornelius, was credited with saving his father during the retreat.

While Hannibal collected his troops as they came down from the mountains, Publius Scipio's expedition retreated to the Legion fort at Piacenza.

In *'The Punic Wars: Rome, Carthage, and the Struggle for the Mediterranean,'* 'Field Marshal Sir *Nigel Thomas Bagnall* wrote, "That night, 2,200 Gallic troops serving with the Roman army attacked the Romans closest to them in their tents, and deserted to the Carthaginians, taking the Romans' heads with them as a sign of good faith."

Through victory, Hannibal attracted tribesmen who thrusted for the downfall of Rome. It was a pattern we see again and again in the 2nd Punic War.

A month after the Battle of Ticinus, Publius Scipio's co-Consul, Tiberius Longus, faced off with the Carthaginians at the Battle of the Trebia. The Romans were defeated again by Hannibal Barca's foresight and battlefield tactics.

In June 217 B.C., four Legions were beaten by Hannibal at the Battle of Lake Trasimene. Realizing they were in trouble, the Senate of Rome sent requests to client states for soldiers. When they contacted King Hiero of Syracuse, he agreed to send men. Rather than send his own soldiers,

Hiero hired five hundred Cretan archers and a thousand peltasts, Thracian light infantrymen.

Whether Hannibal acted alone to start the 2nd Punic War, or in response to orders from Carthage, we don't know. But we do know that Hannibal Barca was a superb military commander.

Battle of Lake Trasimene

The Romans had split their forces. With Legions at Rimini on the Adriatic coast and 66 miles over the mountains at Arezzo (ancient Arretium), the Senate assumed they had Hannibal barricaded in the north. When Hannibal came over the Apennine Mountains to the west of Arezzo, Consul/General Flaminius decamped his army and followed the Carthaginian to Lake Trasimene. In the fog at dawn on the banks of the lake, Flaminius advanced his Legions into an ambush.

To take some of the blame off Gaius Flaminius, historians admit Hannibal's tactics were unexpected. Military historian *Theodore Dodge* commented, "It is the only instance in history of lying-in ambush with the whole of a large army."

Roman Historian, *Quintus Fabius Pictor,* wrote that of the 25,000 Roman troops at the battle, 15,000 were killed and 10,000 scattered. Of the scattered, a considerable number were captured and sold into slavery. As a recruitment tactic, General Barca had the Latin survivors murdered while sending some of Rome's allied troops home to boast of Hannibal's mercy.

Because some might have escaped and for the sake of *Journey from Exile,* I put Jace and twelve files of Cretan archers in the battle. This kept the characters engaged and allowed the fictional Jace Kasia to meet the historical figure of Cornelius Scipio.

The Battle of Lake Trasimene was the third disaster for the Legions at the start of the 2nd Punic War. Unfortunately for the Republic, It would not be their last.

***

I appreciate your emails and adore reading your comments. If you enjoyed *Journey from Exile,* consider leaving a written review on Amazon or Goodreads. Every review helps other readers find the stories.

If you have comments e-mail me.

E-mail: GalacticCouncilRealm@gmail.com

To get the latest information about my books, visit my website. There you can sign up for my monthly author report, see all my books, and read blogs about ancient history.

Website: www.JCliftonSlater.com

Facebook: Galactic Council Realm and Clay Warrior Stories

I am J. Clifton Slater and I write military adventure both future and ancient.

Other books by J. Clifton Slater:

Historical Adventure of the 2nd Punic War

A Legion Archer series

#1 Journey from Exile

#2 Pity the Rebellious

Historical Adventure of the 1st Punic War

Clay Warrior Stories series

#1 Clay Legionary

#2 Spilled Blood

#3 Bloody Water

#4 Reluctant Siege

#5 Brutal Diplomacy

#6 Fortune Reigns

#7 Fatal Obligation

#8 Infinite Courage

#9 Deceptive Valor

#10 Neptune's Fury

#11 Unjust Sacrifice

#12 Muted Implications

#13 Death Caller

#14 Rome's Tribune

#15 Deranged Sovereignty

#16 Uncertain Honor

#17 Tribune's Oath

#18 Savage Birthright

#19 Abject Authority

Fantasy – *Terror & Talons* series

#1 Hawks of the Sorcerer Queen

#2 Magic and the Rage of Intent

Military Science Fiction - *Call Sign Warlock* series

#1 Op File Revenge

#2 Op File Treason

#3 Op File Sanction

Military Science Fiction – *Galactic Council Realm* series

#1 On Station

#2 On Duty

#3 On Guard

#4 On Point

Printed in Great Britain
by Amazon